DATE DUE

Feathers in the Dust

A Hospice Doctor's Tale

David Trevelyan

authorHOUSE®

AuthorHouse™ UK Ltd.
500 Avebury Boulevard
Central Milton Keynes, MK9 2BE
www.authorhouse.co.uk
Phone: 08001974150

First published by AuthorHouse 7/22/2010

ISBN: 978-1-4520-4387-6 (sc)

Some of the characters and incidents in this book are based on actual
experience. Where this is the case, names and key details have been
changed in order to preserve anonymity.

This book is printed on acid-free paper.

Dedication

To Smiffy – one of the finest. It was a privilege to work with you.

Introduction

Many people expect that a hospice must be a sad place to work, a place of suffering and darkness. Those who pass through discover that this is only one side of the coin. It is also a place of light and life and hope and laughter.

Some people suggest that those who work in a hospice must be in some way extraordinary. There are extraordinary people in hospices, but the people who work there will tell you that these are usually the patients, whose courage and patience and resilience can be awe-inspiring and profoundly humbling. Those who feel called to care for them often give much of themselves, but in doing so they receive much back in return. Such care can be emotionally costly of course, and there are casualties. For most, what helps sustain them through difficult times are the teamwork and sense of 'family' that is often found amongst hospice staff; the fact that they can make a real difference; and also, perhaps surprisingly, the humour.

For a long time I thought that someone ought to write a novel about a hospice. For too long now we have been afraid to talk about death and dying, which has replaced sex as the great taboo. For too ma what happens in a hospice is cloaked in mystery and misunderstanding, and this engenders fear. I believe there is a story that needs to be told, and the time finally came when I thought I'd give it a go myself.

Acknowledgement

I am grateful to Dr Richard Hillier for the advice he gave me when I was looking to specialise in palliative care. He also introduced me to the concept of accumulated grief over many years of working with the dying. He shared with me a metaphor, 'hairs of grief', which he in turn had received from Dr David Percy. This became 'feathers of grief' to me, and is something that I have found helpful on innumerable occasions over my career to date.

I am also grateful to the many patients and colleagues from whom I have learned so much, and who gave me the privilege of becoming part of their story.

Contents

Chapter 1
Arrival

I switched off the engine and sat for a few minutes looking out over the gently sloping hillside to the shallow valley below, and across to the patchwork of wooded grassland beyond. It was still late summer, but autumn was just around the corner, and already leaving its calling card in the early morning chill. Wraiths of mist curled up from the shadows in the valley floor and dissolved, shuddering momentarily with panic as they were caught by the rays of the morning sun. Summer would not relax its grip yet. On the far side a bird of prey hovered, suspended seemingly motionless apart from almost imperceptible movements of wing and tail to correct its trim.

I sighed. This was less than a quarter of an hour from the city centre, where I had spent the best part of every waking hour for the last four years in the district general hospital, unaware of such beauty on the doorstep. My world had been reduced to theatre scrubs, ward rounds, long nights on my feet and waking up stiff on the sofa in the doctors' mess, day and night merging under the glare of artificial light, strong coffee and plastic food snatched during the infrequent lulls. Whenever I did emerge zombie-like from the sterile tomb there was the relentless demand of study, sucking whatever vestige of vitality, spontaneity, and originality the hospital had grudgingly spared me. Yet, this was what I had wanted to do. I had finally scrambled over the academic hurdles, ticked the appropriate boxes, and was ready for a surgical registrar post – the next step on the way to being a consultant surgeon.

So what was I doing here? There were plenty of other interesting fill-in posts I could have applied for until the right job came up. What possessed me to apply for the hospice post? I'd always wanted to save lives, not hold the hands of the dying. The irony screamed at me. My psyche needed a spring clean, I needed reinvigorating; I needed to re-connect with life, not marinate in the misery of suffering and death.

I got out of the car and shivered. Perhaps summer's grip would not hold much longer after all. There was a wonderful stillness. I could hear the faint sound of running water wafting up from the valley, massaging and accentuating the peacefulness of the hospice grounds. There must be a stream at the bottom that I couldn't see. The bird of prey suddenly pitched left, hesitated for a moment and then dropped out of the sky. Moments later it emerged from the long grass beyond what must have been the stream and soared off towards the tree line on the far side, a small rabbit suspended beneath it. The rabbit's legs jerked convulsively a couple of times and then it went limp. The sound of another car broke the stillness and I turned to head up the path towards the hospice.

It was a low-set building of fairly modern construction, mainly single storey except for the central block which appeared to be two storeys and had an Alpine look to it, with long sloping roofs on an 'A' shaped frame. The single storey wings were of unequal length, the larger one on the right stretching out along the contour of the gentle hill on which it stood, with windows looking out across the scene that had held my attention for the last ten minutes. A path branched off to the right along the length of the wing, and about half way along there was a paved area, partially enclosed by lattice panels covered in climbing roses, with some tables and a small water feature. The whole building was framed by a background of tall poplar trees, and as modern healthcare facilities go this had a certain elegance.

Along the front of the building, on either side of the path up to the main entrance was a series of planted beds displaying a riot of colour, immaculately kept with neat lines, clipped borders, and not a hint of weeds. It almost seemed too neat, too perfect, the processes of nature tidily controlled, in stark contrast no doubt to the struggle to contain the ravages of nature within the building. Over to the left I noticed a small pond, and sitting on the edge were two plastic garden gnomes, one smiling impishly and dangling a fishing line into the water and the other leaning across and whispering in his ear. I stopped momentarily, briefly taken aback as I saw them, almost winded by the incongruity of the scene. The faintly ridiculous breaking in on the spirituality of the ambience that the morning had so far managed to create seemed to render the latter rather pretentious. I couldn't suppress a quiet chuckle.

I approached the glass-panelled doors of the main entrance and paused on the threshold, taking a deep breath. A large sign crowned the entrance with the words 'St. Julian's Hospice' in dark green on a pale yellow background. The 'a' of Julian was incorporated into a motif which looked like a naive representation of the upper torso of a monk topped off with a halo. The typeface and colouring matched the numerous small directional signs that guided the way from the car park, and presumably reflected the livery of the organisation. As I dropped my gaze again, out of the corner of my eye I noticed a plastic bucket to the side of the entrance. Walking over, I could see inside what looked like half eaten or half digested fish and chips bathed in a yellow liquid. A whiff of a rancid aroma caught my nostrils and I jerked back reflexively. Composing myself once again I pushed open the door and stepped inside.

I immediately noticed the warmth, very welcoming after the chill morning air outside. It was a spacious foyer, light and airy. There was a seating area with comfortable looking chairs and low tables immediately on the left, and beyond this a doorway led into a coffee shop. Along one wall there were glass display cabinets with merchandise of various kinds, mainly arts and crafts, and there was a rack of greetings cards. Indoor plants stood as sentinels in most of the unoccupied corners of the asymmetrical reception area. Directly across from me was the reception desk. A middle-aged lady was sitting at the desk and talking on the phone. She was calmly and patiently explaining something to the caller who was clearly having difficulty grasping what she was saying, as she repeated the same explanation in three different ways during the brief time that I had paused to take in the surroundings.

'Yes, you'll need to speak to your own doctor first and get him to contact the doctors here.' She looked up briefly when I entered and smiled before returning to her distracted caller.

My direct line to the desk was barred by a large bundle of fur on the carpet. A brindle coloured tomcat was lying stretched out on his back, belly uppermost to the world as if sunning himself, hind legs extended and front legs elevated but relaxed with one paw flopped by his right ear and the other suspended above his breast. His eyes were closed and I could have sworn he had a smile on his face as a deep gravelly purring sound surrounded him. He appeared totally oblivious to me and to his rather vulnerable location, as I checked my step and carefully detoured round his not insignificant form. The lady at the desk had by now hung up and she smiled, this time more broadly, as I approached the desk. She wore a metal badge on her lapel with the same motif I had noticed on the entrance sign.

'You'll have to excuse Willie. He does his own thing, and he thinks he owns the place at times. How can I help you?'

'Morning. I'm Dr Trevelyan, David Trevelyan. I'm starting work here today. I was told to ask for Dr Crosbie.'

'Ah, Dr Crosbie is away at the moment, but we are expecting you. I'll just phone through to Matron and let her know you've arrived. They'll be starting the morning meeting very soon.'

As she picked up the phone to announce my arrival

5

my eyes wandered to the wall behind the reception desk. This was dominated by a large framed photograph of the Queen shaking hands with a tall silver haired man who was flanked by what were presumably members of hospice staff. There was a key box below this, and to the right were a series of smaller photographs with names and titles inscribed – Medical Director, Matron, Business Director, and Chair of the Trustees.

'Hello Matron. Dr Trevelyan has arrived. Shall I send him down? That's fine, I'll tell him.' She replaced the receiver and turned her smile to me once again. She pointed to a set of double doors to my right. They had glass panels, but there were blinds drawn down over the glass. 'If you'd like to go through there, Matron's office is the third door down on the left. There are sentries out at the moment, as we are apparently moving someone, but they'll let you through.' She looked down and started writing on something at the desk.

'Sentries?' I asked disconcertedly.

'Yes.' She looked up briefly, and smiled again, then returned to her activity. I thanked her and turned to go, a little bemused.

'Oh, by the way, I thought I should mention. There appears to be a bucket of sick or something just by the entrance. Fish and chips maybe. It's not very nice.'

'Fish and chips? Ah, that will be John. Don't worry.' She smiled and looked down again.

I shrugged and walked across to the double doors that presently barred my way. As I pushed on them they gave initially and then met resistance.

A face appeared at the crack and whispered, 'Hang on a moment please.'

'I'm Dr Trevelyan.'

A blank expression gave way after a few moments to a look of realisation. 'Ah yes, of course. I'm sorry, do come through.'

The door opened a little more and I squeezed through. A nurse, who was the gatekeeper, flashed me an embarrassed smile and motioned me down the corridor. Stationed along the right hand side of this corridor at regular intervals were what looked like linen bins and several other nurses of various designations. As I walked a few yards down it became apparent that they were positioned outside closed doors and preventing their opening. Suddenly, behind me a door opened from what I later realised was one of two single patient rooms at the top of the corridor. Out wheeled a hospital bed, steered by a nurse at each end, and it headed down the corridor towards me.

'Look out there. Mrs Evans is coming through.'

I pressed myself against the left wall as the bed glided past. On it was a nightdress-clad figure lying on her back. She was probably in her late forties, though I later learned that it can be very difficult to tell. Her eyes were closed and mouth half open, and her gaunt face looked porcelain white. Auburn hair was carefully combed and spilled over the pillow around her. The bedclothes were tucked around her upper torso and her arms folded outside across her chest. In one hand she clasped a red rose and on the pillow beside her was a small teddy bear.

It only took a second or so for her to be wheeled past me, but you couldn't mistake the fact that she was dead. I'd heard people talk of a person's aura, and rather dismissed such ideas, but I was brought up short. Beautifully laid out as she was, and as peaceful as she looked, there was nothing but a lifeless shell. It wasn't just that there was an absence of vital force, or aura if you like, that might interact with and influence the surroundings, there was actually a felt deficit, so that her passing by was not a neutral event that could go unnoticed, but one that drew you in and made you aware of something lost, something missing.

For a moment I was shaken. I had seen dead bodies before, and had had patients die before. There are no doubt defences that even the most empathic doctors or nurses erect when dealing with loss and suffering in those for whom they care, in order to protect themselves. The reality of death may be rationalised in a hundred different ways, neatly boxed up and dealt with from a position of detachment. However, this time I was caught unprepared, my defences down. I lingered against the wall, a little bewildered, while the bed disappeared down the corridor. After what seemed like an age, but was in fact only a few seconds, everything erupted in a bustle of activity. The entrance doors to the wing and those along the corridor were opened, linen baskets were moved aside and nurses scattered in all directions. The route of Mrs Evans' final journey along to the room of rest, attended only by the honour guard of clinical staff and laundry, now became a vibrant highway filled with light and chatter and life.

I persevered another few yards until I came to an open door that was marked as the matron's office. She was sitting at her desk, half in profile and humming quietly to herself. I knocked gently. She turned and rose immediately to greet me. She was tall and slim, with russet shoulder length hair tied back in a ponytail and subdued with a couple of broad hair clips. Her delicate face was lightly freckled and she had crows' feet creases that drew attention in towards the most striking emerald green eyes I had ever seen. She had a similar set of faint creases cornering her mouth, and it was immediately apparent why. Her face broke into a rapturous smile that was truly radiant. Before she smiled I would have said she was in late middle age, maybe even nearing retirement, but now I wasn't sure as years appeared to have fallen away from her face and she exuded a youthful vigour. She stepped across and took my right hand in hers and placed her left hand on my upper arm.

'You must be David. I'm Cathy Ryan. Call me Cathy. Welcome. Welcome.' Her voice was quiet, but authoritative, and she had the softest of Irish accents.

'Yes. David. David Trevelyan. Hello.'

'I'm so pleased to see you, so pleased you've come to join us. We've been waiting for you. I knew you'd come.' She gently squeezed my upper arm, and for a moment I thought she might be about to hug me.

Her eyes held my gaze for a few moments, and it felt as though she was looking much deeper within. Yet it didn't feel uncomfortable, in fact quite the opposite. It was one of those moments when people meet and there passes between them something intangible, unspoken, a connection opened up on a subliminal level. It was the first time I'd experienced this. I liked her. You couldn't help but like her. Her openness and informality were disarming and engaging. It was as if she'd known me for years. What is more, she stirred something deep within me, a yearning for opportunities lost, echoes of long forgotten ideals once held passionately, a quickening of hope and hints of possibilities unlimited. This was unnerving!

'I only secured the post a couple of weeks ago.'

It had been a strange transition. I had seen the job advertisement and, seemingly on a whim, had submitted a CV. I was offered the post immediately, after a telephone interview by the medical director. Not the usual procedure nowadays. I was rather taken aback and accepted without really giving it much more thought. It would be a new experience, and would only be for a few months, so what had I to lose?

'Ah, is that right? We've been waiting for you a lot longer than that.' Her smile became more enigmatic. She did not elaborate further. She let go of my hand and arm. 'Have you far to come in on a morning?'

'No. I rent a flat in the city. It takes about ten minutes.'

'Any family?'

'No. I'm unattached. To be honest, social life hasn't had much of a look in over the last few years.'

'That's a shame. A fine young man like you having to look after himself. We'll have to make a special effort to mother you.'

'Thanks.' I didn't know whether that was something I would really welcome or not, but the way she put it made it sound wholly desirable.

'We're about to start the morning ward meeting. Come along and sit in, and I'll introduce you to some

more of the team. Brian Crosbie is our medical director
– but then you probably spoke to him on the phone.
He apologises for not being here to welcome you, but
he's speaking at a conference today. After the ward
meeting, we'll get Sheila our medical secretary to show
you round, and then I've arranged for you to see Roger
our business director. He'll give you some background
on the hospice.' She picked up a folder from the desk
and led the way out of the office and down towards the
meeting room.

As we approached I became aware of raucous
laughter, and a booming voice. I thought I made
out the words 'It's a dog collar, madam,' followed by
more laughter. We turned and Cathy ushered me into
a large room with easy chairs along each wall and a
low-set coffee table in the centre. Most of the chairs
were filled, many of the occupants still recovering
from the outburst of hilarity, ripples of laughter fading
into smirks and smiles. We sat down in two adjacent
armchairs. There was a tray of tea, coffee and biscuits
on the table and Cathy motioned me to help myself.

'Good morning everyone. Let me introduce David
Trevelyan to you all. David's a doctor and he's joining
us today. We're so very pleased to have him, and I'm
sure you are all going to make him feel very welcome.
Shall we go round the room and introduce ourselves?
Let's start with Nick, our chaplain, and no doubt the
cause of all the riotous noise.'

She grinned cheekily and motioned towards the
man sitting on my left. He was a large man, with an
even larger presence. It was difficult to judge with him
sitting down but he was certainly well over six feet tall,

and he had a substantial frame. Maybe early forties, he had a boyish face with ruddy cheeks and large brown eyes, thick bushy eyebrows and tousled dark hair. He wore casual clothes with an open necked shirt, and no sign of the dog collar that appeared to have been the butt of the partially overheard joke. He stretched out a meaty hand and squeezed mine powerfully.

'Good to have you, old boy. Welcome to the madhouse. I'm Nick Hardy. Nick the vic. Hardy by name and hardy by nature. I'm the one who's supposed to remain sane and look out for all these others' souls. The one they come to with all the impossible questions.' He was loud and bombastic, and had a twinkle in his eyes. Then he lowered his voice in a feigned whisper and said, 'Sooner or later they're going to wake up and realise that I'm just as much in the dark as they are, a case of the blind leading the blind.' More booming laughter, that quickly subsided.

'Don't you listen to him,' Cathy interjected. 'He's a treasure, and I don't know what we'd do without him.'

'We'll make some time for a chat in the next few days,' he continued. 'Give you a bit of time first to find your feet.'

'Hello. I'm Sally Marshall, staff grade doctor.' We had moved on to the next chair. 'Apart from Brian, our consultant, I'm the only other full time doctor here, until now that is. Good to have another pair of hands.' She smiled over the top of a mug of steaming coffee. She looked tired, and the reason became evident later in the meeting.

The introductions continued round the room: a senior staff nurse who led the meeting in that she gave most of the handover information; the physiotherapist and visiting physiotherapy student; a social worker; and the remaining doctor present, Lucy Danvers who was a senior registrar. She was immaculately turned out, and she had an air of efficiency about her. Her greeting was short and friendly, but not overly friendly. I concentrated hard in order to remember the names as this was something I was usually very bad at doing. Cathy leaned across to me.

'We normally start by mentioning the deaths over the last twenty-four hours, and then we briefly discuss every patient on the ward, and finish by reviewing those who are being admitted to the hospice today. It gives an update on where we are with each patient and an opportunity to share ongoing concerns with other members of the team. As you'll see it's very much multidisciplinary team working, with professionals from several disciplines contributing to the overall care of any given patient. Thank you everyone, shall we get started?'

'I wonder if I ought to just mention something,' I said. 'I noticed on coming in the main entrance this morning a bucket of what looks like vomit.....'

'Oh, that'll be John,' Sally interjected. 'The bucket is there all the time in case it's needed, but usually in an unobtrusive place. I must say I didn't notice it today, and presumably no one else did.' It was half question, half statement, as she glanced around the room.

'Thanks David. We'll get one of the domestics to sort it out after the meeting before any relatives arrive.' Cathy continued in explanation. 'John Tucker is one of our longer stay patients. He's been with us about two months, and he has also had one or two previous shorter admissions. He's quite a young man and has complete upper gastrointestinal obstruction from a bowel cancer. Everything that goes into his stomach eventually comes back up. He's been like that for weeks, so he must be absorbing something from what he ingests, though I have to say he's looking more and more skeletal. He's essentially homeless, with no family to look out for him, so we are kind of his family now. He's a sweet man. He'll stay with us till he dies, as he's got nowhere else to go. He has some friends who take an interest, and they take him into town periodically for a drink and fish and chips. He knows it will all come back up, but he likes the taste and the pleasure of eating it. He's usually ready to vomit as he returns to the hospice, so we've taken to leaving a bucket out for the purpose – it saves our plants getting a drenching!'

The matter now settled, we proceeded with the meeting. The staff nurse, whose name I suddenly recalled was Gail, kicked off in a business-like way.

'We lost one overnight, Mrs Evans. She died at about seven this morning. Gradual deterioration over the last few days as you know, then became much less well yesterday evening. Breathing very laboured and a lot of secretions. The rattle sounded pretty awful. She was unaware, but her husband Philip was extremely distressed. Tanya had to spend a lot of time with him last night. He's hardly left his wife's side over the last few days and was just exhausted. In the end he just couldn't bear to see and hear her in such a state. His daughter took him home and they asked to be called when she died. Sharon, they'll need picking up very soon for bereavement care.'

14

Sharon was the social worker. Another name reinforced in my memory. 'Will do,' she replied. 'We've got the details. I know the family well. They've had quite a lot of input already.'

'I've seen quite a bit of them too,' Nick added. 'They were a lovely couple, utterly devoted. He's going to take this very hard. He has a faith of sorts, but we spent most of the time talking about his love of fishing. Struck a chord with me, as I used to wave a rod in my early days. Stillwater trout fishing - I once verged on the obsessive. It has got me thinking about taking it up again. It's a wonderful pass-time, out in the open, peaceful, time to reflect and get away from it all. It's also a sacred sport. Listen, have you heard the old saying that God does not count towards man's allotted span the hours spent fishing?'

'No, that's golf isn't it?' interjected Cathy. 'Not that I know much about either.'

'Anyway, it was an interest they pursued as a couple. He'd regularly attend fishing competitions, and she'd always be there right by his side. She said that she didn't always share that interest, but she realised early on in their marriage that it was a passion that wouldn't be tamed, and she might as well be out there with him rather than become a fishing widow. Then she grew to love it herself. They've asked me to do the funeral, so I'll follow him up as well.'

'There was also a transfer to the hospital last night,' Gail continued. 'Mr Jackson hadn't been quite right for most of yesterday, and by the evening he was clearly septic. Temperature of thirty-nine, tachycardic and with a low BP. He's still having chemotherapy and was with us for pain control, so Sally came in to assess him and discuss him with the oncology team. They felt he ought to have active treatment, and he was happy to be transferred. His family were a bit shaken, but fully on board. It was very helpful to have Sally around as she was able to help dispense on the evening drug round. Everything had become very delayed with Tanya tied up with Mr Evans, and an urgent transfer to sort out. We were also one auxiliary down due to last minute sickness. Anyway, poor Sally had rather a late night.'

'Okay. Thanks Sally,' Cathy replied. 'Maybe you can get off a bit early today? I don't suppose we need to hold Mr Jackson's bed, as he may be over there for a while.'

The meeting proceeded with a review of all the inpatients: some clearly dying; others awaiting discharge planning; and some seemingly in limbo, the team as yet unsure as to which way they would go. I sat back and listened. Gail summarised the facts and there would follow a brief discussion. Sally did most of the talking on the medical perspective, referring to the physiotherapist occasionally on uncertainties about a patient's mobility. Lucy Danvers interjected occasional comments and clarifications on medical issues, and Nick and Sharon filled in on emotional, spiritual and family perspectives.

Throughout it all, Cathy contributed little herself but orchestrated masterfully the whole, oiling the flow with relevant comments, inviting contributions when needed, skilfully moving the meeting on whenever it risked getting bogged down over any particular patient or concern. When she did offer insights of her own she immediately commanded attention and she was adept at bringing clarity to matters that were becoming muddied or confused. The respect in which she was held by those in the room was obvious. She was the most defining presence. Authority, wisdom, compassion, warmth and approachability danced in her every gesture, her every word. From time to time she would glance towards me to check I was alright, or she'd lean over and whisper clarification of something that a newcomer might not be familiar with. I was hugely impressed, and at the same time rather humbled.

The meeting ended and the assembly dispersed to get on with the tasks of the day. I was left in the hands of the medical secretary, an elegant woman with a bubbly demeanour.

'This is Sheila. She's one of the originals, been here since we started, and if you ever want to know what's going on with whom in the hospice, Sheila's the one to tell you.' Cathy grinned and left us to it.

Sheila was effusive in her greeting, and set about the task of showing me round with evident enthusiasm. By the time we'd been down to the end of the ward and back to the reception area she had grilled me on my life history, love life and aspirations both personal and professional.

'Oh, you're a surgeon. You'll find it very different here, and you'll learn an awful lot.' It felt like a put down, but I don't think this even occurred to her, and I'm sure it wasn't intended. 'Most people find they love it here, and it's never quite what they expected. Mind you, we've seen some changes over the years.'

She went on to describe the various renovations

and refurbishments, and the fundraising drives that paid for them. I learnt an interesting fact about almost every person she introduced me to, and the tour was somewhat delayed by her exchange of pleasantries with each one.

The central double-storey block housed the reception area, coffee shop, and chapel on the ground floor, and above was a floor of offices. To the rear of the ground floor there was a day centre, with a separate smaller entrance to the side. The wing that I had seen on the left that looked smaller in fact extended out to the rear as well, and this too was largely two-storey. The ground floor housed the kitchen and staff dining room, and above this more office space, a library and a large meeting room. The longer single storey wing extending out to the right from the entrance was, as I had already discovered, the inpatient unit, accommodating sixteen beds in total. There were two single rooms at the near end, then three bays of four beds each, and then a further two single rooms towards the far end.

All the rooms and bays were looking out onto the view that had absorbed me earlier that morning, with the offices and storage areas on the opposite side of the corridor. A large nurses' station and office was strategically placed at the centre of the wing, and the doctors' office was adjacent to this. Other offices, a couple of sitting rooms, a treatment room, and bathrooms occupied the remainder of the corridor. At the far end, beyond the last patient rooms, there was the sluice and also a chapel of rest where bodies were laid out before being collected by funeral directors. There was separate external access to this area so the deceased could be moved out discreetly.

'Now, you'll be meeting Roger, our business director at eleven-thirty, so you've got a bit of time in hand. You saw where his office is. Shall I get you another drink while you are waiting?'

'No thank you, I'm fine.'

'Perhaps you could have a look round the library or the grounds, or just sit and relax for a while. You'll find Roger very interesting. He's been with us a long time, and has been great for the hospice. He's really raised our profile in the community over the years. He's a war hero too – he won the Military Cross fighting in some far flung place as a young man. He's very shy about it all, and doesn't really talk much about it. I'll see you later.'

Sheila headed off towards the ward, stopping for a good few minutes on the way to talk to the receptionist. They parted laughing. I sat down in one of the easy chairs in the foyer and gazed out over the car park. Willie the tom had sloped off and was nowhere to be seen. I sighed. Sheila was right; I was already finding it very different here.

I knocked gently on the door to Roger Forbes' office. As with most of the offices the door was glass-panelled so I could see he wasn't in conference. He was sitting at his desk, slightly hunched over, evidently absorbed in some paperwork. I couldn't see much of his face, but his head was largely bald, the sheen reflecting the overhead light, with some preservation of silvery grey hair along the sides. He looked up, and then glanced at his watch. He looked across to the door again and smiled, gesturing to me to come in. He stood to greet me and extended a hand. The handshake was firm and it lingered.

'Roger Forbes. Do call me Roger. You must be David. Delighted to meet you. Have a seat.' He ushered me with his gaze to a chair to the side of his desk and he swivelled round to face me.

I scanned the walls around the room, looking for any photographs attesting to a previous military career or framed medals, but there were none. I was disappointed, though not surprised. Since boyhood I'd had a fascination with soldiering and military history; with what it must be like to be in combat; with the qualities and circumstances that propel a man or woman to extraordinary feats of courage; and with the bonds that must surely develop between those who have shared such experiences. Deep down, I suppose I still cherished boyhood dreams of being a soldier, and heard whispers of shame that I had never been tested in battle, never faced fear and death in that way. Here was someone who had, and I would have loved to hear tell of it. However, the most highly decorated for their exploits are usually the least likely to recount them. He already had my respect before we'd even exchanged a few words.

Roger continued the introduction. 'Welcome to St. Julian's. Brian Crosbie would normally do the official welcome, but as I expect you know he's unable to be here today. I'm the business director, Brian is medical director, and Cathy, whom you've already met, is the director of nursing or matron. Together we are the unholy trinity, a triumvirate, and it's a model that's shared by a number of other hospices. We are effectively the management team, and we report to the trustees. We've all pretty much been here from the beginning. Next year is the hospice's twenty-first anniversary.' There was a pause. 'What's your background? Have you had any experience of hospices before?'

'No I've never even visited one before. I've worked entirely in hospitals up to now, latterly in surgery. Of course I've been aware of the hospice, and I remember one or two occasions when we transferred patients across here.'

He listened attentively, his hands held together on his lap with fingertips touching, almost in a prayer position, his steely blue eyes getting the measure of me. He smiled again. Perhaps I'd gained his approval.

'Well, I'll need to give you some background. Many hospices grew out of a reaction to the perceived deficiencies in care that the dying experienced in our hospitals. They started popping up all over the place, as it turns out with little thought or planning in terms of population coverage. As with many other places, a group of local concerned citizens got together and lobbied and fundraised for a hospice for the area. I was on the original organising committee, involved in the local business community and with some useful connections. We eventually got it built, and managed to recruit enough staff to run a small inpatient unit. Over the years this grew and we added a day centre.'

'Brian Crosbie was a consultant physician at the hospital and was a supporter from the start. We managed to persuade him to come and head up the medical team. It was a real coup, as he has almost every professional qualification you can think of, and was highly regarded by his colleagues in the hospital. It made a huge difference in getting the local medical fraternity on board. He joined the ranks of the early hospice pioneers and is very well known in hospice medical circles, or rather palliative care as it is now called. Cathy joined us after a few months. What do you make of Cathy?'

I felt a little awkward. I didn't know what I was expected to say. I thought for a while, trying to find suitable words. I was sure I'd be judged by what I said. 'She's very impressive.' I cringed a little inside. Is that the best I can come up with?

'I'll say. A remarkable lady. In many ways she's been the heart and soul of this place. She went abroad in her early twenties to work in a small mission hospital in Africa. She lost her husband after a couple of years, but stayed on for another decade, running it almost single-handed. She once faced down a local warlord who was set upon stealing supplies and killing some members of a rival group whom she was treating. He was apparently so impressed by her that he brought the hospital under his wing of protection and let it be known that if anyone harmed any of the staff or patients, regardless of group or tribe, they would have him to answer to. She came home when the whole place eventually erupted in one of the many bloodbaths that seem to continually stain that beautiful but tragic continent.'

He looked down at the floor, and there was a brief interlude of silence. It wasn't long but it was definitely perceptible, a hiatus in his flow, and for a moment he seemed distant, lost in thought, or was it remembrance?

'Anyway, she heard about us through a mutual contact and came and joined us.'

'Have you been business director from the beginning?'

'Yes. I ran a moderately successful business at the time, and was doing pretty well. There was something that gripped me about the whole idea of hospice. The more I got involved in the planning and setting up the less fulfilling I found my own work. When we opened there was a need for a business director, and I was offered the post. So I sold up and stayed.'

'What was it about the idea of the hospice that so interested you?'

'It was innovative and exciting, something that could really make a difference. I loved the whole ethos, particularly in the early days. It was humbling and inspiring to work with people who were passionate and self-sacrificing. It also seemed a way of giving something back. I'd witnessed and contributed to a lot of death and suffering. Perhaps devoting my time indirectly to caring for the dying has been a means of redemption.' He looked distant, reflective.

'It must be very different from running your own business?' I was curious, and he was being remarkably candid.

'In some ways it is. You are not chasing profit all the time. Like most hospices we are a charitable organisation. It has its own challenges, not least of which is securing enough funding every year to keep going. We get some money from the NHS, but that still leaves almost two million pounds a year to be raised through charitable donations, legacies and fundraising activities. The landscape's changed since I started here. I was a local businessman with some passion and some business sense. Nowadays my equivalents in other hospices are coming through with higher degrees and MBAs. The world of hospice is becoming more like a corporate enterprise, and while it still attracts the goodwill of the public it must not take for granted its generosity. We are now into corporate branding and have to sell ourselves in the marketplace in competition with the many other good causes that are chasing a dwindling pool of charitable giving.' There was a hint of frustration and almost resentment in his tone.

He continued. 'Brian will tell you there have been equally dramatic changes in the way clinical care is delivered. We used to be pioneers working outside of mainstream healthcare, and often flying by the seats of our pants and breaking new ground in care of the dying. Then palliative care became an accredited medical specialty, and with that comes the need for a research base and training programmes, audit cycles and clinical governance. All well and good, but we now live with a tension between the 'old' and the emerging 'new', which is increasingly protocol and guideline driven. We risk becoming less and less distinct from the hospital units that our patients are often seeking refuge from, more interventionist in our approach, focused on sorting out problems and moving people on in order to make way for the next. Even the word hospice now invokes disapproval and we are being encouraged to call ourselves specialist palliative care units.'

He sighed softly. 'All perfectly reasonable and necessary when you rationalise it, but one can't help thinking we are losing something along the way. I'll be retiring very soon, and perhaps it's just as well. Then, so are many of us who were in at the beginning. Brian is very close to retirement too. Cathy has a little longer to go.' The sentence tailed off into a long pause. For a moment I felt a little awkward, as though I was intruding on some private grief.

'Where did the name St. Julian's come from?' I felt a slight change in direction was needed.

'Oh, he was a local abbot. There's a ruined abbey a few miles from here where Julian presided in the Middle Ages. During an outbreak of the Black Death he used one wing of the abbey as a hospital of sorts where those who were affected could be brought to be cared for in their last days. Some of the monks inevitably contracted it and ended up as patients, and most of the rest then fled. Julian stayed on and personally tended the dying, until he too fell ill. Legend has it that he received an angelic visitation during the night, and was totally healed the following morning. As he went through the abbey tending the sick that day everyone that he touched was healed, and the black boils melted away before his eyes. The place became a shrine for a while, and he was eventually canonised. He seemed an appropriate candidate to have the hospice named after him.'

Suddenly he grunted disapprovingly, and rolled his eyes upwards. 'Two of our newer trustees are pushing for the name to be changed. They argue that it sounds too religious, an anachronism in the present culture that might offend or deter some people from coming to us. They are suggesting something blander, less threatening such as 'The Poplars'.' He laughed. 'Makes us sound more like a health spa where a number of dying programmes are on offer!' He fixed me with his piercing eyes and smiled. 'Enough of my cynicism. As you can see, I too have become an anachronism and it is high time for me to move over and let someone else steer us into the brave new world!' He finished with a relish.

We talked for another quarter of an hour or so, about the practicalities of running the organisation, fundraising, statutory requirements, and touched again on my own background. The meeting over, he walked me to the door. 'Well David, we're very glad to have you, and I'm sure you'll enjoy your time with us. My office is open whenever you need to come and talk.' I thanked him and we shook hands again.

I proceeded down the corridor to the personnel manager's office and set about the tedious formalities that attend starting any new post. I emerged into the foyer downstairs an hour or so later, having also spent a little time with the education nurse and then the volunteers manager. By now I was feeling befuddled with information overload and had that rather weary feeling that one has when starting somewhere new, and wishing you were already settled in. I'd much rather get stuck in and do some clinical work.

There was a buzz of conversation coming from the staff dining room. I hadn't ordered any lunch so I bought a sandwich at the coffee shop and took a seat at one of the two long tables among a group comprising some nurses, two of the administrative staff and Nick the chaplain. He introduced me to those whom I had not yet met, and the conversation continued with occasional reference to me in an effort to include me in what was being discussed. I discovered the colour coding of the nurses' uniforms. All wore a light blue uniform with a darker colour edging to the collars, lapels, and cuffs: dark blue for staff nurses, most of whom also wore lapel badges designating where they had trained; and green for auxiliary nurses. This was a fairly recently adopted livery, and gone now were the nurses' caps that had apparently survived in the hospice long after they had disappeared in the hospitals. General opinion at the table was that they wouldn't be missed. All staff wore name badges with the hospice motif.

Nick surfed the ebb and flow of conversation with consummate ease, and punctuated it with his distinctive laughter. He was clearly a people person, a communicator, able to put anyone at their ease. Conversation ranged over a number of disconnected topics: what everyone did at the weekend; some theatrical event taking place in the city; an upcoming fundraising event; updates on spouses or family. I sat and observed mainly, taking in the different personalities, slightly soporific as a result of food and hot coffee in a warm environment after a tiring morning.

❧

'Sheila we need some more sticky name labels for Mr Thompson.' The medical secretary's desk was set up along one wall of the large doctors' office, together with printer, photocopier, drawers and filing cabinets. A staff nurse had stuck her head round the office door and was looking pleadingly. The name labels were used on all documentation and charts relating to a given patient.

'Okay,' she replied with a feigned reluctance. 'What's his prognosis?'

'What does that matter?'

'Well, how long is he going to be with us? Do I print off one sheet or two?'

'Sheila!' The nurse laughed.

'Waste not, want not. We're entering difficult times, you know, and every saving helps.'

'One will do.....for the moment. Thanks.' She disappeared.

Apart from Sheila the office was empty. I had meandered down after lunch and had set about familiarising myself with some of the documentation and procedures on the ward. I had missed the bulk of the ward work, which usually took place in the morning. During the afternoon was when admissions were normally seen, and although there had been none planned for that day it appeared that we were now expecting an emergency admission. Lucy Danvers had gone off to do some teaching at the hospital, and Sally was on the ward mopping up one or two patients who weren't seen before lunch, and talking to some relatives.

I did spend some time with two of the staff nurses on the 'syringe driver round'. Syringe drivers are devices that discharge a syringe of medication over a set time period, the drugs being delivered into a vein or, as is always the case in the hospice, under the skin. It was a simple concept that had apparently transformed care at the end of life, as it meant that patients could receive essential background medications such as painkillers or sedatives beyond the point at which they were conscious or able to swallow, and without the inconvenience of having to give regular injections. I'd come across them occasionally in my hospital experience, but I was soon to discover that they are pretty much standard fare in hospice care. They are usually replenished every twenty-four hours and this was done at lunchtime after the normal drug round.

I watched the nurses making up the drug mixtures and setting up the device. They supervised me doing the same and then showed me how to insert the fine bore cannula under the skin on two patients who were having a change of site, and then connect it all together. Syringe driver management is primarily a nursing task, but as a doctor on the unit I had to be aware of how to set one up. The round finished, I had returned to the office to resume my familiarisation.

Sheila was chatting away, explaining the finer points of hospice discharge summaries, when Sally appeared at the door. 'David, could you give me a hand with the new patient. I need to get a cannula into him, but he is shutting down and I can't find a vein. You are probably more of an expert than I am with your recent experience.'

'Yeah, will do. Though I'm not particularly expert. We used to get the anaesthetists to do the very difficult ones.' I followed her out of the office and into the treatment room, where she was stocking up a tray with fresh supplies of kit.

'He's a man in his late thirties with malignant melanoma that has spread extensively. His bowel is involved and he's bleeding profusely from his rectum, with lot of abdominal pain and huge amounts of distress. He's clearly on the way out and we need to settle him quickly. We've tried subcutaneous diamorphine and midazolam, but it's not working very well, probably because his peripheral circulation is shutting down. I'm not sure an intramuscular injection will be any better. We'll need to get it into him intravenously.'

Diamorphine is a morphine-related painkiller, known as heroin on the streets, and midazolam is a sedative, one that I'd often used in sedating patients for endoscopy or other procedures. She picked up the tray and we hurried down to one of the single rooms.

The distress in the room was palpable. The man was stretched out on the bed, deathly white and sweating profusely. There were some green towels rolled up and placed either side of his hips, but there was also some visible blood-staining of the bedclothes around his upper legs. He was grimacing and moaning loudly, tears mixing with the sweat on his face. Intermittently he would shudder violently. His wife was kneeling over the bed with her face on his upper chest, and a staff nurse stood beside her with a hand resting on one of her shoulders. The nurse was struggling to hold back tears, while the wife was speaking to him calmly and softly.

'Michael, this is Dr Trevelyan,' said Sally. 'We are going to get some medication into your vein to make you more comfortable.' She motioned me to the other side of the bed.

The wife glanced up and acknowledged me. She looked tired, and all colour and emotion had drained from her face. She continued to speak softly and reassuringly. 'I love you my darling. I love you so much. You've been so brave.'

'The children. Tell them I love them, I'll miss them. Oh, I hate to leave you.' Weak sobs punctuated his moaning.

'They know that my love. They know you love them more than anything. You've been a wonderful father.'

I knelt down and took his grey and clammy arm, feeling for a pulse. It was barely detectable. I hung it over the edge of the bed and felt around the front of the elbow for any hint of a vein. Beads of sweat began to appear on my forehead, and my hand was trembling slightly. The heart-rending exchange between husband and wife continued as an accompaniment to my increasingly desperate quest to locate the vein. I struggled for what seemed like an age. I felt choked up myself, an intruder on an intimacy that I had no right to witness. The room became increasingly claustrophobic as I had nightmare images of several fumbling attempts to get the cannula in while he faded away before my eyes in unrelieved suffering. Another nurse arrived with a charged syringe and added to the audience.

'Come on, it's here somewhere,' I mumbled to myself. I couldn't delay any longer. I'd have to give it a go. My fingers stroked the skin one last time looking for the slightest change in underlying anatomy, and then I went for it at the most promising spot. To my amazement, and indescribable relief, I got flashback and advanced the butterfly cannula up into the vein.

'Marvellous, well done.' Sally came over and connected the syringe. The wife looked up at me and nodded. I stood up and stepped back while Sally took my place kneeling at his side and slowly discharged the syringe, a little at a time over the next minute or so, gently massaging up the arm after each small depression of the plunger. She stopped short of the whole syringe-full, presumably happy that she had given enough. He was visibly starting to relax, the tension in his body gradually melting away, the moaning becoming softer.

'I love you Kate. I love you…..' His voice tailed off into a whisper.

'I know Michael. I know. I love you.' Her shoulders dropped and she sighed as he drifted off into unconsciousness.

I quietly and discreetly headed towards the door. I had to get out, there were too many of us in the room, too many intruding on something so terribly poignant. The wife turned her head to me as I reached the door and said, 'Thank you.' Her voice sounded wearier now, but she was able to summon up a half smile. I turned quickly away, tears welling up, and left the room.

I squatted against the wall outside the room, head in my hands and staring at the floor, trying to process what I had just witnessed. After another few minutes I heard a muffled wail followed by soft sobbing. Shortly afterwards Sally emerged.

She looked down at me and said, 'Are you okay David?' I looked up, having by now managed to compose myself sufficiently to engage again. 'Welcome to the hospice. Let's go and have a cup of tea.'

Chapter 2
The Ward Round

Brian Crosbie was tall and wiry, with close-cropped silvery hair and aquiline features. When I first met him that morning I recognised him as the man shaking hands with the Queen in the photograph above the reception desk. As with everyone else so far he had greeted me warmly and we had recollected together some details from my telephone interview. He apologised for missing my arrival, citing coyly the 'tiresome curse of notoriety that meant one was in much demand for speaking and teaching engagements.' As one would expect he had taken the medical lead in the morning ward meeting, scrutinising the prescription charts for each patient that was being discussed, suggesting fine tuning adjustments to some drugs and crossing off others, pausing proceedings periodically to impart some teaching point or anecdote about a particular drug or the symptom for which it was prescribed.

I had already witnessed an incisive ability to quickly garner the facts of a situation and arrive at insightful judgements and observations about patients or relatives whom he may not even have met. He combined an authoritative wisdom with a boyish enthusiasm for his craft, and his enthusiasm was infectious. The meeting had overrun, largely because of his contributions, but he had remained unruffled and unhurried while we all hung on his every word. There was none of the anxiety or pressure to move the meeting on as there had been in the other morning meetings I had attended earlier in the week. Now Lucy Danvers and I were accompanying him on a ward round of all the patients, together with Sarah, one of the two ward sisters.

The first single room was occupied by a lady in her seventies with bowel obstruction from cancer of the ovary, who was gradually getting weaker and was in the last days of life. Pain and nausea were controlled with drugs via the ubiquitous syringe driver, and apart from an occasional foul smelling vomit and profound fatigue she was relatively comfortable. Other than managing small sips of fluid she was too weak to do anything for herself and needed full nursing care. When Brian entered the room her face lit up and she reached out her hand.

'Dr Crosbie, thank you for coming to see me.' She spoke as if to a long lost friend.

'Hello Elsie. That's a lovely smile for an old friend.' He moved across to the other side of the bed, got down on both knees, leaned across with his elbows on the bed and took hold of her hand in both of his.

It was a simple and natural act, and yet in a strange way profoundly moving. I had never seen a consultant do that before. I was so used to the hierarchy of medicine, and ward rounds conducted from the end, or at least the side, of the bed with doctors and entourage standing and looking down, and sadly sometimes talking down, at the patient. It was humbling to see this by all accounts highly eminent and distinguished physician metaphorically shed his status, learning, and power, and bring himself both physically and relationally onto a level with his patient, one vulnerable human being engaging with another. His manner and demeanour and tone exuded compassion and love.

I soon discovered that this was not isolated behaviour with a patient whom he knew particularly well, but was his manner of interacting with everyone in his care. Sometimes sitting on the bed, sometimes kneeling, always at eye level and almost always making physical contact in some way, he engaged person to person with every patient, and the effect was almost mesmerising. He elicited a reciprocal openness and warmth from them.

'Are you comfortable my dear?' he asked.

'Yes, pretty much so. I have a nasty vomit from time to time, but I've no pain. I'm so dreadfully tired. I wish it were over, I wish he'd take me, I'm ready. Is it going to be much longer?' There was tension in her face and a pleading look in her eyes.

'It's been a long road, and we've travelled much of it together you and I. You've been a trooper. I don't think it will be very long now, a few days at most.' A wave of relief broke over her face and she relaxed back into the pillow.

'Thank goodness. Thank you for all your care. The nurses are fantastic, really, you are all so kind.'

'How's Bert?'

'Oh, he's okay; he's coping in his own way. We've had our deep and meaningfuls a while ago, and said all that needs to be said. He's a good man, and we've had a great life together. I worry sometimes about how he'll cope, but the children will gather round and the church is being marvellous. They have a rota to cook him dinners and bring him groceries.'

'I'll try to catch up with him when he's next in.' He stood up. 'Let us know if you get any pain or nausea and we'll tweak the drugs in your pump.' He took her hand again and squeezed it gently. 'Goodbye Elsie.'

'Thank you.' The words were pregnant with meaning and emotion. She said it in the way of someone who knew it would be the last exchange.

We left the room and conferred outside. 'As you'll be aware,' Brian explained, 'when people have a bowel obstruction in the context of extensive abdominal disease surgery is rarely appropriate. But we can usually manage symptoms fairly well. Lucy will be able to go into more detail and give you the up-to-date evidence, as she's recently done a study on malignant bowel obstruction.' Lucy Danvers nodded. 'Any luck with publication Lucy?'

'I've submitted a paper and I'm waiting to hear back.'

'What do you do about hydration and oral intake?' I asked. I was used to using nasogastric tubes, nil by mouth orders and intravenous fluids.

'Patients take whatever they can manage,' Brian replied. 'Eventually it comes down to sips of fluid, but they may find things they can keep down and enjoy. It's remarkable how much they can absorb even when they are fully obstructed. We can't completely eliminate the vomiting, but we can usually control nausea and also reduce the frequency and volume of vomits. Elsie's bowels have not worked at all for almost a month now, but she's remained pretty comfortable, just getting gradually weaker.'

We moved on to the next single room. Three people were sitting round the bed, which was occupied this time by a man. On one side was a woman in her late middle age sitting very close to the side of the bed and resting her cheek on the man's arm as it lay stretched out by his side. On the other side was a younger couple, sitting together a little further from the bed and holding hands. They all looked tired and empty. The man in the bed was unconscious and lying slightly over to his right side towards his wife. He was terribly emaciated, and his skin had the greenish yellow tinge of deep jaundice. I say he was unconscious, but in fact he looked like a corpse in the bed, barely alive, and it seemed incredible that there could still be life in him. His neck was partially extended on the pillow, his mouth half open, and his eyes sunken and closed and with sticky mucus at the edge of the lids. He was taking erratic shallow breaths and each inspiration was accompanied by a loud rattling sound that emanated from deep within his throat. It was a dreadful sight, the weight loss and emaciation that is sometimes a feature of advanced cancer taken to its extreme. The sound from the retained secretions, or death rattle, was profoundly disturbing.

Brian moved across to the far side of the bed and crouched down beside the man's wife. Sarah stood by the couple, while Lucy Danvers and I remained in the background by the door. It felt as if it would be somehow insensitive or intrusive for us all to enter that space around the bed, like voyeurs looking upon the macabre spectacle within it. The wife sat up and Brian spoke something softly to her. She nodded and tears welled up in her eyes. She moved back a little and Brian came in closer and took hold of the man's hand.

'Mr Luscombe,' he said, 'it's just the doctors. We're checking to see that you are comfortable.'

I could see that he was discreetly feeling the pulse at the wrist. For a few moments he gazed in silence at the man's face. I noticed almost imperceptible movements of Brian's lips, and was sure he was saying something under his breath, undetectable to any of us looking on. He replaced the man's hand on the bed and turned back to the wife. 'Is there anything you want to ask?'

'How long is this going to go on? Can't you do something to speed it up and end his suffering?' She broke down into sobbing. 'I can't bear it.' The younger woman at the other side of the bed, who was in fact her daughter, came over and put her arm around her shoulders.

'Come outside and let's have a chat.' Brian nodded to Sarah to come and guide the two women out of the room.

'Will you stay here?' The daughter looked across at her own husband and he nodded.

We made our way across the corridor to a small sitting room and sat down. Lucy Danvers remained outside the door.

'Can't you do something?' The wife had stopped sobbing, and was looking imploringly at Brian.

'I know this is awful for you. It's so hard to watch someone you love get to this state. I know it sounds awful, but I can assure you he won't be aware of it. He's very much unconscious.'

'Are you sure? It sounds like he's drowning.' She started sobbing softly again.

'We are sure,' said Sarah. 'For the last two days there hasn't been a flicker when we've turned him.'

'But you were speaking to him just now as if he could hear you.' The wife was looking at Brian again.

'Yes, I always speak to patients, even when they are unconscious. Unresponsive though he is, he is still a person with inherent dignity and worthy of respect.'

'This doesn't seem very dignified.' It was the daughter this time, and there was a hint of accusation in her tone.

Brian continued. 'I know this seems awful. We cannot do anything to hasten the end, nor would we want to. But neither are we doing anything to delay that. We are simply allowing nature to take its course. We have given, and will give him whatever he needs to make sure he is peaceful and comfortable. I promise you, he is not suffering. And if it's of any comfort, I don't think it will be very long now. His pulse is quite weak.' Brian was on the edge of his seat leaning forward, hands clasped in front of him, his tone authoritative, gentle and reassuring.

'I'm sorry Dr Crosbie. I know you are doing the best for him. We're grateful, we really are. It's just so hard.' Her daughter hugged her tightly.

'You are welcome to stay in here for a while if you'd like. We can bring you a cup of tea.'

They hesitated and looked at each other. 'No, thank you. We ought to get back. I promised him I'd be there at the end.' They got up and Brian held the door for them. The wife squeezed his hand. 'Thank you.' The daughter nodded and mouthed a thank you before they both disappeared back into the room.

We lingered in the sitting room for a moment. Brian looked reflective. 'It is hard for relatives to watch a loved one die. We are not exposed to dying the way people were a hundred years ago. We live in a quick fix society where we expect things to happen instantly, and we don't like waiting. People today don't realise that often dying is a very slow process. And it does involve suffering. You cannot have death without suffering, because none of us exist in isolation. No matter how peaceful and comfortable a person's death may be, others are impacted and have to live with the pain and loss. Even with the most isolated people, without family or friends, there is always someone who is affected by their passing.'

'They clearly feel he is suffering, and that this is not a dignified way to go,' I suggested.

'Like many, they want it to be over because they perceive he is suffering, but in fact it is their own suffering that they are finding hard to bear. And as for dignity? Dignity is a congenial courtesan, paid into service to justify all manner of conflicting viewpoints. Dignity can't be taken from a person, not by illness nor suffering nor circumstance. It can only be relinquished or forfeited, and even then there is a spark of something inherently dignified in every human being.'

'Do you get many families asking you to hasten things along?'

'The desire for it to be over is frequently expressed,

but more rarely do we get families actually requesting that we do something to actively hasten death. Actually, more often we find that there is a general assumption that helping people along is what we routinely do, which is of course entirely untrue. It's a serious problem of perception that we are very conscious of needing to correct, as it may be one of the reasons behind the fear that many people have of coming into the hospice.'

'That and the fact that it's a place where you go to die?'

'Exactly. You'll be aware already that this isn't simply a place where people die. In fact almost half of our patients who are admitted end up being discharged again. They come in for a sort out of their symptoms and many then get home again. Some will end up being re-admitted, sometimes several times, and of course they may end up dying here eventually. The irony is, we are just as much about living as about dying, and it is a shame when people for whom we could do a lot to improve their quality of life shy away from any involvement with us because of fears and preconceived ideas.'

He moved towards the door, signalling that it was time to move on. I wanted to press him further on the issue of hastening death, as I'd found already that we were often using doses of morphine-like drugs and sedatives that would put the wind up most of my colleagues in the hospital, but it was clear that this was not the time to pursue it.

The four-bedded bays were light and roomy, particularly when compared to those in the hospital. At the far end almost the entire wall was taken up by a window opening onto the vista that I had grown to love. Every morning now I sat for a few minutes in the car before entering the hospice, gazing out onto its unassuming splendour. The car park was further down the slope, so the view from these windows, particularly when standing a little way back from the end of the ward, was unadulterated by tarmac and steel. The windows were also south-facing and in the morning, as now, the sun would stream in and interrogate every dark corner, permeating both physical and metaphysical space with warmth and light. Dust particles danced in a frenzy, caught unexpectedly in the glare of its rays like some hapless curfew-breakers, and cards and flowers adorning the tops of bedside lockers seemed braced precariously against their turbulent runs and eddies.

The occupant of the first bed was nowhere to be seen. Photographs of better times defiantly paraded on the bedside table, and a hand-drawn 'get well' card with 'I love you grandma' was proudly attached to the foot of the bed. I always made a point now of looking at these photographs. They gave you a glimpse of who and what these patients were, before their appearance was despoiled by the ravages of disease and treatments. It was the weight loss that was usually the most shocking, and sometimes it was hard to believe that the person in the bed or chair before you was the same man or woman who was so evidently healthy and brimming with life in the photograph. A lifetime of memories lay behind the smiling faces in those photographs; people who had lived and loved and worked and fought and laughed and cried; who had touched the lives of others in a million different ways; who had made a difference, for better or for worse; and whose passing, I was only just beginning to appreciate, mattered not just to those who loved and knew them. And now we too were part of their story, given privileged access to their lives at a time when they were most vulnerable, perhaps most frightened. Often the spark of what they once were before illness seemingly redefined so many aspects of their personhood was still evident, and you'd look at the photographs and think, 'Yes, that figures. I can see that.'

Sarah tidied away some used tissues from the table. 'I should think Mrs Scott is in the smoking room. We called in the family yesterday as she took a turn for the worse and we thought she was on the way. But this morning she sat up and ate a cooked breakfast.' She shrugged her shoulders. 'She's still very frail, though, and can barely move herself around the bed. She gets extremely short of breath on exertion. I suspect this is only a fleeting improvement, and she's already not as good as she was first thing.'

'She's managed to get to the smoking room?' I asked incredulously. I'd seen how unwell she was the previous day.

Brian nodded. 'The need to smoke will recruit previously untapped reserves of strength from within even the sickest patients. Such is the power of addiction. We'll sometimes wheel the bed out the back of the building if people are bed bound and can't manage to sit in the smoking room. We also resort to nicotine patches, particularly in the last days of life when patients may be very weak. Otherwise, nicotine withdrawal may sometimes be a factor in terminal agitation.' He turned to Sarah. 'Presumably she has a patch on?'

'Yes. But she has been a very heavy smoker. Do you want me to get her back to the bed so you can see her?'

'No, let her be. Any particular worries about her?'

'No. Symptoms are well controlled, and family are on board.'

We moved on to the next bed. Mrs Hilda Davies was an elderly lady with cancer of the uterus, or womb. She was looked after by her daughter and had been admitted some days before, having 'gone off her legs'. This was a colloquial term for a sudden deterioration in mobility and there were any number of possible causative factors that could be implicated. In this case it was a urine infection that had caused her deterioration and was the final straw for an already exhausted family. She was acutely confused when she came in, and although her strength and mobility had improved greatly with antibiotics the confusion did not clear completely. It then transpired that she had been intermittently mildly confused for several weeks, and the conclusion was that she probably had early dementia, now more clearly unmasked as a result of her change in environment. She was also partially deaf which added to the potential for confusion. She was pleasantly muddled and would sing quietly when left to herself.

She was sitting in the recliner chair next to her bed. Brian sat on the bed next to her and shook her hand. 'Hello Mrs Davies. I'm Dr Brian Crosbie, and we are coming round together today. How are you feeling?'

'Oh good morning doctor. How nice of you to come and see me. I'm fine thank you.' She wriggled her mildly swollen legs in excitement.

'Well, actually Hilda, you've been having some

tummy pain, haven't you,' Sarah chipped in. 'She's needed several breakthrough doses since yesterday. And I'm not sure she always asks for the extra when she needs it. You sometimes catch her looking quite uncomfortable, and I wonder whether her background dose needs increasing. It was reduced when she came in, in case it was contributing to the confusion.'

The breakthrough doses referred to are the 'as requested' doses of painkiller that are additional to the regular background dose, in her case morphine.

Sarah continued. 'I think we could make you a bit more comfortable Hilda.' She crouched down and squeezed her upper arm.

'Perhaps we'd better feel your tummy, if that's alright.' Brian gestured towards the bed. Sarah helped her stand up and transfer across to the bed while I drew the curtains. As we did so the occupant of the fourth bed in the bay was being wheeled back to her bed, a towel around her head. Brian knelt beside Hilda's bed. 'Where does it hurt?'

'Where does what hurt?'

'Your tummy.'

'Does it?'

'When she's in pain it appears to be in the lower abdomen,' Sarah interjected, saving us from a descent into farce. 'Bowels are working okay.' She had anticipated the next question. I had quickly surmised that bowel habit was something of an obsession in the hospice, and became one of my most frequently asked questions. This was because most of these patients were very prone to constipation, particularly when on strong painkillers.

'Do you sleep well?' Brian persevered, unhurried and gentle. He asked Sarah, 'Does she wake at night with pain?'

'Yes, she's needed breakthroughs during the night.' Sarah didn't have any notes with her, but she was always totally on the ball about the condition and history of everyone in her care. The mark of an experienced sister, I suppose.

'Oh I didn't sleep at all last night.' Hilda sat forward slightly and beckoned Brian closer with a conspiratorial look. 'Of course, the lady across from me had twins last night.' She nodded knowingly and rested back into the pillow.

Curtains round a bed are necessary for dignity's sake during examinations, but provide only a comforting illusion of privacy for conversation. I wondered what the lady across the room made of the news of her two additions. Brian looked at Sarah quizzically. 'She's got a distended abdomen,' Sarah whispered. 'Someone probably quipped that it looked like twins.'

'I'm going to gently feel your tummy,' said Brian. 'You tell me if I hit any sore bits.' Starting at the top of the abdomen he deftly and systematically covered all four quadrants, all the time fixing his gaze on her face to look for signs of discomfort. She winced as he felt her lower abdomen. 'That's the spot, isn't it? Hilda I'd like to get my friend here, Dr David to feel this as well, if that's alright.'

Doctors at the hospice tended to be referred to by title and first name, or simply first name. Brian was the exception in that he was always introduced to patients as Dr Crosbie, almost the only deference to his seniority and experience. Even then he would often end up on first name terms with patients. I'd noticed that Lucy Danvers usually corrected her introduction to her title and full name. This general informality seemed to be to most patients' liking. The only time it was reported to have caused confusion was when a previous doctor introduced as 'Dr Geoff', was mistakenly interpreted by a rather deaf old man as 'Dr Death', and was subsequently referred to as such to his friends and relatives over the next few days. All of them apparently accepted unquestioningly that such a doctor should stalk the wards of a hospice. Strictly speaking, in my own case it ought to be 'Mr David Trevelyan', as I had passed my membership exams for the Royal College of Surgeons, but that would have confused patients. Besides, titles meant little to me, and I could never quite understand why one would study for five years to gain the title of 'Doctor' only to give it up at the first opportunity.

I took Brian's place and felt the abdomen, taking care over the area that I'd seen was tender. There was a large underlying craggy mass that was clearly her enlarging tumour. Brian resumed the dialogue. 'I can see why you've been getting pain Hilda, but I'm sure we can get that easier for you.' He made some adjustments to the prescription chart.

The consultation with Mrs Davies was punctuated by the background noise of the lady diagonally across from us being returned to her bed space, her exchanges with the auxiliary nurse who was helping her, and sounds of rummaging in her locker. The nurse had by now left her, when she suddenly remarked, 'Oh

Marjorie, have you had one of those jacuzzi baths yet? You must, my dear, they're to die for!'

I looked at Sarah and she looked at me and brought a hand up to her mouth to stifle a laugh. We waited with bated breath to see whether there would be any response. Brian remained focused on Mrs Davies, seemingly oblivious to the incident. There was a moment of silence, then some humming, and then the same voice again, a little distractedly, said, 'My, those of yours flowers really are lovely.'

'Well Hilda, is there anything else we can do for you today?' Brian continued with the business at hand.

'No thank you doctor. That's very kind.' Mrs Davies was helped back to her chair and the curtains drawn back, with some trepidation as to the state of the poor lady opposite.

Marjorie Dixon was lying on the bed looking like a frightened rabbit. She was a slight lady in her fifties. She had an obviously distended abdomen that her loose fitting jumper did little to conceal, and which was all the more striking because of her slender frame. She had been transferred from the hospital the previous day, having very recently been diagnosed with terminal cancer of the pancreas, and was shell-shocked and extremely anxious. This wasn't surprising as she'd had one traumatic experience after another over the last three weeks. She had been admitted to hospital as an emergency with severe abdominal pain, and because of her remote location had required evacuation by air ambulance. She had a smallholding and bred chickens which were apparently her pride and joy. The Macmillan nurse recounted that when the air ambulance arrived the down-draught from the rotors sent all the chickens in a nearby pen somersaulting through the air, bundles of feathers flying in all directions, some clearing the fence and landing several yards away and others splayed in various postures of indignity against it.

After initial treatment at the hospital there was a long wait for a bed on a ward, then delayed scans and complications following diagnostic endoscopy. After all this she was given the news that she had cancer of the pancreas that had spread to the liver and throughout the abdomen, that nothing could be done to treat it and that she had only a few weeks to live. Her wish was to see her home again, but she feared she would never leave the hospice.

Brian paused before crossing to greet her, as Lucy Danvers rejoined us. 'Sorry to leave you unannounced,' she said. I had to take a call from Jenny of the Macmillan team. She was ringing about John Watkins. He's running into trouble again at home, escalating pain, and lots of distress in the house. I don't think it's easily manageable at home so I've asked her to send him in.'

'That's fine, thank you. I've been expecting something like that. I'm surprised they've managed so long since we last discharged him.'

He turned his attention back to Mrs Dixon who was staring wide-eyed at the assembled entourage. Before approaching the bed he bent over and smelled the large bouquet of flowers that were arranged in a vase on the table. 'Hmm. I love the smell of freesias. These really are lovely flowers.' He flashed a quick smile at the lady in the next bed. 'Are freesias your favourite?'

'Yes. Yes they are.' She smiled nervously. 'I grow them myself. We manage to cultivate several varieties. I exhibit at flower shows occasionally.'

He approached the bed and clasped her hand. 'Hello Mrs Dixon, I'm Brian Crosbie. May I sit on the bed here?'

'Yes, of course.' She moved her legs across a little.

'I hear you've really been through the mill recently. I can't imagine how you must be feeling.'

Her gaze dropped to the bedclothes. 'Yes.....it's been awful.' Tears welled up and she stifled a sob. 'I'm sorry,' she said. Sarah proffered a tissue, and she looked up and took it. 'Thank you.'

Brian took her hand again, and held her gaze. 'I promise you, we are going to do our very best to make you feel better and get you home again.'

'Oh. Do you think that will be possible? That's all I want.' She half smiled through her tears and her face brightened.

The conversation continued for a few minutes, about husband and family, what she understood about her illness and current symptoms. There followed an examination of her abdomen that confirmed the presence of fluid causing the distension. Although distended, her abdomen wasn't tight or causing much in the way of discomfort at the moment, but the fluid could be drained in a few days time when it was. This would be a very straightforward procedure, but the fluid would inevitably come back over a matter of weeks, and the drainage may need to be repeated in the future. Brian concluded with a summary of the support that was available through the hospice and at home.

'Do you have any particular beliefs that help you when facing something like his? Are you a lady of faith?' he asked.

'I'm not a regular church goer, but I suppose I do believe in God and I've been praying a lot lately.'

'We'll ask our chaplain to stop by and say hello, if you'd like that. He'll happily talk about anything under the sun, and matters of faith of course.'

'Thank you. Yes, I'd like that.'

'There are also all sorts of complementary therapies that might be helpful, if you are into that sort of thing. Sarah can arrange that for you if it is of interest.' He stood up to leave. 'Oh, and you might want to try one of our jacuzzi baths. I understand they're rather good!' He winked and she smiled broadly.

The fourth lady in the bay had now almost finished sorting herself out after the trip to the bathroom, and was sitting on the edge of her bed combing her hair. She had breast cancer that had spread to the bones, and she had been admitted with nausea and vomiting. Blood tests had revealed that she had raised a calcium level as the cause of her symptoms. This is a complication of advanced cancer, but it usually responds to treatment. She had improved dramatically over a period of a few days, and was really rather well despite her advanced disease. She had attended an outpatient appointment at the hospital during her time with us, and she was going to start a course of chemotherapy in the near future. As she was feeling better again, she was going home the following day. She was an exuberant character who had adopted a mothering role towards the other ladies in the bay, being a friend to all, offering help, advice and encouragement, and generally looking out for them. Such patients sometimes needed careful management, as they could be a positive influence in the bay but could also cause problems, especially when their good intentions exceeded their sensitivity. We lingered only briefly at her bedside, Brian exchanging some small talk and clarifying plans for follow-up care.

The next bay was at the moment a male bay. With three open wards and the need to keep them single sex, the hospice was sometimes restricted as to whom it could admit even if there were empty beds. However, the availability of the single rooms meant that some clever juggling of beds could take place to accommodate the shifting demands. Where possible patients who were in the last days of life were prioritised for single rooms, but these might also be needed for those with particularly disfiguring problems or other specific needs. We paused before entering the bay.

'I see John's in here. How long has it been now?' Brian looked to Sarah. This was the John of fish and chips fame.

'He's been with us two months now on this admission. But he is deteriorating. He's spending more time resting on his bed, and sometimes when you see him asleep you do a double-take, wondering whether he's still breathing.' Sarah had a soft spot for John.

'Goodness knows what's keeping him going,' Brian mused.

'Good nursing care, attentive friends, sheer determination.....and fish and chips.' She laughed, and continued. 'Bless him. I think these last few weeks with us have been the first time in his life that he's felt nurtured. He's still a stubborn old sod sometimes though. He'll do it his own way, right to the end.'

'Is he still going out?' Brian asked.

'Yes, but for shorter periods now. I think he'll drop dead one day on the way somewhere.'

'His friends are presumably prepared for that.' It was a statement from Brian rather than a question. 'Are his symptoms still controlled?'

'Yes. The doses in his syringe driver haven't changed for about three weeks now. He's on pretty big doses of diamorphine and midazolam.' She handed Brian the prescription chart.

John was lying on the first bed on the left, fast asleep. Brian stood watching him for a while. 'No need to wake him. I see what you mean. When he's asleep like that all the life seems to drain out of him. How long has Willie been sleeping on his bed?' The big tom was curled up behind the bend of his knees.

'We've found him there over the last couple of days.' Sarah reached down and stroked the back of his neck. Willie opened an eye momentarily and started purring. 'John hasn't made much of him up to now. I didn't think he was a cat sort of person, but he seems quite happy to have him on the bed.'

Brian looked knowingly at Sarah. 'Well, we'll see.'

Willie's presence on the bed had been attributed some significance in the morning meeting the day before, and I had pressed Sally about it later in the day. Willie had been with the hospice for about six years, having turned up out of the blue in the entrance foyer one day. He had a collar with identification tag and his owners had been contacted. He was collected and taken home, but reappeared at the hospice the following day. This went on repeatedly until his owner gave up responding. Willie had adopted the hospice.

No one was absolutely sure, but he was probably around ten years old now. He was doted on by some of the staff, who attended to his every need, and by a good number of the patients over the years. He wandered around the hospice and its grounds with an air of nonchalance and sometimes defiance, particularly in the car park stand-offs with approaching vehicles. He displayed characteristic feline independence, sometimes aloof and reserved, at others affectionate and playful. He could be decidedly grumpy and one proceeded cautiously in evicting him from a chair or desk when that was the favoured spot of the moment. At times he was a highly visible and solid presence, lounging in full view, a definite statement, impacting on those around him; at others he flitted ethereally like a shadow, showing up unexpectedly and then disappearing just as quickly, a spirit permeating every part of the hospice. Very occasionally his behaviour would change radically and he would latch on to a particular patient, sleeping on their bed and never leaving their side. Usually these were patients who, it transpired later, were in the last few days of life, as though he had some sense of this and some reason to connect on a deeper level. As we watched them sleeping back to back one could imagine a silent communication between kindred spirits.

The next two beds were empty, one of them being readied for the urgent admission that was expected later. Relaxing on the fourth bed was a man in his seventies who had lung cancer. He had been admitted ten days before with pain, sickness and loss of appetite. Adjustments to his medication and a course of steroids had transformed the way he was feeling and he was keen to get home as soon as possible. His wife was by the bedside and he was sharing something from one of the cards he had received.

'Hello doctors. How are you today?' He pre-empted our introductions.

'Fine, thank you. And how are you?' Brian shook his hand. 'This must be your good wife. How do you do? I'm Brian Crosbie.' She took his hand enthusiastically.

'Dr Crosbie, Fred's told me all about you. I can't thank you all enough for the wonders you've done. You've given me back my old Fred. We were in a real state before he came in. And he was terrified of coming in, needed a lot of persuading, didn't you Fred, but in the end I think he felt so awful he'd have agreed to anything. Well, look at him now.' She could barely contain her delight.

'That's right. I never thought it would be like this. You've been fantastic, all of you. I shall tell everyone.'

'I'm very glad we've been able to help. I understand you're keen to get home now?'

'Yes please. Oh, that's not to say I don't appreciate it here anymore, but it's not the same as home.'

'I quite agree. Do you need any extra help at home?'

'No, I think we'll manage with what we've got at the moment, thank you.'

'There's an existing care package that we can reactivate once he gets home,' Sarah commented.

'Fine. We'll need to sort out your medicines to take home and arrange some transport.'

'Oh, don't worry about the transport, I can get the bus. There's a direct one from here. Doris uses it to come in to visit.'

'Hmm, I'd rather you let us get you home with proper transport. I don't much like the thought of you on the bus with a week's supply of your morphine and other medicines. We can get our volunteer driver to take you in our minibus.'

'Okay. Thank you.'

'Doctor, is there anything I can do about his eating. It is better since he came in but he's still not eating much at all. I try everything I can think of to get him to eat, I cook all his old favourites, but he just picks at everything. He's lost so much weight, and I throw so much food away. I get a bit cross sometimes, don't I Fred?' She reached out quickly and took Fred's hand.

'It's no good Doris. I try to eat, but I just can't be bothered most of the time.'

'Is there anything we can do doctor?'

Brian leaned forward. 'What you are telling me is not unusual, believe me. Part of the problem is that one of the ways we care for people is to feed them. You Doris are probably thinking that if he could only eat more, he'd feel stronger, fight harder and live longer. The trouble is it just doesn't work like that. When you have a cancer, particularly one that has spread like Fred's has, the way the body uses food changes, the appetite goes and the weight comes off. Even if you were to eat three good meals a day you probably wouldn't put on any weight. On the other hand, forcing yourself to eat, Fred, when your body can't cope with it may make you feel worse. You need to look at food differently now, and you need to throw away your scales! Eat for pleasure rather than because you have to, don't worry about what is healthy or unhealthy, and try eating small amounts more frequently instead of large portions at meal times. And, for goodness sake, don't let eating become a source of stress and argument. You need each other more than ever at this time, and you want to focus on the things that are important.'

'Thank you doctor. That makes more sense now. We'll do our best, won't we Fred?'

'We'll be fine my love. Thank you Dr Crosbie.'

After more shaking of hands we moved on into the corridor. 'Feeding is one of the commonest issues that we find ourselves having to deal with,' Brian remarked. 'Understandably, people worry about weight loss and loss of appetite, and are often concerned about eating the right foods in order to fight the illness. So strong is the drive to nourish that we sometimes have problems with relatives trying to force food or fluid into semi-comatose patients who are nearing death. Actually, there is usually little that can be done to counter the loss of appetite and weight.'

'Steroids presumably help,' I ventured. Steroids, like syringe drivers appeared to be ubiquitous in hospice patients.

'Steroids will often give a short-term boost to appetite and well-being, but it usually only lasts a few weeks. There's a lot of research going on at the moment into the mechanisms underlying the weight loss that we see in advanced cancer, and it's possible that some treatments may be available in the future.'

We moved on to the final bay. Before we entered it,

Lucy Danvers handed Brian a sheet of paper, which he perused before handing it back. He nodded. 'I thought that would be the case. Does he know yet?'

'No. He's expecting to be told today.' It was the result of a CT scan for Duncan Pritchard, one of the patients we were about to see.

'Is his wife in at the moment?'

'Yes. I think I saw her in the coffee shop. I'll fetch her.' Sarah disappeared off towards the entrance foyer, while we pressed on into the bay.

Mr Cox was a man with end-stage cirrhosis of the liver. He had a gaunt face, thin arms and legs, pot belly, yellow skin with characteristic small red blotches like spider's legs, and that slightly vacant 'spaced out' look characteristic of encephalopathy. He had been admitted for drainage of ascites, the fluid that accumulates in the abdomen. That had been done a few days before, but it was rapidly re-accumulating and he was extremely fatigued and weak. He was probably slipping away.

Mr Warburton, who occupied the next bed, was over at the hospital having some radiotherapy to his lower back. He had prostate cancer with bone deposits that had been causing a lot of pain.

The curtains were drawn around the third bed. Some family members were gathered around a man who was unconscious and clearly nearing death. We stayed in the background while Brian knelt by his bed for a while. I watched him as he held the man's hand and gazed at his near lifeless face. Again, I was sure he was whispering something under his breath. He got up and spoke something in hushed tones to the nearest family members, before we took our leave and moved on to the next bed. By this stage Sarah had rejoined us.

Mr Pritchard was sitting in the recliner chair and his wife was now seated next to him, their hands clasped on the arm of the recliner. Brian didn't dwell too long on the usual pleasantries, as it was obvious what was uppermost in their minds.

'Duncan, can we just clarify where we are at the moment. The colon cancer came back in the liver back in November last year and you had some chemotherapy that seemed to work very well. You had another scan in July that showed it had progressed again in the liver and you've completed another three cycles of chemotherapy.'

'Yes, that's right. I have another appointment with oncology next week, when they'll decide whether or not to continue with chemotherapy.'

'So you came into the hospice before the weekend with abdominal pain and vomiting, which I gather has now settled?'

'Yes, I'm feeling fine again. I was worried I wouldn't feel well enough to attend for my scan earlier this week, but I was okay.'

'I have the results of the scan, and could go through those with you if you would like.'

He looked at his wife. She put an arm round him and said, 'Come on darling, we've got to know.'

'Yes. Please tell us what it found.'

'Can I ask what you are expecting it to show?'

'Well, I'm worried things will be a lot worse. That pain really frightened me, and I've noticed that I've been feeling more tired lately.'

'I'm afraid it isn't good news.' Brian paused. He paused for what seemed like an age. He maintained his posture, leaning forward, kind eyes earnestly scanning the faces of the couple in front of him. Tears began to well up in the wife's eyes, and Duncan squeezed her hand.

'Come on darling. It's okay. We were expecting this.' He looked back at Brian and said, 'Please go on.'

'I'm afraid the scan shows that the cancer has spread further.' There was another pause.

A heavy silence lingered for what seemed like minutes but was probably only a few seconds. Everything within me wanted to break it, to say something that would ameliorate the awful reality and its implications that were settling on these two people. Duncan stared blankly into nowhere, trying to process what was happening to him. Finally he spoke again. 'Please go on. I'd like to know.'

'I'm afraid the liver is much worse.....and the cancer has now also spread within the abdomen and to the lungs.'

'Oh God! I haven't got long, have I?' Tears were now streaming down his wife's face, but his own had regained composure, almost a sense of peace.

Brian nodded slowly. 'It's moving on very quickly.'

'And I don't suppose there will be any more chemo-therapy. There's not much point in going next week, is there?'

'I can't imagine they'll be offering any more. I'm really sorry.'

Brian was measured and calm, gentle and unhurried. He gave the impression of having all the time in the world, and for this moment these people and the unutterably awful enormity of what they were trying to take in were the sole focus of his attention and energies. It was as though a spotlight was illuminating this scene of three people in shared space and shared pain, and everyone and everything in the background faded into the shadows. My mind flashed back to some scenes of breaking bad news on previous ward rounds in the hospital wards and outpatient clinics. I recalled patients being told that they had cancer almost as an incidental comment and then left falling apart on their own as the entourage moved on to the next ward. I cringed inwardly at some of the things I'd heard said, and the off-hand way people's shock and grief had sometimes been managed. In any specialty there are good communicators and bad communicators, but what I was witnessing now reinforced just how bad those bad ones were.

'I know that this is devastating for you, and you'll need time for it to sink in properly. Are there any immediate concerns that you want to talk about?'

Duncan sat up a little and inhaled deeply. 'Umm. We'll need to tell the children. Yes, we'll do that as soon as possible. And I need to make a Will.' He sighed. 'I've been meaning to do it for a while, but it's one of those things you just keep putting off.'

'Is there anything else we can do for you at the moment? Anything else you want to ask?'

'No. Not just at the moment. There will be more questions, I'm sure, but not for now.'

'Okay. We'll talk again.'

'Thank you Dr Crosbie.' He turned and embraced his gently sobbing wife, and we left them holding each other.

We moved on to the last two single rooms. In the first was Deirdre, a woman with motor neurone disease. She was in her early fifties and had been diagnosed only a few months before. Her disease had initially affected predominantly her swallowing and speech, but it had progressed rapidly and she now had some weakness of the limbs and respiratory muscles. She had a feeding tube directly into her stomach, having lost the ability to swallow anything. She had been admitted largely for respite and a review of her home situation. She lived alone, a divorcee, and was determined to remain independent, but it was becoming increasingly difficult for her to manage. She had a daughter who did her best to support her, but she had a full time job and family to support. Deirdre was no longer able to speak, and instead used an electronic communication device whereby she typed a message on a small keyboard and a synthesised voice spoke out what she had written. Consultations were often quite long and involved because of this, and I was rather relieved to find that she was fast asleep when we entered her room. She usually needed a visit separate from the ward round in order to give her the time that she needed.

Brian stood and watched her for a while. She was sitting in the chair with her neck twisted and her chin resting on her chest. She had a bib covering her upper chest and this was damp from the saliva that dribbled almost continuously from her mouth. Her neck muscles were not strong enough to maintain normal head posture, and because of this she had developed a pressure sore on her chin where it contacted the chest. She had been given a supporting collar, but she didn't like it and up to now had refused to wear it. She was very strong minded and could appear cantankerous and stubborn at times, but most of those caring for her were very fond of her.

Sarah spoke her name softly to see whether she was awake. There was no response. Brian motioned not to wake her. 'How on earth has she been managing alone at home?' He shook his head, and looked at Sarah. 'Was she managing her own feeds?'

'Just about, but it was becoming more difficult as she's losing function in the hands and arms.' Deirdre briefly opened an eye, and it was apparent that she was awake but she ignored us and continued in her repose. Brian and Sarah hadn't noticed.

'That pressure area's very quickly going to become a problem. See if we can talk her round to wearing the collar, or at least have some more cushioning under the chin.'

'We'll work on it,' Sarah replied. 'Last time I mentioned it was the first time I've been sworn at by a machine.' Sarah spoke her name softly again, but there wasn't a flicker from Deirdre. She obviously wanted to be left alone.

In the next room was a lady who had malignant melanoma and an open wound in her groin. The tissues of the groin and thigh were breaking down as a result of cancer infiltration and infection. The wound was very malodorous and despite the best efforts of the nurses with various dressings and air fresheners there was always a lingering smell. She bore the whole thing very stoically and remained incredibly cheerful in the face of the gradual disintegration of her upper leg.

We didn't go in to see her as her dressings were being changed at the time. I was again relieved, as the smell was not something that one easily gets used to, and one that I preferred to avoid just before lunch.

Brian thanked Sarah and we made our way back to the doctors' office. We passed the drinks trolley on the way as it was being steered into one of the bays by an elderly lady volunteer. This was a bit of an institution in the hospice, and a very popular one, offering a free tipple to patients as an aperitif before lunch. The lady greeted Brian warmly and paused while he asked after her husband. The lunch trolley had already taken up station at the other end of the ward and steaming trays were being shuttled to and fro between the bays. We arrived at the office to find Sheila talking to a stocky middle-aged man with dishevelled black hair who was perched on the edge of the desk. He was wearing a checked open necked shirt with a cravat, and a tweed sports jacket with a stethoscope dangling out of the side pocket. He jumped up on seeing us enter.

'Hello Gordon! Good to see you. How are you?' Brian reached out and shook his hand enthusiastically. There was an obvious camaraderie between them.

'Hello Brian. Hi Lucy. I'm fine, thanks. I had a great holiday.' He had a Scottish accent, probably Edinburgh.

'And how's GP land?' asked Brian.

'Oh, you know. The usual. Mad as ever. My desk is buried in paperwork, and I'm ranting against the latest round of diktats from the powers on high. I spend more time these days turning well people into patients than I do looking after the genuinely sick. It's a great relief to come here and regain some sanity!'

'You mean a different kind of insanity!' Sheila interjected, and they all laughed.

'Gordon can I introduce our new colleague to you, David Trevelyan.' We shook hands. 'David joined us this week, and he's in at the deep end already. David, this is Gordon Mackay. He's a senior partner at one of our local GP practices, and he helps us out here.'

'A pleasure to meet you. I do a couple of afternoons a week, Thursdays and Fridays, so these two can go off and do other important things like teaching and research, and give the hospital the benefit of their wisdom.' He winked at Lucy Danvers. 'I also cover the on-call on a Thursday night and some weekends. I'm not as expert as the rest of the team, but I'm learning all the time. And this lot keep a close eye on me to make sure I'm not killing anybody!' He grinned mischievously.

'Don't you believe it,' retorted Brian. 'It's Gordon who keeps us on our toes. It's very easy to become inward looking and a bit nihilistic in this job, and he brings a fresh perspective from someone who is at the coal face of acute medicine, and whose patients don't all die!' There was more general laughter. 'Gordon, the ward is pretty quiet, but we're expecting John Watkins back in this afternoon. His pain's out of control again. I think we're reaching the stage of thinking about spinal analgesia, so it might be worth contacting the pain team at the hospital. See how he is when he comes in. Is it okay if Lucy gives you a quick handover? I've a couple of phone calls to make first, but I can meet you all in the dining room for lunch?'

They nodded in agreement, and disappeared into the nurses' office to look at the notice board that had a ward plan indicating the names of patients occupying each bed. Brian turned to me and asked, 'How are you finding it so far David?'

'Well, I think I'm finding my feet. It's a very different emphasis, and I'm not familiar with some of the drugs and doses, but I think I'm picking it up quite quickly.'

'Good. The major adjustment is to the different emphasis in care and the way that can affect treatment decisions. How are you coping with the death and dying?'

'It's all pretty intense at times. I expect you get used to it and develop ways of dealing with it.'

'It is a difficult line to walk sometimes. We need to engage with it in an empathic way in order to be of any use. Much of the time all we have to offer is ourselves. But at the same time we need to be sufficiently detached in order to cope with the constant exposure to suffering. Every death we witness, each time we draw alongside the suffering, lays a feather of grief on our shoulders. An individual feather doesn't weigh much at all, but accumulate a lot of them and they can start to weigh you down. You need to have ways of offloading. Do you have any ways of offloading?'

'Perhaps I'll have to develop some more.'

'It's not the kind of work that everyone is suited to, and even among those who are there are casualties. The doctor you replaced had to leave because of burnout. He was an excellent hospice doctor, caring and compassionate, a first rate clinician. He suddenly succumbed to the stress and couldn't face the work any longer. The alarming thing was that to us it seemed to come out of the blue. He'd apparently been struggling for a while, but we were unaware of it.' He paused. 'Think about it. And if you ever feel it is beginning to get on top of you, do say something, won't you?' He smiled and left the room.

I sat down and set about writing in the patients' notes, to the background accompaniment of Sheila tapping away on the keyboard.

I stood in the room of rest and looked down at John Tucker's lifeless form on the bed. He had died that morning just after dawn. The nurses had recently checked that bay but were alerted to go back by Willie running out and past the nurses' station. His death was announced in the morning meeting together with some brief details of his last hours. He'd seemed no different the evening before, and had appeared to sleep peacefully during the night. He just slipped quietly away, unnoticed in dying much as he had been unnoticed in living. There was a moment of silence, everyone's gaze averted to the floor, lost in thought or silent remembering. It wasn't long or formal, but it was definite and collective, and I recognised it again and again over subsequent meetings as the way the passing of someone who had particularly impacted the team was marked, an instinctive and communal sacrament of respect. I had now come to inspect the body in order to complete the death certification paperwork.

He had been washed and laid out, the bedclothes neatly tucked around him and arms folded across his chest. He looked serenely peaceful, washed by the dappled light of a partially overcast morning, the creases that had marked his face somehow smoothed out, his hair neatly combed across his forehead. There was soft music playing in the background. The door opened and Sarah came into the room. She stopped abruptly when she saw me.

'Sorry David, I didn't realise you were in here.'

'Don't worry, I've finished.' I turned to go.

Sarah headed across to the window. 'Oh. They've forgotten to open the window.' She started unlatching it.

'To let some air in?' I suggested, as I headed to the door. There wasn't any particular smell yet, as he'd only been dead about four hours.

'No. To let his spirit out.' She started humming.

As I approached the doorway I saw Willie standing looking into the room. He miaowed softly, gave a swish of his tail and sauntered slowly up the corridor.

Chapter 3
Relatives

You couldn't miss it as you walked into the room. No matter how hard you tried to focus on her face, your eyes were always initially drawn to the mass sitting atop her chest, grotesquely distorting the contours of her body. Celia was a lady in her sixties who had a rare form of cancer, a type of sarcoma, which had spread to her right breast and had long escaped the confines of the normal breast tissue. The tumour was large and predatory, and as she lay in the bed on her back, which increasingly was the only position in which she could get comfortable, it appeared to dominate her like some misogynistic parasite, pinning her down and plundering the very essence of her womanhood.

As the tumour grew larger she grew progressively weaker, the strength and energy sapped from her body in order to satisfy the voracious appetite of the monstrosity that was gradually subsuming her. To add the final insult the skin and tissue over the tumour was now beginning to break down and ooze a foul smelling bloodstained liquid that soaked through two dressing changes per day. The one mercy was that she experienced remarkably little in the way of pain. Despite the ravages of illness you could still see, like a watermark on crumpled paper, the elegant and beautiful woman that she had been and that still looked out from the photographs by the bedside. She bore her condition with inspirational courage and dignity, a quiet acceptance, and with deep gratitude for any service or care rendered.

However, perhaps more inspirational still was her husband, Denys, who rarely left her side. He attended to her every need, helping out with her care, and largely taking responsibility for her changes of dressing. He spoke to her tenderly and lovingly, constantly affirming his 'beautiful Celia', reassuring and encouraging while never denying the reality of what they were both facing. He would sit by the bed holding her hand and reading to her when she was too tired to continue reading herself. He'd hold up the mirror for her to apply some token makeup every morning, her own defiant gesture against the undermining of her femininity, and help steady her hand when the effort became too great. He only left her side during those times when she was asleep, and he'd quickly return and sit gazing into her face, sometimes stroking the hair off her forehead or speaking softly into her dreams.

They shared an open and relaxed intimacy and devotion that I had not previously seen, and in all the times I attended them there was never a hint of bitterness or regret, never a tear or frown. The future didn't seem to impinge upon their present; rather they appeared wholly absorbed in the moment and with each other. I always came away from the single room that she had occupied for two weeks now with almost a sense of envy. I wondered whether I would ever love or be loved that much.

Today their example was glorified by the contrast with the family scene in the bay that I had just left. Florence was a slight lady, also in her sixties, with cancer of the stomach. She had been admitted on the premise of controlling her symptoms, but in truth it had been to get her away from her family situation and give her some respite. She lived on a farm with her husband and grown up son, and while they did the farm work it seemed she was expected to do everything else. There was little allowance made for her deteriorating health and increasing fatigue, and in her passivity she didn't appear to expect any. Husband and son would turn up every day just before lunch and sit by her bed, husband staring at her and son reading the newspaper. Occasional monosyllabic exchanges would take place and they would leave after an hour or so, but not before seeking one of us out to ask when they could expect her home as 'the house needs keeping.'

There was a daughter who always turned up separately and was clearly very close to her mother. She had flown the nest a long time before, by her own account in order to escape the oppressive atmosphere, and this with her mother's blessing, but you could see that she was now racked with guilt about leaving her mother to cope on her own. Florence, for her part, was uncritical and uncomplaining, seemingly resigned to her situation and unquestioning about a relationship in which love and devotion had long since given way to duty. We did what we could to prolong her stay with us while we worked at persuading them to accept some extra help in the house.

As I emerged from the single room I was aware of a rumpus further down the corridor. Raised voices and expletives were emanating from one of the bays. I hurried down to see what was happening and entered onto a scene of utter pandemonium by the standards I'd come to appreciate in the hospice, though reminiscent in its choler of a few incidents I'd witnessed in the hospital. The drinks trolley was parked near the bed in the far right corner, which I knew to be occupied by a man with liver cancer. His wife, a rather beefy and coarse woman, was standing on one side of the trolley and leaning across with her face inches away from that of the elderly volunteer on the other side, who was deathly pale and wide eyed in terror and shock. The wife was yelling at full volume at the hapless lady, who was starting to shake a little and looked as though she might be on the point of fainting. The man on the bed was trying to say something to pacify the situation, but he was clearly too frail and exhausted to put in much of an effort and fairly soon he sank back onto the pillow. Another younger woman, presumably his daughter, was reaching up from a chair by the bed in a rather ineffectual attempt to draw her mother away. The other patients and one or two visitors by the other beds were looking on in shocked disbelief at the scene unfolding before them.

An auxiliary nurse came into the bay close on my heels and made straight for the volunteer who was now looking very precarious on her feet. The wife continued her tirade, pausing only to take breaths, her face becoming progressively more puce. 'You fucking stupid idiot! Bloody alcohol is what has got him into this mess. What kind of moron are you?'

Her husband's cancer had developed on a background of alcoholic liver cirrhosis and the offer of a lunchtime drink had obviously lit this woman's touch paper. Months, perhaps years of pent up anger seemed to have erupted and was being unleashed on the poor victim before her. I moved in and made to separate the two of them, while the nurse put her arms round the volunteer's shoulders and shepherded her to a nearby chair. She collapsed onto it sobbing. The wife's attention now focused on me as the surrogate target.

'Mrs Jenkins, may I ask you to please calm down. We have some very sick people in here.' She glowered at me.

'Yes! And my husband is one of them. I won't calm down sonny. He's a fucking alcoholic. What kind of place is this, offering drinks to an alcoholic?'

I backed off a little and tried not to look threatening, desperately trying to remember my conflict resolution training. 'I'm very sorry that you have been upset, really I am. Can we come away to some other place and talk about it?' She seemed to grow bigger, and I sensed I wasn't getting very far. I remembered that the family came from one of rougher areas of the city, where arguments tended to be resolved with fists.

'Come on Mum, let it go.' The daughter's attempt was rather half-hearted, even pathetic. In fact she was suppressing a smile, and I guessed she was probably enjoying the spectacle. I was trying to see where the panic button was located in the bay without making it too obvious that I was doing so, when I heard a familiar Irish accent behind me.

'My, my, what a commotion!' Cathy walked calmly

and purposefully across the bay towards the wife, touching me lightly on the shoulder as she passed.

There was almost a tangible relief in the bay in the wake of her progress across the floor. She bore a presence that seemed to permeate the atmosphere and dissipate the mounting tension. The wife appeared to shrink in stature and the heat faded from her face as Cathy approached her and gently took hold of her arm. 'Mrs Jenkins, I can see there's been a bit of a misunderstanding. Come with me and we'll have a chat about it, shall we?'

My jaw dropped as I watched the wife meekly allowing herself to be led away. She looked puzzled and slightly vacant, winded by the wave that had broken over her. Cathy winked at me as she passed. 'Val would you take Agnes and get her a cup of tea please? I'll come and have a chat with her in a minute.' She disappeared out of the bay, followed shortly by nurse and volunteer.

I checked on Mr Jenkins and apologised for any distress we'd caused him. He was too exhausted to say much other than that it wasn't a problem for him at all. I reassured the remaining patients before escorting the trolley back to its station.

When I got back to the nurses' office there was a buzz about the incident with Mrs Jenkins. Val, the auxiliary nurse, had deposited Agnes in the coffee shop with the volunteer coordinator, a cup of tea and a scone, and had returned to duty on the ward where she was now sharing every detail of what had happened.

'Almost savaged by the Rottweiler I hear David?' Tina was another of the auxiliary nurses, feisty and fresh, and wonderful with the patients. We enjoyed a healthy camaraderie and a frequent exchange of banter.

'Yes. I thought it might turn nasty at one point. Mind you, it already had for poor Agnes. I'm not sure she'll ever want to man the trolley again.'

'David, did you see Mr Phillips?' Sally was in conference with one of the staff nurses at the far desk. 'Apparently his daughter rang wanting to speak to his doctor. We were both out on the ward so Sheila suggested she phone back later.'

'Which daughter was it?' Lorna chipped in, a little alarmed. She was the staff nurse who was responsible for that bay. 'Was it the step-daughter or his real daughter? He was estranged from his real daughter for a while and doesn't want us to communicate any information about him directly to her. There's a lot of bad feeling and bitterness there and some complicated family dynamics. Wife, ex-wife, mistress are all on the scene. I think he's playing them all off against each other.'

'Current mistress,' Val interjected. 'He's been a right lad, by all accounts. He was a bit of a ladies' man in his time. He was telling me all about it in the bath yesterday.'

It's a fact that many patients are most open with the auxiliary nurses, sharing deeply of themselves in those exchanges and conversations while receiving care or being toileted and bathed.

Val continued. 'I really like him. He's got a wicked sense of humour. He says he thinks they're all hovering, waiting for his money, like vultures at the carcass. But he's going to surprise them all because he's leaving it all to the hospice!'

'Well,' Lorna replied, 'I'm getting very confused

about what I'm supposed to say to which member of his entourage. I'm a bit worried someone who isn't aware of the problems is going to put their foot in it.' She turned back to her paperwork.

'Right,' I said. 'Presumably we've documented it all in the notes? I'll remember to be careful.' I sighed. 'What happened to normal families?'

'What's normal?' said Sally.

'Well, my family's normal, I think. We all get on pretty well, and at least we're all talking to each other. I'm discovering that reality is a lot stranger than fiction sometimes.'

'You bet. Soap operas and sitcoms have nothing on this place!' retorted Tina.

'David, did you get round everyone at your end of the ward?' Sally beckoned me over.

'Yes, all sorted for the moment. Mr Campbell is on the way. I should think it'll be today. Family have been called in. How about you?'

'I didn't get very far. I've just spent about an hour and a half with Deirdre. She's refusing to have anything else down her tube. She says she's had enough, and if she can't manage at home she'd rather not be anywhere. Her daughter's distraught, but Deirdre is adamant.'

Deirdre was the lady with motor neurone disease who had been in a few weeks before. We'd managed to get her home again after she finally agreed to have some help in the house, but she had deteriorated further and the situation at home had become untenable. Her daughter had even given up her job in order to support her mother at home, but the physical burden of caring was now too much. Everything in terms of medication and nutrition was going through her feeding tube, and her refusal to have anything further put down the tube meant that she would probably die within a few days.

Sally continued. 'We'll need to put up a syringe driver as she's been on morphine, and she'll soon need some sedative. At least she's agreed to have the driver.'

'It's getting a bit messy ethically, isn't it?' I asked. 'She's effectively starving and dehydrating herself to death and we are easing her passage.' It seemed decidedly uncomfortable. 'Are we sure she knows what she's doing?'

'Well, communication is painfully slow as she has to use her machine, but I've been through it several times and I'm convinced she's competent to make the decision. She has a right to refuse any treatment, and tube feeding is deemed in law to be a medical treatment. We can't force anything on her.'

'Do we need to get a psychiatric opinion? What if she's really depressed?'

'She probably is, but not in a way that would respond to treatments. She's dying, and some would say pretty horribly. I offered to get someone else to talk it through with her and she told me, or rather the machine told me where to go! She wouldn't cooperate for any assessment, and in practice what could we do even if she was depressed? She's terminally ill.'

'It just doesn't feel comfortable. We're now going to sedate her.'

'You need to separate the act of refusing the treatment from palliation of her symptoms. We're now faced with someone who is more than likely in the last days of life, regardless of how she's got there. She may need something for agitation, distress, secretions just like any other of our dying patients. We are providing symptom control, not assisting a suicide.'

'Right, I think I see what you mean. I'll need to go away and ponder this.'

'Would you be able to finish off my end of the ward? I've said I'll spend some time with her daughter now.'

❦

'Dr David, when I'm at home will I be able to have sex again?'

The question took me completely by surprise, and threw me off balance. I'd seen Belinda several times since she had been admitted and nothing on this subject had even been hinted at. I usually tried to have one of the nurses accompany me when seeing patients, but this afternoon I had set off on my own to finish the bays that Sally hadn't managed to complete. It was probably the fact that there was no one else looking on that finally made her comfortable to open up on a new level.

Belinda was a lady in her forties with cancer of the cervix. It had spread to her bones and into her lungs, and she had a large deposit of cancer at the top of her vaginal vault. The tissue was fragile and prone to bleeding. Sexual intercourse might be uncomfortable and would be risky. I desperately tried to conceal my sense of awkwardness, and say something positive and natural.

'Umm.' That's all I could come up with. I cringed inwardly.

'My husband doesn't really get intimate any more. He barely hugs me. Don't get me wrong, he loves me to bits. I think he's afraid.....afraid I'll break or that he'll hurt me.' There was a forlorn sadness in her voice. 'The thing is, I need him, and I need that intimacy, now more than ever. I'm feeling so alone, so dirty, untouchable.'

I swallowed hard. 'The thing is Belinda, having sex isn't completely ruled out, but it isn't without problems. You've had a lot of pain from the pelvic bones, so any weight on that area might be very uncomfortable.' I tried to sound as matter of fact as possible. She looked pleadingly into my eyes, desperate for my approval, as if I had the power to grant or withhold this request to fulfil her deepest need.

'That wouldn't matter. I'd accept that,' she said.

'The other thing is that there would be a risk of bleeding from the tumour at the top of the vagina. You'd have to be very careful, but you'd only know by trying.' She looked down, and I could detect the disappointment.

'Thank you.' The window onto this deeper level of her emotional pain closed again.

The consultation continued a little longer, covering arrangements for her discharge home later in the week and follow up thereafter.

I came away with a profound sense of guilt. She had trusted me enough to open up about something so intimate and I felt I had let her down, unable to give her the unqualified release that she had hoped for. I couldn't go on to see the remaining patients yet, I had to regain my composure. I walked back up the ward and leant with my elbows on the nurses' station with chin in hand. I glanced through the numerous thank you cards that were strewn across the top of the station, a litany of effusive gratitude and goodwill from relatives and friends, the names of their loved ones therein a roll-call of recently discharged and deceased patients, many of whose faces were already beginning to fade in my recollection. This was a shitty job sometimes. Cancer is a shitty disease. I sighed softly, lost in thought.

Sarah came up and stood on the opposite side of the station. 'Are you okay David?'

I sighed again. 'Not really. I've just been to see Belinda.' I recounted the conversation we'd had and my complete sense of inadequacy.

She thought for a moment. 'Umm. All's not lost. There are ways and means.'

'What do you mean?'

'It's not just about penetration. And there are positions that don't result in deep penetration. The spoon position for instance.'

'The spoon position?'

'Yes. Lying on their sides with husband behind.' She demonstrated with her cupped hands. 'That way she doesn't take any of his weight either. Penetration is less deep and there's much less chance of bleeding from the tumour.'

'That hadn't even occurred to me. I was so befuddled by her asking the question.' I blushed.

'Don't worry. Shall I go and have a discreet chat with her?'

'Would you? Thanks.'

She patted me on the shoulder. 'Listen David, it's a tribute to you that she felt able to open up to you. Don't beat yourself up.' She smiled and headed off down towards the bay.

I lingered for a while at the station. Claire, one of the staff nurses came up. 'David, Mr Campbell died about half an hour ago. The family are keen to have the paperwork before they go rather than having to come back another time. Would you mind seeing him now and doing the death certificate?'

'Yes, that's fine. Is he still in his room or has he been moved?'

'He's still in there, and the family are in there too, but they know you've got to examine him.' She continued on down towards the sluice. 'Oh, and prepare yourself. It's a bit surreal in there.'

I knocked gently on the door to the single room and pushed it open. Six relatives of varying ages were seated around the bed, drinking tea and eating scones. The late Kenneth Campbell was sitting propped up against the pillows, chin on chest and his tam-o-chanter cap on his head cocked at a jaunty angle. A flag of St Andrew was draped across the back of the bed. There was a lively banter going on, interspersed with laughter, with comments and jibes periodically directed to Mr Campbell as if to include him in the conversation.

'Good afternoon doctor. Come to do the business? Don't mind us, you just carry on. Kenny will give you no trouble.' The thick Glaswegian accent belonged to one of Mr Campbell's brothers.

I squeezed through the opening that he made for me by drawing his chair back slightly and set about listening on the chest for heart and breath sounds that I knew would not be there. I'd always been so meticulous in the hospital on the rare occasions when I'd had to confirm a death, but these days it was beginning to seem an unnecessary formality. It was obvious to me and everyone else that he was dead. Going through the motions today seemed to add to the farce of the situation that I was witnessing.

'Isn't that right Kenny? Hey, do you remember that time in Ibiza.....'

I tried hard to concentrate on listening above the chatter going on behind me. After the required minute I checked his pupils and folded my stethoscope into my pocket. I turned to go.

'So what's the verdict doctor? Och, you're not going to tell us it's all been a mistake, are you? Our Kenny's always been a prankster, but he's been holding his breath a long time!' There was general laughter.

'Thank you. I'll sort out the certificate.' I smiled, and exited the room as gracefully as possible.

As I came out I bumped into one of the volunteers bringing another tray of refreshments, a fresh faced youth probably doing some volunteer work in the hospice to enhance his CV or as part of his Duke of Edinburgh Award. 'This is for the man in this room,' he said. It was more of a question that a statement. I took the tray from him.

'I think it's best if I take that in. Thank you. I'll see to this.' He handed over the tray and ambled off towards the kitchen, none the wiser. The mind boggled at what he would have made of the scene within. I braved it once more and returned to the office to complete the death certificate.

A little later, as I was finishing Sarah came up beside me and pulled up a chair.

'Belinda's fine. We've had a talk and she's much happier.'

'That's a relief. I hope she doesn't feel I've betrayed a confidence.'

'Quite the opposite. She's very grateful that you listened and took her seriously.' She smiled enigmatically. 'There's one thing though. She's asked if you could talk to her husband about it. Put him in the picture and sort of give him permission......'

'Oh, you're kidding?'

'She thinks he'll be less embarrassed and will talk more easily about the whole business if it comes man to man. She trusts you and wants it to come from you.'

There were two large ice cream tubs full of packets of tablets and bottles of potions. I sorted through them painstakingly, correlating each one with the extensive list of medications that her husband had furnished. It had been a bizarre consultation. Vanessa was a lady in her thirties who had breast cancer that had spread to her liver, bones and her brain. She was deteriorating quickly and the likelihood was that she wouldn't be leaving us again. She had presented with a small breast lump about eighteen months before and had declined the usual conventional treatments. She and her husband were opposed to orthodox medicine, preferring instead to use dietary and alternative therapies. He had packed her off to South America to some clinic where she had received some bizarre treatments, no doubt at significant cost.

Six months later her cancer had grown substantially and she finally agreed to have surgery. At operation she was found to have cancer in her lymph glands as well, but she declined hormonal treatments, radiotherapy or chemotherapy. Since then she had been under the care of someone in London who was peddling some experimental 'natural' therapies, convinced all the while that they were working despite increasing pain and malaise. She had finally agreed to be admitted to hospital a month before and the diagnosis of extensive disease was confirmed. She did agree to some radiotherapy for pain control, but declined chemotherapy, which was too late anyway.

Apart from some medication for pain and sickness she was currently taking sixty-two tablets and capsules and three suppositories per day of 'natural' remedies. She was finding it increasingly difficult to swallow such a dispensary and I got the impression that she was getting tired and beyond caring, and only acquiescing in the face of her husband's undiminished evangelistic fervour about their health beliefs. I fumed inwardly. I'd never had much time for alternative treatments, but had always reasoned that if that's what people were into that was their business. However, I'd never come across anyone taking such an extreme position before. Here was someone who might have been cured if she'd had appropriate treatment from the start. It seemed a tragic waste.

Sally came into the office looking flustered. 'I've just spent another age with Deirdre's daughter. She's really struggling with what's happening. Sharon and Nick are involved, but she caught me as I was leaving the ward. I think she's latching on to anyone who can give her time.'

'How's Deirdre?' I asked.

'Just hanging in there. She's too weak to communicate now, but seems reasonably settled. Have you seen the new lady?'

'Yes. Vanessa Meakin. It's quite a tale.' I recounted the background and my frustrations. 'I can't believe someone would take such an irrational position.'

'Ah. People and their beliefs. Maybe I'm getting too long in the tooth, but not much surprises me any more.'

'Have you come across any similar situations before?'

'I've come across some very strange health beliefs. In some people I think this sort of thing is merely a form of denial, but many people have beliefs of all kinds that may not seem rational to others. Faith reaches beyond what can be materially demonstrated and may be held in the face of what others would see as evidence to the contrary. For some it is simply a lifestyle choice or a cultural norm that is different to our own.'

'But in this case her beliefs have actually led to harm,' I protested.

Sally thought for a while. 'How do we know for sure? She may have lived longer than she would otherwise have done. She may well have progressed and died anyway, and had to put up with side effects of conventional treatments on the way. Don't underestimate the power of belief – after all the whole placebo effect relies on it. Everyone to his own, that's what I've come to accept. Take Joyce Riley for instance.' Joyce was another of our current inpatients. 'Her religious beliefs are sustaining her during a slow and unpleasant dying process with an equanimity and serenity that I know I wouldn't find within me. Now I'm an agnostic at best, but I can't deny the power of what is at work in her. That's not to say that I haven't seen others die equally serenely who had no such faith at all. But if that's what works for her as she faces the reality of death, then all power to her elbow! When it's my turn to return to dust I'll need plenty of gin and any pharmacological agent to which I have access to numb the reality of what's happening.' She laughed.

'What do I do about all these drugs that Mrs Meakin has been taking?'

'Does she still want to take them?'

'She seems to. I'm just not happy prescribing this rubbish. I've no idea whether there are any interactions with other drugs she might need; they can't possibly be helping at all; and I feel that if I prescribe them I'm endorsing them as legitimate treatments.'

'Well, the alternative is to just give them all back to her and let her self-medicate them. Presumably her husband has been administering them up to now? The drawback with that is that we can't keep an eye on what she's having. As she deteriorates she'll struggle even more to take them, and the point will be reached when she'll need permission or direction not to try taking them any longer. If we are controlling the administration that might be easier than if her husband is doing so. Distraught people find it harder to make those sorts of decisions and to let go of things they are convinced might be helping.'

I mulled this over as Sally set about rewriting a drug chart. One of the staff nurses came in and asked, 'David, were you going to see Mrs Meakin's parents? They're here expecting to see a doctor.'

'Oh yes. She asked me to pick them up when they arrived. Can you show them to the small sitting room and I'll be along in a second?' I finished writing up an entry into her notes and then found her parents. They were sitting together holding hands and looking lost. We got through the introductions.

The father spoke first. 'Doctor, thank you for seeing us. We won't take up much of your time. We know that Vanessa is very poorly and we are fully expecting her to die soon.' The mother started weeping quietly. The father squeezed her hand and continued. 'Sorry. It's very hard to see your child suffer and die. It's not right, not the way things should be. She had so much life left in her.' He paused and looked to the floor, fighting to hold his composure. 'It's all the harder when you know it might not have been necessary if she'd had the right treatment.'

'Presumably you know the background?' It was the mother. Her body seemed to tense with a surge of emotion that invigorated her for a moment. 'We pleaded with her, but she wouldn't listen. We can't help blaming Mark, her husband. I'm afraid there's bad feeling there now.'

'I can see that it's hard,' I offered hesitantly, 'but she presumably made her own choices. She must have understood what she was doing and the possible implications?'

'We're not sure she really did. She was under his influence, you see. She never had these strange health ideas till she met him. She's always been eager to please and we can't help thinking that she went along with it all for him.'

'But in the end, wasn't that her decision to make?' I was sounding like Sally.

The father sighed, and continued. 'None of this

matters any more. What's done is done. Doctor we just wanted to ask that you do all that you can to make sure she doesn't suffer. He's still pouring all kinds of stuff into her, and she just can't manage now. He won't be keen on her having the usual medication that I presume many people need to help them at this stage. We're just asking, please will you give her whatever she needs. We can't bear to think of our baby suffering.'

He was in tears now, and I was almost choking up myself. I steadied myself. 'I promise you, we'll do whatever we can to make sure she's comfortable.'

'Thank you so much.' They got up, shook my hand and left the room, his arm around her sagging shoulders.

I returned to the office and flopped down at the desk. I looked again at the collection of pills and potions, and thought for a while. I nodded my head and started laboriously writing them up on the prescription chart.

The morning meeting had begun with some good news, though it had little impact on me. Roger Forbes attended the meeting once a month as he felt it was important to keep in touch with the issues that the clinical team faced. This morning he announced that there had been news in the last week of two substantial legacies that would be coming the hospice's way. Suddenly a potential deficit budget was looking a lot healthier. The hospice depended in large part on such legacies, but they were unpredictable both in timing and amount.

Neither Cathy nor Brian was at the meeting, and Sally was having a day off, so Sarah was leading and

Lucy Danvers provided the senior medical input. Nick, Sharon and the physiotherapist made up the complement. Late autumn rain lashed against the window, driven by a howling wind, a Faustian symphony of noise and menace, and the gloom outside seemed to me to permeate the room despite the overhead light and the two table lamps. I felt a heaviness probably born out of tiredness following a difficult few days.

While nowhere near as physically tiring as the long hours on the hospital wards, this kind of work had its own stresses and could be very draining. My mood hadn't been helped by the complete drenching I'd received in getting to work. I had then received a tongue lashing from the bereaved husband of a young woman for whom I had completed a death certificate the previous morning, only I had inadvertently omitted to sign it. He had presented it at the Registry Office later that afternoon to be told that it was not valid. We had arranged for him to attend first thing this morning to have it signed, and my perceived incompetence had been a switch to unleash a torrent of pent up emotion that was looking for a convenient outlet. I came away emotionally battered and bruised, but acutely aware that this was nothing compared to what he was enduring, having lost his wife and mother to his two young children. Nevertheless, it all contributed to a sense of weariness. Perhaps it was time I had a break.

Everyone else in the room seemed their usual selves, chatting animatedly. Sarah kicked off the meeting. 'We had an admission yesterday. Mrs Shaw, a fifty-six year old lady with bowel obstruction from a carcinoma of the ovary. She's actually okay, symptoms reasonably well controlled, but she's apparently deteriorating steadily. The main concern for us is her husband who has been totally dependent on her for almost everything. Her Macmillan nurse is very worried about how he'll cope as he has very few practical skills around the house. She did everything, from keeping house to managing their financial affairs. Apparently he can barely make himself a cup of tea without her direction. You'll need to be involved ASAP Sharon. We'll need to support him emotionally, but also practically, and maybe teach him a few life skills while there's still time.'

'Oh the variety in hospice work!' Nick exclaimed.

'Yes,' Sarah replied, 'and he's going to be quite hard work. He's already being very demanding of nurses' time, constantly coming to find us for something or other. He's absolutely devoted to her and everything has to be just right.'

'Perhaps that might be another area we can branch out into,' Roger added. 'St. Julian's life skills training. It could be a money spinner!' He grinned mischievously.

'Be quiet Roger!' Nick retorted, with feigned consternation. 'The family is a unit of care, remember. His needs impact on her needs.'

'Just teasing Nick. I'm proud that we are still prepared to care 'outside the box'. It makes us what we are.'

'I'll pick them up today.' Sharon brought us back to business.

'Moving on. Mr Bradshaw is dying and the family are very keen to have him home. The son in Australia is arriving back today, and the other son and daughter are dropping everything to support their mother in looking after him at home. We'll need to fast-track his discharge today and alert the community team.'

'I've done the prescription for the drugs he'll be taking with him, and the discharge summary is with Sheila. I just need to phone his GP.'

'Thanks Lucy. Sharon, you've been involved. Are there likely to be any bereavement issues?' Getting someone home quickly to die required a well-coordinated flurry of activity, and Sarah was a seasoned conductor of this orchestra.

'I don't think so. I've had some input, and they seem to be pulling together in the way we wish everyone would. They seem a lovely family.'

'I've spent quite a bit of time with them at various stages,' Nick added. 'I've said I'll visit them at home tomorrow.'

'Okay. Joyce Riley remains very comfortable. Again it's just a gradual deterioration there. She's definitely less well than last week. Nick, you were involved yesterday.'

'Yes, there was a disturbance in that bay yesterday. Her minister and several friends from her church gathered around the bedside to pray. They were doing so rather loudly and then broke into singing hymns and choruses. All very nice, but a bit insensitive to the other patients and families in the bay. Her minister came to see me later, very embarrassed and apologetic. He realised it was not appropriate and that they had just got carried away.'

'Was Joyce upset?' I asked.

'No, not at all. She found it a great blessing, and isn't aware that it caused problems. We won't mention it to her.'

The meeting moved on through the patients in the bays, most of whom were fairly straightforward. The major symptom management problem of the day came with Mr Justy, a man in his early sixties with lung cancer that had spread to his liver and bones.

'Since the weekend he's experienced increasing pain in his left groin and hip. We were mobilising him quite easily, but now the slightest movement is excruciatingly painful. He's needed a lot of analgesia over the last couple of days, and it's making him drowsy but not really getting on top of his pain. The trouble is he's pain free at rest, but the slightest movement of that leg brings it on.'

'Has he fallen at all during that time?' Lucy Danvers was frowning. 'It sounds like he might have a fracture.'

'No, he hasn't fallen. Nor have we been aware of any sudden 'cracks' when moving him. The truth is we can barely move him now anyway, it's just too painful.'

I scanned his notes to see if I could shed any light on the matter. 'The last bone scan didn't show any disease in the left hip or pelvis. Plenty in the spine and in the right hip, but nothing in the area of his pain.'

Bones weakened by cancer deposits can break more easily, sometimes with minimal impact or just on moving awkwardly. His level of pain was suspicious of a fracture, but there was no obvious reason for this to be the case.

'We'll review him this morning after the meeting,' said Lucy Danvers. 'It sounds like we need to get an X-ray of that hip.' The discussion moved on to the patients in the last two single rooms.

'Moving on to Deirdre. She's very close now. I'd be

surprised if she doesn't die within the next day or two. Sharon, how are you getting on with the daughter?'

'She's bearing up. I've spent a lot of time with her. She did ask if she could speak to a doctor this morning. Apparently there's something she desperately needs to ask. The only time she could make before this evening is immediately after the meeting. I hope that's alright?'

'That should be fine,' said Lucy Danvers, looking over at me. 'David, would you be happy to see her briefly? I'll have a few things to tie up regarding Mr Bradshaw's discharge.' I nodded.

Sarah continued. 'Mr Lewis has been moved up into a single room, largely because of the numbers of visitors we're having to cope with. He has a large extended family and they rather take over the place when they are here. We've spoken to them and asked if they can limit the number of people attending at any one time, for his sake as much as anyone else's.'

'Any symptom problems?' Lucy Danvers was looking through his chart.

'He's had some nausea overnight and pain control isn't as good as it has been,' Sarah replied. 'He'll need a review today.'

Coffee mugs gathered in, the meeting ended and we filed out of the sitting room. The rain continued its assault on the window, though the wind had steadied a little by now and a constant drumming replaced the violent crescendos of the storm driven percussion. As I emerged into the corridor I met Belinda who was being pushed in a wheelchair by her husband. She was on her way home. They stopped as they saw me and she stretched out her hand.

'Dr David, I'm off home. I just want to thank you for everything. You've been so kind.' Her husband also shook my hand, and he mouthed silently the words 'thank you.'

It was only a moment but it seemed suspended in time. The noise of the rain and the activity of the ward faded away in that moment, in the handshakes. Something seemed to pass between the three of us that no one else around was party to. I nodded and smiled, curiously reassured. 'You're welcome. It's been a privilege. You take care.' I watched as they disappeared slowly down the corridor. The smallest things. There was a lightening in my spirit, the breath from a butterfly's wings facing down the tempestuous wind bearing leaden clouds. What a difference we can make.

I found Deirdre's daughter in the coffee shop and invited her down to the small sitting room. She looked tired and gaunt, her hair tousled after another night in a recliner chair by the bedside and eyeliner smudged after another precipitation of tears. She sat forward in the chair and clasped her hands in front of her.

'Thank you for seeing me now doctor. There are some things I have to go and sort out this morning, and I was afraid that my mum might die before I got to speak to anyone about this.'

'That's absolutely fine. How can I help?'

She shifted awkwardly in the chair. 'It's a bit of an odd thing to mention, but it's very important to my mum.'

'Go on,' I said, trying to put her at her ease.

'My mum has always had a fear of not really being dead and then waking up in the coffin. She locked herself in a trunk when she was very small and the experience scarred her deeply. She's terrified of finding herself trapped and unable to communicate that she's still alive. She made me promise that when she dies I would slit her wrists, to make absolutely sure that she was dead. The thing is I don't think I could do that even if it were feasible. Doctor, can you do that for her when she dies?'

There was a pause. I repeated slowly what she had told me while holding her gaze. 'So, your mum is frightened that we'll think she's dead when in fact she isn't, and that she'll then wake up later in the coffin. And she'd like someone to slit her wrists to make sure she's dead?' I'd adopted this technique after the incident with Belinda, as a way of coping in situations in which I was taken aback or caught off guard by questions or statements. It gave me time to process what I had just heard and hopefully mask any resulting surprise, awkwardness or dismay.

'Yes,' she said. 'I know it probably seems weird, but it is really important to her.'

There was another pause, while I mentally rehearsed my response. 'I'm really sorry, but I'm afraid we can't slit her wrists, or mutilate her body in any way after she's dead.' Her gaze fell to the floor and her shoulders sagged. 'However, I can assure you that we will make absolutely sure that she's dead before we pronounce her so.'

'Can you really be sure? How do you tell?'

'We have a set routine of examination that we usually go through, including listening for a heartbeat and sounds of breathing. We can also check the pupils, and if necessary look with an ophthalmoscope at the back of the eye.'

She looked up. 'And you'll do all that.....and make sure?'

I leaned forward and met her gaze again. 'I promise we'll make sure she's dead. I'll do more than I normally would in terms of checks. We will make absolutely sure.'

'Will it definitely be you who does it?'

'It will almost certainly be me. But, with your permission, I'll share this with the rest of the team so that, if for some reason I am not around, whoever does it will be aware of your concerns.'

She nodded her head, hesitantly at first while seemingly pondering what I had said, and then more definitely, presumably satisfied with the compromise. She stood up and shook my hand. 'Thank you, doctor. That's all I needed to know.' She gave me a wan smile and then turned to go.

'Mrs Tompkins.' She stopped and looked round. 'We often make promises to those we love that we simply cannot keep. She won't ever know.'

'I know she'll never know. But I will.' She shrugged and left the room.

Deirdre died the night of the following day. It happened around midnight and her body was collected by the undertaker overnight, and before we arrived at the start of the day. This was standard practice, as we had an arrangement with the local coroner that an expected death could be certified by nursing staff if it occurred out of hours, rather than calling in the on-call doctor. The information about her daughter's concerns had failed to reach the night staff, and as a result her body was not kept until morning and the extensive verification I had promised did not take place.

'Please don't send him across to the hospital. He had an awful time there, and we were so relieved to get him here. Please don't put him through that again.' The anguish on Lynette Justy's face was mirrored in the tension in her body. Her son, in his late twenties, sat on the sofa next to her, his face fixed and impassive.

I had got to know this family quite well over the two weeks that Trevor Justy had been with us. He was a personable man with an easygoing manner and a wry sense of humour. A well travelled diplomat he had regaled us with tales of secret machinations and daring-do in foreign places. He had a lovely family, devoted wife Lynette, son Harry and a daughter Becky who worked in Paris and had visited once since he had been admitted.

He had been diagnosed with advanced cancer about three months before, and had been admitted to hospital as an emergency with spinal cord compression. The cancer deposits in his spine had destroyed some of the vertebrae and had started to press on his spinal cord, causing weakness in the legs and problems with bladder control. He had received a course of radiotherapy but had not regained full power in his legs. He was also experiencing continuing problems with pain in his back, and had been transferred to the hospice for pain control and rehabilitation with a view to getting him home again. He had had a rather stormy time in the hospital, with a lot of pain and perceived deficiencies in his nursing care at times. The whole episode had left him and his family scarred, and I could understand their distress at the prospect of another admission.

Lucy Danvers and I had gone to assess him together earlier that morning. He had developed excruciating pain in his left hip and groin on the slightest movement. Basic nursing care was now extremely difficult to provide without causing him considerable distress and the increasing doses of morphine-type painkiller that he was requiring were making him drowsy and confused at times. When we saw him I was shocked at the change in his appearance and condition even since the day before. He was grey and clammy and very drowsy. There was no obvious outward sign that he had fractured his hip, and any attempt to examine the leg immediately woke him from his stupor and invited an anguished cry.

We faced a dilemma in knowing what to do for the best. Although he had not been imminently dying, his prognosis was poor, perhaps as little as a few weeks. A transfer to the hospital for investigation would be extremely uncomfortable for him, and if a fracture was confirmed the next decision would be whether or not to operate and fix it. This would provide the best chance of controlling his pain adequately, but the risks associated with such an operation would be higher, given his general condition and advanced disease. The alternative would be to keep him at the hospice and do our best to keep him comfortable, but in all likelihood the only way to do this would result in sedation and he would continue to deteriorate and die within a short time.

I felt strongly that we should give him a chance. We set out the options for him as best we could in the circumstances, and although drowsy he didn't appear confused at that time, and we felt he was able to understand the nature of the decision we faced. He indicated that he would like to transfer to the hospital for investigation. This was enough to convince Lucy Danvers in what was a difficult call to make. Because I knew the family I offered to speak to them when they came in later that day.

'I know this is distressing, but at the moment we don't really know why he's in so much pain. If we are able to confirm whether or not he has a fracture at least we'll know what we are dealing with, whether or not it is possible to fix it. At the moment all we are doing is giving him more and more painkillers, with limited effect, and they are causing excessive side effects.'

'I can't bear to see him suffering so much. I don't want him to have an operation, he's too weak,' replied his wife. Lynette's eyes were pleading. Her son looked blankly at the floor. I felt I needed to be blunt.

'The way things are at the moment, he will deteriorate and die quite quickly, and we are still struggling to make him comfortable.'

'Can't we just give him whatever he needs to be out of it, and let him die?' she said. 'I just can't bear to see him like this.'

'We are very uneasy about just sedating him at the moment, particularly as we don't know for sure what is going on and whether something definitive could be done to alleviate the problem. I was able to speak to him quite frankly this morning and he said that he would like to give it a go at the hospital. We must respect his wishes.'

Lynette closed her eyes and let out a deep mournful sigh. Her son cleared his throat and said, 'Is he going across today?'

'Yes. We are waiting for the ambulance.'

'So we should know later today what is happening? If nothing can be done can he come straight back here?'

'Certainly. We'll hold his bed open.'

He put his arm around his mother. 'Thank you. Is it okay if we stay here for a few minutes?'

I left them to their own thoughts and sadness. I hoped, I was convinced, that this was the right decision, yet I felt as if I had somehow betrayed this family that had opened up to me and let me in. As I emerged from the sitting room I bumped into Nick. We walked together back towards the doctors' office.

'How did it go David?'

'Very difficult. They really don't want him to be messed around any more. It's a difficult call. I hope we are doing the right thing.' I sighed.

'The right thing isn't always easy to discern. That's part of what makes this work challenging – and rewarding. The more I see of it, the more it seems to me that medicine, and end-of-life care in particular, is as much an art as science. You can only do your best, given the circumstances and information you have. When you've worked here for a while you can often trust your gut feeling as to the right thing to do. What's your gut feeling about this?'

'I think we are making the right call,' I replied.

'The rest of the team are behind that decision. So we go with it. And no looking back, even though we'll sometimes get it wrong. Changing the subject, have you got any time off coming up?'

'Yes, I'm off next week. I'm heading up to Scotland to meet up with some friends from my medical school days. I'm really looking forward to it. It's the first real break I've had since starting here.'

'Good, glad to hear it. You've earned it. We can't keep giving out in this sort of work without being topped up ourselves.' He slapped me on the back and turned to go. 'I'll look in on the Justys.'

As I watched him saunter down the corridor humming to himself and exchanging banter with one of the cleaners I smiled. I had a sneaking feeling that he hadn't bumped into me by coincidence.

Friday came at last after what had seemed like an endless week. Such is usually the case when one is tired and hanging on for a holiday that is just around the corner. I had that wonderful 'demob happy' feeling that banishes fatigue and lifts the spirits. I was on first name terms with most of the staff, and Joy in particular, who was one of the cleaners, always made a point of greeting me in the mornings as I walked past. This morning I was more effusive than normal and stopped to chat while she sorted through her trolley. I explained my itinerary for the following week and she shared fond memories of her own trips to Scotland to visit her sister. Shafts of thin winter sunlight burst out of the entrance to each bay like waterfalls of silver onto the current of activity along the length of the corridor. Things were running a little late and the drug trolley was still making slow progress towards the far end, but the nurses attending it were laughing over some shared confidence, and appeared careless about time that was biting at their heels.

My wave of euphoria broke during the morning meeting when Cathy informed us that Trevor Justy had died in hospital the previous evening. After his transfer two days before, an X-ray had confirmed a nasty fracture of his left hip. He underwent surgical pinning of the fracture later that night and was reported to be doing well post-operatively. However, he had obviously had some sudden event that led to his demise. His passing was marked in the usual way in the meeting and there was general agreement that we had done the right thing, before we moved on to the business of the day.

I was completely deflated, and felt once again the weight of tiredness that had lifted in the excitement over looming holidays. More than sadness, I felt disappointment and a little angry. I thought of the family and wondered how they were coping. I wondered whether the daughter had managed to get over from Paris in time. I wondered whether we had made the right call. I wondered whether I was any good at this job.

I waded through the routine ward work, taking a lot longer than I normally would. Sally took the other half of the ward. Gordon would usually have been in for the afternoon but he was away at a conference. Lucy Danvers was at the hospital and called to say that she was sending over a lady in her fifties with spinal cord compression who had not responded to treatment and whose legs were almost completely paralysed.

Mrs Hogarth arrived in the early afternoon, accompanied by her sister, and was settled into one of the bays. Accompanied by one of the staff nurses I went along to admit her. I spoke at length to them both together and then her sister sat outside the curtains while I completed the examination. As I was finishing Mrs Hogarth took my hand and beckoned me closer. 'Doctor, I can't make sense of this. I feel fine apart from these legs. Why won't they work?'

I knelt down by the bed. 'What did they tell you in the hospital?'

'I was told that the cancer has spread to my back.'

'That's right, I'm afraid it has. The cancer is pressing on your spinal cord and that is what has caused the weakness in the legs.'

'Will I ever walk again?'

'I'm sorry, but no. Almost certainly not.'

At that moment there was a scream from outside the curtains. 'Why did you say that? Why did you tell her that?' The sister was clearly distraught and was exclaiming loudly to all who cared to listen. 'I can't believe you said that. Why did he say that? Why would you take someone's hope away like that? What kind of place is this?' The staff nurse quickly went outside the curtains, while I pulled them back. She put her arm around the sister's shoulder and ushered her out of the bay. The sister kept looking back at me and shouting, amidst sobs, 'Why did you tell her that?'

I looked uneasily at the other patients in the bay, all of whom were now fully caught up in the drama. I wanted the floor to open up. I turned back to Mrs Hogarth who was crying quietly. 'I'm sorry to have to break such news to you, I really am,' I said.

'No. Don't worry. Thank you.' She reached for the box of tissues.

Tina the auxiliary nurse appeared beside me and put

an arm around her. She nodded to me and mouthed, 'It's okay. I'll deal with this, you go.'

I trudged wearily back to the office, shell-shocked. I explained what had happened to Sally. 'I thought she was aware of what was happening. Lucy said she'd spoken to them both. Surely, they knew already?'

'Don't worry. You couldn't have done anything differently. She asked a straight question and you gave an honest answer. Listen.' She pulled her chair up closer. 'You write up the notes and then head off. Take an early afternoon. I can hold the fort here. You go and enjoy your holiday.'

I was too stupefied to protest. I finished the notes, said goodbyes to Sally and Sheila and slinked away up the ward. As I passed Cathy's office she jumped up from her desk and came out to greet me. She put her hand on my shoulders and scanned my face with her deep emerald eyes. Then she drew me closer and gave me a hug.

'You're doing just fine. You go and have a great week.' She shooed me away and went back inside her office. A moment later she called after me. 'Oh David, I need to give you something.' She came towards me holding out an envelope. 'Mrs Justy came in early this morning to collect some of her husband's effects and she asked me to give this to you.' She smiled and turned away once more.

I sat in the car and looked at the envelope for a while before opening it. Inside was a letter from Lynette Justy.

Dear David,
As you know, my darling Trevor passed away last night.

I just want to thank you on behalf of our whole family for the loving care you showed both him and us throughout his time at the hospice.

I also want to thank you for making the difficult decision to send him up to the hospital for the X-ray. Although we weren't keen on him having the operation he was very clear that that was what he wanted. He came through without any problem and yesterday he enjoyed a day completely free from pain and the side effects of the drugs. He was back to his old self and we had a lovely day together as a family, including Becky who arrived from Paris in the morning.

The ward staff were very kind, and our last memories of him are positive and happy, filled with laughter and love. And when his end came it was sudden and swift and without suffering. This is a far cry from what we would have had to witness if he had not had the operation.

We can't thank you enough for all you have done, and we shall always be in your debt.

With love and best wishes,
Lynette Justy

Chapter 4
Out of Hours

The headlights swept off the end of the wall and fanned out across the valley below as I swung around into the car park. They caught a fox, momentarily transfixed by the sudden intrusion into its world, its shadowy face framing oversized balls of luminescent green that stared back like some psychic alien's. It turned and slinked away into the shadows. I switched off the lights and was plunged once again into the enveloping darkness that so eerily transforms the most familiar of surroundings, distorting perspective and distance, disorientating and beguiling the senses with false expectation. I got out and shivered. It was almost perfectly still. I could hear the gentle laughter of the stream in the valley below that seemed so much closer than usual. Above was a clear sky, and as the effects of the light washed out of my eyes there gradually emerged a star-strewn vista of breathtaking proportion. I leaned against the car for a few minutes, lost in the wonder of it, the chill air chasing away the last vestiges of sleep.

The phone had shocked me into consciousness. Even after so many years of being bleeped or phoned during the night it still had the effect of a lightning bolt through the body and a moment of transient panic as I oriented myself to where I was and what I was hearing. I was probably out of practice, as middle of the night phone calls had been relatively rare during on-calls for the hospice. When they happened it was almost always a request for a verbal prescription for medication or some advice on what to try next for someone with terminal agitation or pain who was not responding to the prescribed doses. There was very rarely a need to come in to the hospice, perhaps to assess a patient who had deteriorated unexpectedly and for whom some active treatment might be appropriate, or when the nursing staff needed a reassuring presence.

I had developed an enduring respect and admiration for these angels of the night. There were two staff nurses and two auxiliary nurses looking after the whole unit from about eight thirty in the evening to seven the following morning. Distressed patients and families, agitated patients, patients dying on their shift, and availability round the clock to take telephone calls from other professionals, patients and their families were all potentially part of any given working night, and all done in defiance of natural circadian rhythms. These night nurses shouldered a greater level of responsibility and theirs was the power to determine the degree to which the on-call doctor had a disturbed night. When they asked for, or seemed to hint at the need for, your actual presence you didn't hesitate to come in, as you knew that they would not do so lightly. This was the first time I had had to come out during the night. It was two in the morning. One of the patients had become extremely confused and aggressive and, importantly, was mobile enough to do some damage if not restrained adequately.

I made my way up the path towards the main entrance. It was marked out in the darkness by small lights set along the edge of the paving, like an emergency escape route in a commercial aircraft. The sign over the entrance was illuminated as was the foyer within. I rang the bell and waited. I could see Willie sitting on the other side of the door. Presently Tanya came to let me in, and as she opened the door Willie darted out into the blackness. Some unsuspecting field mouse was soon to meet its demise, I mused.

'Hello, David. Nice to see you – we don't often get to. Thanks for coming out.' I followed her down the dimly lit corridor. 'He's actually a little calmer, but we are being careful not to get too close as he seems to react to that.' We paused outside the bay. 'I think he'll be fine if we can get some haloperidol into him. He started revving up on the evening drug round and refused his regular dose, and he's become progressively more agitated. Pain doesn't seem to be the problem. I think he's getting more flashbacks. He's convinced we are trying to cut his throat. I would have given him an intramuscular dose but I wasn't certain we would be able to do it safely.'

'Has he posed a threat to the other patients in the bay?'

'No. He's actually remained around his own bed area, as I think he feels safer there – more easily defended perhaps. Thankfully there is only Mr Finney in the bay with him and he's diagonally opposite. He's managed to sleep through most of the activity.'

Ian Stanley, the man in question, had cancer of the stomach and was in the hospice for pain control and psychological support. He was an ex-soldier who had fought in Korea and had been through some very harrowing experiences, including ferocious hand-to-hand combat. Over recent weeks, as he had deteriorated physically, he had started to experience vivid flashbacks and nightmares. They had responded somewhat to medication but this was a bad relapse. With my interest in things military I had got to know him quite well, and had grown fond of him.

'Could you get me ten of oral haloperidol and his usual night sedation and I'll see if I can persuade him to take it.'

'Will do. Nicky and Paula are in there with him at the moment.' She scurried off towards the drug cupboard.

I entered the bay and surveyed the scene. The far end of the bay was fully lit, while at the near end the lights were dimmed. Paula, the other staff nurse, was sitting on the edge of the bed directly opposite Ian's. Nicky, one of the auxiliary nurses was sitting by Mr Finney's bed. He was snoring softly, seemingly oblivious to the activity in his vicinity. Ian was sitting semi-clothed in his chair, holding his head in his hands and whimpering quietly.

I nodded to Nicky and Paula and approached the end of the bed, slowly and carefully. I spoke his name, softly but firmly. He tensed up and lifted his head to look at me. He looked like a cornered animal, eyes wide and wild, body taut like a coiled spring, any sudden sound sending shudders through his frame.

'Get away from me! Get away!' he growled, his voice a mixture of menace and fear. 'I'll kill you if you lay a hand on me, you yellow bastard.' I stopped and crouched down, opening my hands for him to see I wasn't carrying anything.

'Ian, no one is going to hurt you.'

'Yes they are. They're trying to kill me.' He jabbed a finger aggressively towards Nicky and Paula.

'Ian, listen to me. No one is trying to kill you.'

'Yes they are. They're going to cut my throat. Just like Billy. I saw it. A bayonet slashed him from ear to ear. He tried to scream but nothing came out. I saw it. They've got blood on their hands.'

'Ian, do you remember me, who I am? I'm Dr David, remember?' He looked at me hesitantly, perhaps a glimmer of recognition piercing his fog of delusion. 'This is the hospice, remember? This is Nicky and Paula, they're nurses looking after you. No one is going to hurt you.' I spoke calmly and authoritatively, holding his gaze. 'Ian, my legs are going to give way if I stay crouched like this for very long. I'm just going to sit up here on the end of the bed, okay? You are in no danger.'

I very slowly edged over and sat up against the footboard. I was in his space, so far so good. At that moment he suddenly tensed again and his eyes darted towards the door. I glanced round and saw Tanya approaching with a medicine pot.

'It's okay. Tanya is bringing something for me.' I put a hand up towards Tanya, motioning her to come no nearer. 'She's just going to put it on the table over there until I need it.' I nodded to her and she left the medication and retreated out of the bay.

Ian relaxed slightly as she disappeared out of the room, and then turned his attention back to me, eyeing me with distrust and suspicion. 'Dr David. Dr David. I know you? I know you.'

'Tell me about Billy.' Tears welled up in his eyes and his shoulders slumped momentarily, before he resumed his taut readiness. 'Ian, tell me about Billy.'

For about half an hour he gave, in fits and starts, a jumbled account of a battle, of friends lost, of horrors he had seen and horrors he had committed. As he expunged the demons that had no doubt been tormenting him in his darker moments over decades the tension gradually ebbed from his body and he slumped back into the chair. As I witnessed his catharsis I felt humbled and moved. I wanted to gather him in an embrace and tell him it was okay. He was quiet for a while and then started gently sobbing.

'I'm so tired. The nightmares. I want them to stop. I'm so tired.' I cautiously reached over and placed my hand on his arm. He didn't recoil at all.

'I know you are Ian. It's okay, really it is. I understand. We understand. Let us help you.' He looked up, his gaunt face displaying none of the energy that had so recently contorted it, eyes distant and almost lifeless. 'Let us help you to bed.'

He nodded his acquiescence. I nodded to Nicky, and we helped him into bed. Paula had left us a while ago when it was clear that the situation was being diffused. 'Ian, you missed your medicine earlier. I have a couple of tablets here, one to help with the nightmares and one to help you sleep. Will you take them?' He stuck out his hand and I tipped them in, and we helped him to some water.

'Will you stay for a while?' he asked. I nodded.

Nicky left me sitting by the bed, and dimmed the lights. I waited another half an hour or so, until I heard the soft rhythmic breathing of one who is fast asleep, and crept out of the bay. I felt drained and extremely tired. The adrenaline that accompanies the urgent call-out and deceives the body into believing that night is day had long since worn off, and was now replaced by a craving for sleep. I gave a long and deep yawn that seemed to take over my whole body and completely incapacitated me for a few moments. I rubbed my gritty eyes and wandered down to the nurses' office. Tanya was on the phone and Nicky was pouring out a mug of tea.

'Well. That's that,' I sighed.

'Well done David. Have a cup of tea.' Nicky handed me the mug. 'Unless you think it will stop you getting to sleep when you get home.'

'Thanks. No, I'll need something to keep me awake driving back, and I don't think I'll have any trouble getting off to sleep again when I'm tucked up.'

Tanya came off the phone and looked serious. 'Well, that was a Mr Huxtable, who is due to come in tomorrow, or should I say later today. I think anxiety will be high on the problem list. He was ringing in a panic about his oxygen. He has home oxygen which he's been using in short bursts only. He woke up an hour ago and put it on, and then fell asleep without taking it off. Now, an hour later he has woken up with the oxygen mask still on, and he was worried he might suffer as a result. He has opened all the windows and stuck his head outside, from where he was ringing us on a mobile phone. He wanted to know whether it was safe to switch on a light.' She looked at us intensely and sucked air between her teeth. I suppressed a smile.

'And what advice did you give nurse?' I asked.

She drew herself up to look important. 'Well doctor. I was pleased to be able to strongly reassure him that he was not going to be poisoned. I further reassured him that he had done exactly the right thing in opening all the windows, but that now on such a cold night as this he might be better coming in and shutting them all again, and getting back into his warm bed. I confirmed that it was safe to go back to sleep,' she lifted her chin to look even more imperious, 'but if he did smell any oxygen at any time he would be well advised to phone the gas board.'

She managed to hold her composure for a couple of seconds, before she creased up and all three of us collapsed in paroxysms of laughter. The release was wonderful. There is nothing like laughter to dissipate tension and restore perspective. I had come to appreciate the black humour that was often a part of hospice life, a humour that was life affirming and hopefully never went so far as to violate respect for the person, or so it seemed from the perspective of the context of love and care in which it was so vital a part.

After a while I managed to regain my composure enough to comment. 'You're kidding! Surely not?'

'I kid you not. I didn't really say the bit about the gas board – I'm not that wicked!' She smiled mischievously. 'Oh we get it all during the night you know. Some calls go on for up to an hour. People often feel most lonely and afraid at night.'

Paula came in, with a slightly puzzled expression on her face. 'Something happened?'

'A funny phone call,' I said.

'Ah, tell me all later. Mrs Gibson wants the toilet and we'll need to hoist her.' They got up and went out.

'Thanks for coming in David. You head off home,' said Tanya, waving as she rounded the corner.

I made a brief entry in Ian Stanley's notes, and then headed out to the car. As I left the building I noticed Willie on the paved area to one side. He had caught a mouse and was playing with it and tormenting it by allowing it to run a few steps before pouncing on it again. On another occasion I might have intervened, but I was too tired. I drove home still chuckling at the image of the poor man in his pyjamas hanging out of his window with a mobile phone.

There's nothing quite like getting back into bed when you've been called out during the night. I luxuriated in the enveloping warmth and slowly drifted off. My sleep wasn't very deep or satisfying. There were too many disturbing intrusions by images of battle and hand-to-hand combat. One man's suffering is a universal suffering.

Although I never particularly like having to work weekends, at the hospice they tended to be pretty relaxed compared to previous experiences. One drifted in mid morning and had a quick verbal run through the patients with the senior nurse on duty. Then one wandered round the ward seeing mainly those whose symptoms were not controlled or who specifically needed review. In some ways weekends were particularly satisfying as they afforded more time to spend with individual patients and catch up on relationships that the busyness of the weekdays might have relegated to a subscript. There were fewer phone calls, rarely any discharges, and no planned admissions, though unexpected urgent admissions could keep you from home till late in the day, largely because of the vagaries of ambulance transport at weekends. Families tended to congregate from places afar, and speaking to the doctor was sometimes an assumed necessity, and indeed prerogative. I didn't mind, but one had to be careful that the whole day was not dominated by such discussions, and it could be especially irksome if these were repetitive and if much of this time could be redeemed by family members simply communicating properly with each other.

This weekend was a tiresome imposition. It wasn't my scheduled on-call weekend, but I'd had to step in at short notice when Gordon took ill on the Friday. I was doing the Saturday and Brian was taking over for the Sunday. The ward was relatively quiet and uncomplicated, and the morning was not onerous. Lunchtime and early afternoon were occupied trying to sort out an urgent discharge for a patient whose family wanted to take home to die. Despite the complications of obtaining drugs to take home at a weekend, and arranging district nurse input to replenish his syringe driver once there, it was necessary to act quickly and decisively as Monday might be too late.

The nurses managed to intercept any marauding relatives and thus enabled me to concentrate on the task in hand. We were, rather unusually, expecting an admission that had been arranged late on the Friday for a lady with chronic lung disease, and she was expected to arrive early afternoon. We had just seen our discharge and his family off the premises when the new admission arrived. I returned to the office for a late lunch as I knew it would take ten minutes or so for her to be settled in to her bed. I browsed through her notes and the note from the GP while munching on a sandwich.

Dr Anstey was a seventy-five year old retired GP who had end stage emphysema. She had been housebound and totally dependent on oxygen for the last three years, and had repeatedly declined hospital admission. She was being looked after at home by her older, and very frail, husband with support from her two daughters. Her breathing had deteriorated further over the previous week and care had become more difficult, leaving her family exhausted. She had requested admission to the hospice, and the expectation was that it would be for terminal care.

When I went to see her she appeared semi-comatose, and at times restless and grimacing. She managed an occasional whisper through her oxygen mask before being overcome by breathlessness. I planned to stop her oral medication and start a syringe driver with small doses of diamorphine and sedative to ease her breathlessness. Her husband and two daughters were with her during the afternoon and were fully expecting her to die within the next few days.

Later that afternoon I was in the office finishing off some entries in notes when Sarah hurried in. 'David, I think you'd better come to see Dr Anstey.'

I looked quizzically. 'Something wrong?'

'You'll see.' I joined her in the corridor and we proceeded briskly towards the relevant bay. 'Her family left about an hour ago.'

Dr Anstey was lying on her left side. She was blue and shivering, her breathing laboured and pulse barely palpable. Her oxygen mask was lying on the bed next to her. My natural instinct was to pick up the mask and replace it on her face, and a few months before this would have been my immediate response. However, I very quickly realised that she had removed the mask deliberately.

My next actions were driven by a new instinct that surprised me and overcame my conscious decision-making. It surprised me because up to now I had struggled at times with the change in emphasis in approach to care that is required when looking after the dying and I wasn't aware that I had yet progressed to any level of maturity in this.

'You've taken off your mask. Do you want me to put it back?'

She slowly shook her head and whispered 'No.' I squatted down by the bed, took her hand and brought my face up close to hers. She opened her eyes briefly.

'Dr Anstey, you've taken off your mask. Do you want me to put it back?'

She managed to speak out 'No,' then, after several seconds of respiratory effort, 'Let me go.'

'Do you want to be more sleepy?' This was a horrible way to die, gasping for breath. The question followed on completely naturally – it wouldn't have done so not long ago.

'Yes.' It had a finality about it. It was in fact the last word she spoke.

I looked at Sarah. 'Midazolam?' I squeezed the dying woman's hand and stood up to confer. 'What dose shall we go for? I don't want to give too little. She needs to be unaware as soon as possible.'

I thought for a moment. In my previous medical incarnation I would never have given a sedative at all to someone who was so short of breath and with such low oxygen levels for fear of stopping them breathing. Yet this was now the most natural thing to do. After discussion with Sarah we agreed on a dose, and she disappeared off to draw up the medication. I drew up a chair and held her hand again. It was blue, cold and clammy. Sarah returned and administered the injection.

'I'll phone the family.'

I sat by the bed and watched her die over the next half hour. Her breathing pattern relaxed measurably after a few minutes and I got no response to gentle prompting. I watched her face, before strained and contorted, now relaxed and peaceful. Sarah came back a couple of times to check I was okay, and the first time sat with me for a while. Over the last few minutes the breathing pattern changed again, occasional silent gasps for air like a suffocating beached fish. After a while I became aware that there had not been any such gasps for some time, all effort had ceased, her body motionless and deserted. Out in the corridor I heard the chatter and laughter of children running down the corridor to visit grandpa in the next bay, followed by an admonition by a parent to keep the noise down. I noted the time of death and straightened the bed clothes around her. Her family had not arrived in time but appeared about ten minutes later, appropriately sad but not unduly surprised.

I sat pensively in the office, ruminating over what

had just happened. It had been the first time I had sat for a prolonged period and watched someone die. Even working in the hospice it wasn't that usual for the doctor to be present at the moment of death, this most commonly being the experience of the nurses. I also became increasingly uncomfortable about what had taken place. It felt somewhat surreal, and what had seemed so clear in the execution was now clouded with doubt in the reflection upon it.

It now seemed clear to me that she was much more aware on admission than she was letting on, and that the whole thing had been premeditated on her part. She knew that the hospice was a safe place to choose her end and was presumably aware that we would not let her suffer. I had not performed a rigorous examination because this is often unnecessary in someone who is close to death, but now I felt foolish to have been duped and I also felt I had been used. On the other hand part of me felt a certain respect for this woman who had very much managed her own illness and had now maintained control over her own death.

However, I also wondered whether I had been complicit in some act of suicide, and as my thinking went round in circles my ethical reasoning was getting more and more blurred. Had I hastened her death in giving her the sedative? What else could I have done? There had been only two other options when I found the mask off – to have replaced it against her will, or to have watched her die in distress. Surely, both of these would have been ethically wrong?

Sarah came in and touched my shoulder. 'The family are just spending some time with her, and then we'll move her down to the room of rest. Are you alright David?'

'I don't know.' I sighed. 'I feel confused.....and a little used.'

'Yes. She knew what she was doing alright. She was a doctor after all.' She smiled, and then looked concerned when I didn't reciprocate. 'We did the right thing though. Really we did. She needed sedating.'

I shrugged. 'I guess you're right. It just all feels very strange.'

'Do you want to talk about it?'

'No. It's okay. I just need to digest it, that's all.' Now I smiled. 'I'll do the paperwork, so they can take the certificate away with them.'

I pushed the episode to the back of my mind and completed the work of the day. Come late afternoon there was just one relative to see before I could leave the nurses to it. The son of a gentleman who had been admitted the day before had travelled down to visit him, and was keen for an update. A prickly and rather rude young man, he wouldn't be 'fobbed off with second hand accounts from the nurses,' but wanted to hear it 'from the horse's mouth.' I was after all being paid to be at work today, and no doubt quite handsomely. Little did he know. Medicine was one line of work where the rate for on-call, or overtime, was less than that for normal working hours.

He was waiting for me in the small sitting room. He stood up and shook my hand very firmly before sitting down again. He was smartly dressed and very definite in all his movements, so that they appeared slightly exaggerated. He had an air of self-importance and I did not at all warm to him. Just as I was about engage him a phone rang in his pocket and he proceeded to answer it without any regard to the circumstances. I waited for what seemed like several minutes while he dealt with some domestic matter with his wife whom he had obviously left at home with the children. He ended the call perfunctorily, and with little courtesy or warmth for the speaker on the other end. Then without a word of apology he folded his arms across his chest and launched into an account of his own assessment of his father's condition.

He sought clarification on a number of points, and I gave him our best assessment of his condition and our proposed care. I found myself getting increasingly irritated by his manner and his opinionated interjections. I began to wonder whether he had some medical knowledge, though this was clearly partial and flawed.

'Okay. So you are going to sort out his pain and do your best to make him comfortable, but let's face it, he's obviously very unwell and deteriorating. His quality of life is awful. When are you going to help him on his way?'

'I beg your pardon?' I could feel myself getting hotter. I didn't know whether I was more angry or shocked. His presumption was all the more galling because of the arrogance with which he stated it.

'Well, everyone knows it's what you do here.'

Monday morning came around too quickly. I hadn't been working on the Sunday, but had been disturbed by phone calls from the ward several times during Saturday night over a patient with terminal agitation who was proving very difficult to settle despite substantial doses of medication. As a result Sunday was only any good for resting and recovery, and much of what I had hoped to get done remained undone.

When I arrived on the ward there was a subdued air in the nurses' office. It transpired that there had been a major blunder by one of the night staff. A patient had died around six that morning, and the nurse tasked with ringing the wife to inform her, no doubt tired and frazzled after the difficult night, had inadvertently picked up the wrong file and phoned another patient's wife. This second patient was also in the last days of life, so news of his death was not a terrible shock for the woman, but it was rather premature. The error was realised a few minutes later and the embarrassed nurse had to ring back to say it was all a mistake. The wife had taken it very graciously but the poor nurse was distraught. I had come to realise that the nursing contingent in the hospice was a close knit group and the misfortunes and distress of one tended to be felt by others. I offered what sympathy and consolation I could and repaired to the doctors' office.

Sheila was in fine form, and was chatting ani-matedly to Sally about her weekend. They greeted me enthusiastically and asked how the on-call went. I said something bland that did not invite further probing, and they resumed their girlie talk. The notes for the recently deceased man were on the desk and I got out the death certificate book and cremation form before heading off to the room of rest to view the body. When I returned Brian was sitting where I had been, swivelling to and fro on the chair and laughing about something with Sheila and Sally.

'Morning David! Thank you for doing Saturday. We had family down, so it would have been awkward for me to cover both days. I hear you had an interesting time. Sarah was very complimentary about you. Well done.'

'Thank you,' I replied. 'Yes, we had a difficult time settling Mr Paxton. I presume he died yesterday?'

'Yes. He was very settled by the time I came in yesterday morning, and he died peacefully mid afternoon. Family were very grateful for all we've done. I was still here, as we had some more excitement yesterday. Mrs Caldwell came in as an emergency with hypercalcaemia. She was very dehydrated and terribly sick.'

Mrs Caldwell was a lady with breast cancer that had spread to her bones, and she had been in with us before. Sometimes such bone disease can cause excessive amounts of calcium to accumulate in the blood. These raised calcium levels, or hypercalcaemia, can cause dehydration and lead to a number of symptoms including nausea, drowsiness and confusion. As he continued recounting the tale I saw again that boyish excitement of one who truly loved his profession, which was so endearing.

'She was so dehydrated I couldn't raise a vein to put the drip into, so I had to do a cut-down onto her ankle. I haven't done one of those for many years! By all accounts she's much better this morning.' He beamed proudly.

A cut-down is a procedure whereby an incision is made over the place where a large vein is known to run, in this case on the inner ankle, and the vein is exposed so that the cannula can be inserted directly. I had never had to perform one, even in my time as a surgeon, as we tended to insert an intravenous line into one of the big veins deep in the neck when the superficial veins in the arm were under-filled and difficult to locate. But this would have been too major a procedure to carry out in the hospice. We chatted in the office for a little longer before the morning meeting summoned us, and we continued as we walked together.

'Brian, could I meet up with you some time to talk about Dr Anstey?' I was still preoccupied and troubled by the events of the Saturday afternoon.

'Certainly. Let's talk after the meeting.'

The meeting concluded and Brian and I stayed behind in the room. I recounted in detail the events of Saturday afternoon and my misgivings about the whole affair. He thought for a short while, looking at me earnestly and benevolently. 'I think you did exactly the right thing. I wouldn't have done anything different myself. What specifically worries you about what you did?'

'Did I assist in her suicide? And did I hasten her death?'

'It is important to separate her actions from your own. Suicide is an act of intentionally killing oneself. The removal of her oxygen mask was certainly a deliberate act that would most likely accelerate her death. So she deliberately allowed herself to die, and whether or not one regards this as suicide depends on the distinction, if there is one, between killing and allowing to die – and indeed opinions are divided on the moral distinction between the two. However one views it morally, legally what she did was to discontinue a potentially life-prolonging treatment, and this is something anyone is entitled to do provided they are competent to make that decision. From what you have described I would be in no doubt that she knew exactly what she was doing. To have replaced that mask against her will would have violated her autonomy.'

'If we now look at your actions, you were faced with someone who was dying, and dying badly. It was ethically right to act to relieve her suffering by giving her an appropriate dose of sedative. The dose you gave was entirely reasonable. Did it hasten her death? It is possible, but unlikely to have done so. If you had given a much bigger dose then it might well have done. If the dose you gave did shorten her life, and of course one cannot prove or disprove that categorically, then it is still ethically acceptable because your intention was to relieve her distress and not shorten her life, and the measure you took was a reasonable and proportionate response to her degree of suffering.'

'You mean I'm covered by the principle of Double Effect? I suppose we rely on that a lot in what we do.'

'Why do you say that?'

'Well some of our patients are on pretty large doses of morphine-related drugs and sedatives, doses that would have scared me when I worked in the hospital, and these often have to be increased in the last days of life.'

'Many of our patients are on big doses, but the thing to remember is that they have got to that point very gradually, and dose increases have been only to match their symptoms. When used appropriately like that, these drugs are safe and there is no evidence that they hasten death. In fact quite the opposite is the case sometimes. If we give an adequate level of sedation, for instance, to someone who is very breathless, we may actually extend their life as their resources are no longer being expended on the stress response and their distress. You've seen yourself how people can take days to die even when they are unconscious and not taking anything by mouth.'

I felt like a light was being switched on in my understanding, and a lifting of a burden. 'I think I see what you are saying. I've kind of wrestled with it since I got here, partly because I've had to deal with all my preconceptions about what happens in a hospice. What I did on Saturday seemed instinctively right, but I was tying myself in knots trying to rationalise it.'

'Are you happier about it now?'

'Yes. Yes I am. Thank you.'

'Don't carry these burdens yourself. Remember what I said about feathers.' We stood up and he slapped me gently on the back. 'You are a natural at this kind of work. Everyone speaks very highly of you. Have you considered changing your long term career plans?'

The suggestion took me completely by surprise. I must say I hadn't, though I was finding the job extremely fulfilling. To receive this compliment from such a deeply impressive man left me a little disorientated. I quickly dismissed the thought.

'I haven't really thought about it.' I had been keeping an eye on the medical press for suitable surgical posts.

'Well, perhaps you should.' He smiled and turned to go.

'Brian. Would you mind if I ask you something else?'

He checked and looked expectantly. 'Fire away.'

'I've noticed on several occasions when we are with someone who is unconscious, you seem to be saying something very quietly under your breath. I've been curious. Do you mind me asking what that's all about?'

He fixed me with a penetrating look, searching rather than threatening or discomfiting. After a pause his eyes relaxed and he smiled. I sensed I was about to be welcomed through a gateway beyond another layer of trust and be given deeper insight into the workings of this man who grew progressively in my esteem and admiration.

'You are very observant. At those times I am speaking a blessing over them. It comes from the Old Testament of the Bible, from chapter six of a book called Numbers. 'The Lord bless you and watch over you, the Lord turn his face towards upon you and be gracious to you, the Lord lift up the light of his countenance upon you and give you his peace.' There can be great power in a blessing spoken over someone.'

'Do you have a Christian faith?' I ventured.

'You could call it that, though I don't much like using that term. It has too many connotations for people, many of them misunderstood or negative. I prefer to say that I try to follow Jesus. And those feathers I spoke about – I give mine to him.' His eyes gleamed with an intensity that was alluring. 'See you later David.' He turned and headed off towards his office.

I stood for a while, again slightly disorientated, not sure what to make of what I had just been told. After a few moments I shrugged and returned to the doctors' office. Sarah was giving something to Sheila. I smiled rather distractedly.

'Everything okay David?' Sarah asked.

'Yeah. I think so. I've just been speaking to Brian.' I quickly changed the subject. 'Sorry to hear about the cock-up this morning. Was Paula alright?'

'She'll be fine. It could happen to anyone, a moment's distraction when you're tired. The wife was absolutely fine about it.'

At that moment Sally came in and grinned at Sarah. 'I'm afraid you were a little premature. She's not dead yet.'

'What do you mean? Betty? She is.' Sarah had apparently come in a short while ago to tell Sally that Mrs Higgins had died.

'No she isn't. She took a breath, and she still has a pulse. Very weak, I'll grant you, but still there.'

'No, that can't be right?'

'I assure you Sister, she's not dead yet. At least she wasn't thirty seconds ago when I left her. Fiona is with her.'

'Oh shit!' It was uncharacteristic of Sarah to swear. 'Her husband broke down and his daughter took him off to have a cup of tea. They think she's died!'

'Don't worry. She's very close. Minutes at most. I wouldn't get them back.'

At that moment Fiona, one of the auxiliary nurses came in. She nodded. 'She's gone now.'

'Thank God for that! Sorry. You know what I mean.' Sarah blushed. It was the first time I had seen her flustered.

'I'll go and make absolutely sure for you, Sister. You go and have a gin and tonic!' Sally was having a great time. She disappeared with Fiona.

'Gin and tonic? I need one. It's been one of those mornings!'

Sheila stood and fanned her flamboyantly with an open file. Sarah gave her a friendly shove and scurried out of the office. I spun round on the chair and reached for the daily diary, trying to gather my thoughts, marvelling at the ridiculous incongruities of this place, the daily insanities that kept one sane. My reveries were interrupted by Sally's return.

'No doubt about it now. She's popped it.' She started leafing through Mrs Higgins' notes, and then got up to dig out the death certificate book.

'How was your weekend Sally?'

Sally was extrovert and fun, dependable and down to earth, but tended to avoid anything too self-revelatory. I liked her but couldn't really say I knew much about her. I knew she was divorced and had no children, had a male friend of uncertain intimacy, and seemed to have a gaggle of girlie friends. One sensed that she bore scars that I expect only a handful of close friends had been allowed to see.

'Pretty good, thanks. Rather overdid it on Saturday night with some friends, and felt it the next morning. Yesterday was a lovely afternoon and I had some gardening therapy.'

'What keeps you in this kind of work?'

'Oh, you're getting a bit deep for a Monday morning!' She thought for a while, before continuing. 'Sometimes I wonder. I guess I like the fact that we can really make a difference. I also love working in this team.' Her tone became more teasing. 'Of course, my natural empathy and caring nature suit me totally to this kind of work!'

'What do you make of Brian?'

'He's a lovely boss. An inspirational doctor.' She paused and looked thoughtful. 'Sometimes I find him a bit unnerving.' She was silent and distant for a moment. 'Oh David, I've been meaning to ask. Would you be able to swap on-call nights this week? I've been invited by some friends to go to a concert.'

'Yes that's fine.' She returned to her writing.

I was limbering up to head onto the ward when Sally let out an exasperated cry. 'That bloody cat! He's pissed on my handbag again!'

Sheila looked around in feigned horror. 'Has he. The monkey!' She started to giggle.

'No Sheila, he's not a monkey, he's a cat, and a bloody pain in the arse cat.' She reached angrily over to a box of tissues and started to wipe the bag.

Willie had recently started spraying at various locations in the hospice, and had taken a particular liking, or dislike, to Sally's handbag. She had been caught out a number of times, but not often enough, it would seem, to remember to put the bag out of reach. I made a hasty retreat out of the office and went to find one of the nurses in order to start the ward round.

We started with one of the bays. Trudy, the staff nurse, gave a brief summary of the issues with each patient from her perspective before we went in to see them. The first was a man with lung cancer who had been admitted the day before. 'Mr Corrigan came in yesterday. He's been quite unsettled really. Doesn't seem relaxed, very tetchy when we're giving care. Says he's comfortable, but I get the feeling he's very angry.'

'Okay. Let's see if we can get to the bottom of it.'

He was lying in the bed, half on his side with one leg out of the cover, and with his nasal prongs from the oxygen supply perched on his forehead rather than in his nostrils. I sat by the bed and turned off the oxygen concentrator machine, as the oxygen wasn't getting anywhere near his lungs and he clearly wasn't missing it.

'Morning Mr Corrigan. I'm Dr David Trevelyan. How are you feeling today?'

'You're a doctor are you? Good. Well I'll tell you I'm fed up. Absolutely fed up. I came in here to die, and I want it to be over. When is someone going to give me what I want?'

It had been a bad call to swap nights with Sally. This was the second time in as many weeks that I had had to come back in after hours. I had received a call at about ten in the evening from a very distressed night nurse. There had been a major drug error. A woman who was prescribed long acting morphine in the evening had inadvertently been given her own dose and that of the previous patient on the drug round, amounting to a substantial overdose. The error had happened, as most do, through a lapse in concentration. An overdose of this proportion could lead to serious side effects and possibly stop her breathing. I had driven in through blustery wind that had a biting chill to it and a hint of rain.

Tanya was nurse in charge again, and her mood was subdued as we walked down to the nurses' office. 'I'm really sorry David. We don't normally dispense medication unless the patient is there to give the pot to immediately. I was briefly tending to another patient in the bay while Lesley was dispensing Mrs Dewey's tablets. I checked them with her, but the curtains were round the bed and when we looked we realised that Mrs Dewey wasn't there after all. She was in the toilet as it happened. I went over to knock on the door and check she was alright. Lesley had put the pot on the top of the trolley rather than underneath and when we went to Mrs Blakeley she needed help to sit up the bed. When we got back to dispensing her drugs I did it into Mrs Dewey's pot by mistake.'

'Don't worry. I'm sure she'll be fine. Have you told her about the mistake yet?'

'No. I didn't want to worry her until you were here to reassure her.'

'Is she alright at the moment?'

'Yes, no ill effects so far.'

'It's a slow release preparation. The effects will be delayed and gradual. I'll go and explain what's happened.'

I made my way softly into the dimly lit bay and sat on the end of the bed. Ida Blakely was a delightful woman in her seventies with bladder cancer.

'Hello Mrs Blakely.'

'Good evening Dr David. You're not still here are you? Gosh you do work long hours.'

'I've come back in to see you, actually.'

'To see me? That's very nice of you.' She reached out and grasped my hand briefly.

'I'm afraid we've made a blunder with your tablets tonight. We've given you more of the morphine painkillers than you usually have. It was a big mistake, and I'm really sorry.'

'Oh dear. Will it make me poorly?'

'I don't know. It may do, which is why I have come in to see you. It may make you very sleepy, and it could affect your breathing, but we have a medicine that is like an antidote. If you start to get any problems then we'll give you that.' I paused to let it sink in. 'I'm really sorry that we've messed you around like this.'

'Oh, please don't fret. Anyone can make a mistake. The nurses here are lovely, and very busy sometimes. I hope they won't get into trouble.'

'You're very gracious. I'm sure it will all work out fine. I need to put a drip into your arm in case we have to give you any of that antidote.'

'That's fine. Go ahead and do whatever you have to do.'

I headed for the treatment room to get the cannula and stuck my head into the nurses' office on the way. 'She's fine at the moment. I'll put in a cannula in case we need to give naloxone.' I proceeded to put in the drip and secured it with a bandage. When I returned to the nurses' office there was no one there, so I sat on the edge of the desk and looked up the appropriate dose of the drug in case we needed to give it. I noticed a plate filled with cold roast potatoes sitting on the table by the window. I was still trying to figure out what they were doing there when Tanya came back in.

'What are those for?' I asked.

'Those? They are for the badgers. Have you not

seen the badgers yet? We have a group or set, or whatever you call a collection of badgers, that lives out the back there. We put out old bread and sometimes leftovers from the kitchen. Come next door and have a look. They were there earlier. They tend to come and go several times. We also get a fox that comes down to investigate but he usually keeps well clear of the badgers.'

We moved to the small office next door which was not illuminated so we could see out unhindered by reflections from the interior. We waited a few minutes and sure enough we spotted a couple of large badgers waddling along the gentle slope just in front of the tree line. 'Whow! I think that's the first time I've seen a badger, apart from road kill victims that is.' Tanya left me and I stood transfixed for several more minutes, before I too returned to the office.

'Tanya, could you check her respiratory rate every half hour, and wake me if it drops too low. I've brought some overnight kit and will bed down here.'

'Oh David, that's so good of you. Thank you. You can use the camp bed. There are no relatives needing it tonight.'

'That'll be fine. I'll sleep in the doctors' office.'

She headed off to get the bed and some linen. I sat down at a desk and started to write in Mrs Blakeley's notes. I was interrupted by the phone.

'Hello. St. Julian's Hospice.'

A gravelly voice answered my greeting. 'Ah hello. My name's Travis, Brian Travis. I've not been in with you, but my Macmillan nurse said I could ring at any time if I had a problem.'

'Right. I'm Dr Trevelyan. How can I help?' I was a little hesitant.

'Well. I've run out of the little blue tablets that I had to help me get to sleep.'

'Little blue tablets? Can you remember what they are called?'

'How do I know? You are the doctor. They're blue and small.'

'Okay. Well there are lots of different medicines that might come as a blue tablet. You think it's a sleeping tablet?'

'Yes. And I've run out. I was about to get into bed, and I usually take it with a glass of milk when I've got into bed. Only I've found the box and it's empty.'

'Right.' I was trying not to let my tone betray my incredulity.

'Can you get some out to me? Only I probably won't be able to sleep otherwise.'

I took a deep breath. 'I'm afraid we can't supply tablets to patients out in the community. We can only give them to people who are being looked after in the hospice.'

'Well what am I supposed to do about tonight?' He sounded much put out.

'You won't come to any harm if you miss a dose tonight. I'd suggest that you get a repeat prescription from your own surgery tomorrow.'

'But what if I need something tonight?' He seemed aghast.

'Well, in an emergency you can telephone the on-call GP service, but I don't think a requirement for a sleeping tablet would qualify as an emergency.'

There was a pause at the other end. 'You're supposed to be the bees knees, you lot. But you're bloody crap!' He hung up.

I looked at the receiver, flabbergasted, before shaking my head and replacing it. At that point Tanya came back in. 'What was that all about?'

'You don't want to know.'

'We've put everything in the office for you. You get some sleep. We'll do half-hourly checks.'

I settled down in the doctors' office. Before getting into bed I had another look out of the window to see if I could see any more wildlife. The badgers had gone. The wind had dropped and a light drizzle was falling. A camp bed can seem remarkably comfortable when you are tired. I drifted off quite quickly.

I was shod in walking boots and climbing a steep mountain slope. It was damp under foot and my feet kept slipping, but I made gradual progress towards the summit. From the top I looked out across a large field of wheat. I stepped off and started walking through the swathes of wheat, waist high and golden, as golden as the bright sunshine that beat upon my back. A girl stood a few yards off, in a green floral dress and with golden hair tied back with a band of the same material. She was calling out to me, softly, so that I couldn't make it out at first. As I drew closer it became clearer. She was smiling and saying, or almost singing, words in a language I didn't recognise, and as the mellifluous sound broke over the senses I felt wrapped in the pale blue sky and a lightness that gave way to a heady euphoria.....

'Morning David.' I opened my eyes and stretched in the bed. Pale sunlight was beginning to chase away the early winter dawn. Tanya was standing by the door with a tray.

'Would the doctor like some bacon and egg, tea and toast?'

'Yes please. I propped myself up on my elbow. If I'd known the service was like this I'd sleep here more often!' She set the tray down on the desk.

'A special treat. To say thank you for your support last night. I'm sorry we haven't got a silver service as they used to use in doctors' messes!'

'Ha, ha! How long ago was that? I presume she was alright?'

'Fine. Breathing nice and steady all night. She's just waking now. A little groggy, but no harm done.'

'Gosh. I'm surprised. I'd have thought she'd run into problems after an overdose like that. Thanks very much for the breakfast.'

I polished off the food and sorted myself out with a wash and brush-up. The ward was coming to life. The breakfast trolley was on station at the far end of the corridor. One of the auxiliaries was pushing a patient towards a bathroom in a wheelchair. Beryl, one of the cleaning ladies, was heading into the sluice. I made my way down to Mrs Blakeley's bay. She was sitting up in bed and drinking from a beaker of tea.

'Morning Mrs Blakeley.'

'Morning doctor. Are you in here already? Gosh, do you never get away?'

I smiled. 'How are you today? Any ill-effects from the medication?'

'Well I don't know about any medication. But I'll tell you something – that was the best sleep I've had in months!'

Chapter 5
Staying and Leaving

Expectation can be a cruel and brittle betrayer. Once exposed and shattered its shards can pierce the most armoured heart, bleeding anger, confusion and dismay. Hope, on the other hand, is far more malleable and adaptable. Hope can be battered and bruised, squashed and seemingly extinguished, yet take the tiniest flicker and see it fanned into flame like a phoenix from the ashes of despair. Hope beguiles us from our pain and our fear, and for the dying can be a great dissembler cloaking them like opium from the certainties that they do not wish to face. But it is also the great enabler, the DNA of human resilience and endeavour.

I had come to see that managing hope is a major task of those who care for the dying, facilitating a progressive transferring of hope from something that is no longer realistic or attainable to something that will sustain through the inevitability of decay and death. Sometimes this seemed to me to be manipulative and disingenuous, but the hunger for hope craves satisfaction, and I was often both amazed and humbled at what sustains in the direst circumstances. For many, hope finally comes to rest on dying in a safe and loving environment where they are not alone. For most a hospice is such a place, a way station on the journey, a place of safety and affirmation. What transforms hope into expectation is faith – faith in the source and object of that hope, leading to trusting expectation.

This felt like a betrayal of trust, a trampling upon faith. The look of confusion on the wife's face changed, by degrees, to one of dismay. Her son just looked stunned. 'You're saying he'll have to go to a nursing home? But he's dying. We promised him he'd never go to a home.' Her voice was almost breaking.

'He is very poorly, but his condition is stable at the moment. He's not dying imminently. His symptoms are well controlled and now he just needs nursing care. Home isn't going to be practical, and the only other option is a nursing home.' I sounded so matter of fact. The nub of the issue was that he was not dying quickly enough to stay in the hospice.

The wife continued. 'Can't he stay here? A hospice is where people go to die. We'd pay if necessary. He won't get the same care anywhere else.' Her tone was one of bewilderment and desperation.

'I'm really sorry, but we can't routinely keep people for several weeks if they don't actually need hospice care. We have a limited number of beds and if we held on to people who couldn't go home we would not be able to respond to other people who are in crisis and who need a bed.'

It sounded so logical, so clinical, and so reasonable. The deepest cuts usually are. There was a time, I was led to believe, when there wasn't such a pressure to move people on. The hospice was just that, a place of rest where care wasn't measured in terms of medical interventions but companionship on the last phase of a journey, where suffering was relieved as much in its sharing as in the prescribing of medication. But healthcare had moved on and care was increasingly measured in terms of outcomes. While this change was natural, and the results in many ways more equitable, something very important risked being lost along the way. Moreover, it falls to clinical staff, who have gained trust and given of themselves to patients and families, to abandon the watch in Gethsemane, don the mantle of Judas, and betray with a kiss.

'Of course, we realise that other people have needs, but our concern is for my father.' The son had recovered his balance and sounded frustrated. 'The care in a nursing home won't be as good as it is here, will it?' There was a hint of accusation in his tone.

'There are some very good nursing homes.' I didn't answer his question. The truth is that however good the home it would not replicate the level of care in the hospice. 'Sharon here will talk through the options with you.'

Sharon, the social worker, was ready to step in and take over the discharge process. 'I can give you a list of nearby homes and will sort out the funding arrangements for you. We can talk about it now together with your husband, or I can arrange to meet up with you another time.'

'Does he know about all this?' the wife asked.

'He knows that home is not going to be feasible, and we have mentioned nursing homes as the alternative. We wanted to speak to you first before talking about it in depth with him.'

'He's going to be devastated,' she said. Her son put his arm around her shoulder.

'I'm sorry to have to put you all through this,' I said. 'Setting this up is going to take a little time, and if he deteriorates in the meantime then arrangements can be put on hold or cancelled.'

This was a genuine possibility and it had happened on several occasions in the time I had been at the hospice. Prognosis is often very difficult to assess accurately, even in people who are very frail. A lot of effort that eventually comes to nothing is something that Sharon accepted cheerfully as an inevitable consequence of dealing with such vulnerable patients and their families. Often it was actually a huge relief when someone did deteriorate after all and the family could be let off the hook.

There was a time of silence while they processed the implications of what I had obviously surprised them with. Finally, the wife looked at Sharon and asked, 'Could we spend some time with him and talk to him about it first, and meet up with you later?'

'That's fine. I'll get some paperwork together.'

I nodded at Sharon and took my leave, the 'thirty pieces of silver' weighing more heavily than any number of feathers.

As I stepped out into the corridor I almost bumped into Sheila, who was holding a large card and an envelope with money in it. 'David, have I caught you yet for Helen's leaving card and present?'

Helen was the second nursing sister, and she had been with the hospice for about twelve years, but she was about to retire. She had trained as a nurse over twenty years before, following an acrimonious divorce, and came to the hospice after some years on the medical wards at the hospital. She was much loved by all and her leaving was a sadness to be faced, and no more so than by the auxiliary nurses for whom she had always had a particular concern and who idolised her in return.

'No you haven't. Here, let me contribute something.' Collection envelopes were frequently doing the rounds of the hospice, for significant birthdays and staff departures, but on this occasion I gave more generously than usual. 'There you are. If you remind me later I'll write in the card.'

I traipsed rather forlornly back to the doctors' office. Gordon was flicking through some notes and grunting. 'Something wrong Gordon?' This phlegmatic Scotsman was rarely flustered.

'I've just seen Marilyn Drabble. It's the same old story. She's drowsy and confused. The GP increased her morphine and she got in a muddle again about her tablets, and has no doubt overdone it.'

Marilyn was one of our 'bungee jumpers', as Gordon termed them. These are patients whom we sort out and send home feeling well, and who then keep ending up back with us in a state, usually anxious, in pain and unable to cope. Marilyn was a particularly frequent bouncer, as she really wasn't capable of looking after herself at home in her flat, even with extra help coming in, but insisted every time on going back. Her only family nearby was a sister, who did her best to keep an eye on her, but she was usually on her own overnight.

Marilyn had bladder cancer that had spread within

the pelvis, and mobility was progressively limited by swelling of her legs and general weakness. Her main symptom was pain in the back and legs, and her management was complicated by her psychological responses to pain and illness. She had severe pain at times there is no doubt, but she also tended to express distress or anxiety of any kind as pain. She would wail and moan and complain of severe pain but could often be distracted and settled without resort to extra painkillers. This was fine while she was in the hospice, but when she was at home the automatic reaction of anyone attending her – and this would often be on-call doctors in the middle of the night – would be to increase her painkillers. At other times she would take extra doses herself, and then get confused. Although very exasperating at times and very demanding, there was something about her that was very endearing and I was fond of her.

Gordon continued. 'Mind you, she's not as good as when we last saw her. I think her disease is definitely moving on. She could walk a short distance with a frame during her last admission, but now, even allowing for the effects of medication, I think she'll probably only manage to transfer with help.' I knew Gordon had a soft spot for her too.

'Well, we'll patch her up and send her out again,' I offered. 'Sounds like she might finally have to accept a nursing home?' I sounded unconvinced.

'Ho-ho! I wouldn't count on it!' Gordon shrugged. 'We'll see where we are in a week or so.'

'Have you seen Derek Widdell's notes? I've just had the nursing home talk with his family.'

'I think one of the nurses has them next door. How did it go down?'

'Like a lead balloon, as usual.'

'Well, can't blame them really.'

The nurses' office was a bustle of activity. It was the period of overlap between shifts. In one corner some auxiliary nurses were having a handover from one of the staff nurses. A couple of nurses were writing in notes, Tina was on the phone and Sarah was clearing up dirty mugs onto a tray while chatting with Sheila. From what I could overhear, they were planning some sort of leaving do for Helen.

'She doesn't want a big fuss, and has specifically asked not to have a night out. I thought we'd do something low key here on the ward one afternoon? Could you arrange a cake and nibbles with the kitchen?' Sheila nodded. I found the notes I was looking for on one of the desks.

Tina was raising her voice on the phone. 'I've told you already. No you can't speak to her. And please don't phone again!' She slammed the receiver down and swivelled round, to the attention of everyone in the room. 'Ruddy perverts!'

'Tina, are you okay? What was that all about?' Sarah had stopped mid sentence to express her concern.

'It's this sponsor a nurse campaign that the hospice is running. Somehow a rumour has got out that whoever pledges the most for a given nurse will get the opportunity to take her out for an evening. As if that wasn't enough, a photo of Abby has appeared somewhere in the literature and some bright spark gave out her name. She's apparently the pin up of the local pubs. It's raising a lot of money by all accounts, but we keep getting hopefuls ringing up and asking to speak to her. That's the third call we've had this week.'

One of the auxiliaries chipped in with her account of several calls by someone called Andy, and this led to further exchanges that were a mixture of amusement and outrage.

'How does Abby feel about it?' I said it on the pretext of bringing some sanity back to the situation, but I wondered whether I sounded a bit too concerned.

'Well, as ever, Abby is pretty laid back about it,' said Tina. 'I think she's spoken herself to a couple of callers. She takes it all light-heartedly, and says that at least it's raising money for the hospice.' I suddenly felt very self-conscious and hoped I wasn't blushing.

It had been an epiphany for me, a few days into my second week in the job. I headed into one of the bays to take blood from a patient before the morning meeting. As I looked up I saw her sitting on the edge of the bed helping an old lady to drink tea from her beaker. She was smiling that intoxicating smile that I had thirsted after ever since. She was half in profile, her figure silhouetted by the golden sunlight that filled the space around her and effervesced on her blonde hair. It was shoulder length and she had it, as it often was, tied back in a ponytail. A lock had escaped and was hanging down on her cheek till she hooked it back behind her ear with a half-hearted brush of her finger and a slight tilt of her head. I'd seen her do that dozens of times since and even more in my daydreams. I came to know every contour of that cheek, the gentle sweep of her eyebrows and the line of her delicately proportioned nose leading the eye to the fulsome lips that I ached to melt into, and that easily parted into a smile.

I stopped short for a moment on the threshold of the bay, transfixed in breathless suspense. Warm water rippled from my head to my toes, and I was paralysed in the ecstasy of revelation, aware only of my heart pounding and the scene played out in slow motion before me. She helped the lady put down the beaker on the table and looked towards me. She smiled again and said good morning. Rapture upon rapture! I am undone! I am lost, and my only desire is to be found by her.

I suddenly realised I was staring wide mouthed at her, and my legs were feeling decidedly wobbly. I quickly composed myself and returned a hello, before proceeding, head down, towards the intended patient. I knelt down and set about taking the blood, all the time glancing round furtively, hopelessly beguiled by her presence. My hand was trembling. I missed the vein twice. There was much apologising, my face blushing, my brow sweating. The task eventually accomplished I slinked out, forcing myself not to look round. I made it back to the treatment room and flopped back against the worktop trying to restore my composure.

I had been smitten with her ever since. I quickly found out her name. She was probably in her mid twenties, and was one of the staff nurses. I never saw a ring on her finger, though these days that didn't mean anything, but it fuelled a crazy hope and pathetic yearning. I bumped into her in the office, on ward rounds, and in the staff restaurant, and we exchanged pleasantries, but I avoided too prolonged a discourse as I was sure I'd betray the tumult that she stirred in me. Whenever I brushed against her I would catch my breath and experience a glorious frisson that echoed the intensity of that first epiphany. I would watch her unobtrusively, captivated by her every move and every word.

The patients loved her. She seemed to combine an inner strength with an alluring vulnerability. I'd seen her with apron covered in excrement, hands covered in blood, face covered in sweat and hair dishevelled, and she was always stunning. It came as no surprise that she aroused such interest in the male population of the environs, and I found myself curiously jealous and protective of her honour. I hoped I hadn't given anything away by my display of concern. The last thing I wanted was any awkwardness between us, inflamed by gossip no matter how well meaning. I picked up the notes and did an about turn out of the room, looking as casual as I could.

Sharon was in the doctors' office talking to Gordon. She looked up as I came in. 'Hi David. Thanks for your help with the Widdells.'

'No problem. How did you get on?'

'They seem to be coming round to accepting the reality of the situation. I think he'll get continuing care funding, so there won't be any financial implications for them. His wife has requested some pre-bereavement counselling, so I'll set that up.'

Continuing care funding meant that ongoing care at home or in a nursing home would be paid for by the health service, and was usually assessed on level of need and prognosis. If a patient didn't qualify for this then the funding had to come from social services, and it was then means tested. This could have significant financial implications for the family.

'Can I have the notes once you've finished with them?' Sharon continued.

I held them out to her. 'Here, you take them first. I need to rewrite a drug chart. You can leave them on the desk when you've finished.'

'Thanks.' She took them and went next door to the nurses' office.

I liked Sharon. She was one of three social workers in the hospice team, though the other two worked part time. She also headed up the bereavement service. She was very down to earth, and seemingly unflappable. Her work involved her daily with distressed families and patients, and she often bore the brunt of circumstances ranging from the heated to the tragic, from the banal to the surreal. She dealt with everything thrown at her with equanimity and a sense of humour. She was particularly adept at diffusing seemingly fraught and confused situations with a few carefully chosen, and often very witty observations. She was somehow able to be all things to all people, yet be compromised by none.

When Gordon and I headed to the staff dining room a little later we joined Sharon at one of the tables. I had already, as I always did, scanned the room immediately on entering to see if Abby was there. She wasn't, and I hadn't seen her all morning, so I guessed she was on a late shift.

'Sharon, you know Mrs Barclay who died a few weeks ago. Have you had any bereavement contact with her husband? He struggled so much during those last days. He seemed like someone who might have real problems in bereavement.'

'Yes, he came in to see me the week before last. He's actually doing really well. It's almost as if he went through it all, the struggle to let go and move on, during those long vigils. When she finally died he felt a sense of release. He has little recollection of the anguish of those days, and is getting on with life buoyed by the memories of the good times and the passion they shared. It was really uplifting to talk to him.'

'It's good to hear that. I was really fond of them both.'

Gordon paused between mouthfuls of mashed potato. 'Your books will list all sorts of risk factors for complicated grief,' he made inverted commas signs with his fingers, 'or those who'll struggle in bereavement, but in fact most bereaved people haven't read the books. It's often very difficult to predict. Isn't that right Sharon?' Gordon relished pointing out the deficiencies of theories in the face of the messy reality of healthcare and humanity.

'There's certainly truth in that Gordon,' she replied. 'You can sometimes anticipate problems with particular bereavements, but people will often surprise you.'

'What's the longest you've had to support someone?' I asked.

'I've someone on the books at the moment that I've been seeing for about three years. I don't see her very often now, and I'm about to stop regular follow up. She's coming out the other side, and has just met someone else, which is really lovely to see.'

'Do you ever get any really bizarre reactions?'

'Occasionally. Nothing much surprises me nowadays. Only last week I was visiting a middle-aged lady whose sister died a few weeks ago. They were inseparable, and she had looked after her sister throughout her illness. Now she has died she has kept her room almost like a shrine. When I visited we sat in there with candles lit all around the room. After talking for a while she said that she often hears her sister speaking to her from the 'other side'. After a silent pause her mobile phone went off, and the ringtone was 'someone's calling yooooou.....'.'

Gordon almost choked on his mouthful, and then erupted into raucous laughter, as did those sitting at the adjacent table who had obviously overheard the anecdote.

'Gosh, how did you keep a straight face?' I asked incredulously.

'With great difficulty! But I did.'

'How do you cope with all the distress that you have to wade through?'

'As with all of us, I just learn to do it. And I have ways of offloading. How about you David, how are you finding it?'

'Well, I'm coping better than I expected I think. You walk a fine line between empathy and being overwhelmed sometimes. I'll tell you what I have noticed though. I was never one to get weepy over films before, but now I find myself crying more easily when I watch or read about something tragic or inspiring. I was watching a film the other day in which a family pet dog had to be put down and before I knew it there were tears streaming down my face. I was glad I was on my own or else I'd have felt a right twit!'

'Ah don't worry about it.' Gordon had adopted

his avuncular tone. 'Emotions must come out, and pressure has to be relieved. It's like a dyke effect. We do very well to hold everything back when we're in our professional roles, but holes will appear somewhere, and if we try to plug one hole then another will open up somewhere else. In fact they need to or else the day will come when everything floods over the top. A good cry now and then with friends is better than falling apart at work or burning out.'

'Did I hear something about floods? Can I interest any of you in our canoeing challenge?' Jackie appeared over my shoulder and sat down next to me with her lunch tray. She was one of the fundraising team, a bright and bubbly young woman who was always indomitably cheerful. She had an infectious enthusiasm that seems to be an essential requirement for a fundraiser, and she could charm anyone into doing things they would never have dreamt of doing. I had managed to avoid being pressed into any fundraising activities so far, as they all seemed arduous, messy or embarrassing to varying degrees. Now I was cornered.

'David, how are you? I've been meaning to catch up with you. Please, please, please, pleeeeease can I persuade you to take part in one of our fundraising events. It's such an encouragement to everyone when the hospice staff get involved, and especially the doctors. Gordon took part in our fashion show in the spring, didn't you Gordon?'

'Aye. And I looked great in a ball gown! Go on David, there's no escape.'

'Yes, do David.' Jackie was closing in for the kill. 'Look you can take your pick of the list. Walking on hot coals, the twenty mile coastal canoeing challenge, the half marathon, the karaoke talent show, the parachute jump.....'

'Okay, okay I'll do it. I'll do the parachute jump.' At least it wasn't embarrassing, wasn't painful and would be over pretty quickly. Moderately scary, as I wasn't very good with heights, but I'd always rather fancied giving it a go.

'Oh thank you. You're a star!'

'I did one a couple of years ago,' said Sharon, winking at me. 'It's great fun, you'll enjoy it. Jackie, have you got many doing it this year?'

'Five so far, and David will make six. There's Andrew from fundraising, one of the volunteer drivers, two members of the public, and now two from the hospice clinical staff.'

'Who is the other?'

'Oh that's Abby, one of the staff nurses.'

The notice had sent shock waves through the hospice. Willie had been given his marching orders. The spraying had become more of a problem and, fuelled by some mutterings from certain quarters and then by two complaints, and in particular one from a visitor to the hospice, it had finally been designated a health and safety issue. Despite several trips to the vet Willie continued unrepentant to shower unsuspecting handbags and other items left on the floor in his territory. The nefarious feline would have to go, and was simply waiting for a suitable home to be found. Several members of staff were devastated. Willie had for so long been such an integral part of the hospice that it seemed inconceivable that we should now be seeking to get rid of him.

For a while a resigned despondency hung over the place, while those most fond of him consoled each other with whispered frustrations and silent tears. Soon the passive resignation turned into hopeful activism and a petition was circulated requesting a reprieve. Signatures were obtained from staff, patients, visitors, volunteers – everyone who had come into contact with Willie and who valued his presence and personality. When Helen handed me the clipboard and pen, I signed the petition as much because I knew it was important to her as because of my own fondness for Willie.

'There you are. I don't suppose it will do any good though.'

She shrugged. 'Well we can only try. Thank you.'

I reflected on why this had caused such a rumpus, and wondered whether in some ways this was more than just a battle to save a friend from being re-homed, but it represented something deeper. Perhaps it echoed a battle for the very soul of the hospice itself, a fight for its maverick and free-spirit character and values against the constraints and impositions of an increasingly bureaucratic system. I sighed softly as Helen moved on to find more signatories. It was difficult to see how this oasis would survive unchanged in modern healthcare.

I returned to the letter I was reading. I had been invited to interview for a surgical registrar post up country. I had spotted the advertisement earlier that month and it immediately aroused my interest. It was at a prestigious hospital and would be a real leg up on the career ladder if I were to secure it. I was pleasantly surprised to receive the letter of invitation, and was musing on how best to prepare for it. I needed to read up on recent journals, as I had let that slip a little over the last few weeks. Perhaps I'd also contact my previous consultant for some advice and interview tips.

As I rounded the corner from reception and entered the ward I heard the wailing coming from the first single room that had become a characteristic punctuation to the usual background noise. Marilyn was having a bad morning again. I stuck my head around the door. She was unattended so I went in and knelt beside the bed. She was sprawled at an angle across the bed, anchored by the hugely swollen right leg that was the site of most of her pain.

'Hello Marilyn. What's the matter?'

She opened her eyes and smiled, then grimaced. 'Oh, hello David. It's everything. The pain was bad last night. This leg is so big now, and I can't move very easily.'

We talked for a while about her sister's latest news and some of the visitors she'd had over the last few days. She was easily distracted from her distress.

'I want to get home again, but I just don't see how I'll manage.'

This had been a major breakthrough for Marilyn, to acknowledge her limitations and face the fact that home was really no longer feasible. The option of nursing home had been raised on numerous occasions, but she had always been adamant that she would not go to one. There was a case conference planned for later that day to decide what we should be planning for in terms of discharge. Marilyn knew this and it was probably fuelling her distress. Normally these meetings would include the patient, if they wanted, and relevant family or carers, but this was a preliminary one for hospice staff in order to decide whether we should offer to keep her here indefinitely.

'I know Marilyn. This is all very difficult for you. I'll come back later today to talk about options. Is that alright? In the meantime, do you need anything for pain at the moment?'

'No I think it's passing off. Thank you David. Will you talk to my sister?'

'Yes, of course.'

I left the room and as I headed down the corridor I could hear the soft wailing starting again. As I approached the nurses' station I saw Helen talking to Cathy. The tone and expressions were a mixture of mirth and exasperation.

'What's up?'

'Honestly, David, sometimes I wonder,' Helen replied. 'You know we have that large rack of information leaflets in the foyer. Well it appears that there are, or rather were, some leaflets from one of the local undertakers about planning a funeral. Now, quite what the wisdom is on having such leaflets on open display is one thing. Anyway, it appears that Gloria has taken them all and has been going round handing them out to all the other patients and engaging them in conversations about their preferences. There is a list of questions such as what you would like to wear in the coffin, what special things or jewellery you'd like with you, what you would like your family to do around the time of death, and much more!'

Gloria was a lady in her late fifties with lung cancer. She had become somewhat uninhibited and was displaying some odd behaviour, leading us to suspect that the cancer might have spread to her brain. It didn't surprise me that she would be the agent of such a prank. I could visualise some of the effects this might have had. Cathy shrugged and chuckled.

'Oh dear. Is anyone distressed?' I asked.

'Well, certainly not in her bay! It's a riot of hilarity, each of them vying for the most ridiculous thing to have in their coffin, and animated discussions about what outfit to wear! I haven't checked on the other patients yet.'

'Oh well. I suppose for some people it will be helpful to think about that sort of detail. It certainly opens up conversations about death and dying.'

Helen took her leave and carried on down to the next bay to assess the damage. Cathy motioned me to come closer. 'You know what Helen said when Gloria asked her what she'd like in her coffin? She said her ex-husband – still alive!' I laughed. Cathy continued, 'We'll be sorry to see her go. She's a good girl. Passionate.' Referring to someone who is older than oneself and who is about to retire as a good girl seemed slightly amusing, but coming from Cathy it sounded completely appropriate. 'You are not hatching any plans to go yet, are you David? We wouldn't want to lose two of you at once.'

How could she know about the interview? Does she know? She couldn't know, as I hadn't told anyone. All the same, I felt awkward and disloyal. I reached into my pocket to make sure the letter was still there.

'I've nowhere to go to at the moment.' It was a truthful statement.

She smiled that endearing smile that always lit up her face. 'I don't know whether Brian has spoken to you yet, but we'd like your input at the case conference today. Brian can't make it, and anyway you've got to know Marilyn quite well.'

'That's fine, very happy to contribute.' We parted.

When I came into the doctors' office I found Brian talking to Nick, while Sheila was listening attentively, her face a picture of concentration. I had come in on the end of a conversation that seemed to centre on the Book of Names. This was a book of remembrance that was kept in a glass display case in the chapel. It was effectively an ornate day-to-a-page diary in which relatives could, for a fee, have their loved one's name entered for the particular date on which they died. Every day the page was turned and the names of those who had died on previous anniversaries of that date were displayed as an act of remembrance.

'We don't have a system in place for checking that, it's true,' Nick explained. 'But it's not the sort of situation that one would expect to arise!' He was obviously dismayed.

'Clearly. It's very unusual. Well, we'll see whether he's right.' Brian sounded thoughtful. He looked across to me. 'Hello David. Here's a strange one for you.'

'Something wrong?'

'In the Book of Names for today is written, among others, that of Percival Fleming.'

'Percival Fleming?' I obviously looked puzzled. 'How? Why? He's not dead.....at least he wasn't when I saw him this morning.'

'Quite. And there's the mystery.'

'Well how did it get in there?' This seemed decidedly spooky.

Nick took up the narrative. 'The Book of Names is managed by the fundraising department. Relatives pay the required donation and one of the team who is particularly good at calligraphy updates the book accordingly. It appears that Mr Fleming's son arranged for Percy's name to be entered for today's date. No year is entered, just the name on the anniversary date that they died. The person who administers the process doesn't necessarily ask what year they died as that information isn't needed. When this instruction was received there was no reason to suppose that the name in question was still alive and in the hospice.'

'But why would the son do that?' I asked, perplexed.

'In my conversations with Percy he has consistently said that he believes he is going to die soon, and over the last few days he's narrowed the prediction down to today. Presumably his son too was convinced.'

'But he's fine today. He's the last patient we have in at the moment that I would have predicted would die today. We are starting to think about discharge arrangements.'

I knew Percy quite well. He seemed very level headed and not one to be superstitious. He hadn't mentioned any of this to me over the last few days. Apart from being disconcerted, part of me was a little hurt that he hadn't shared these thoughts with me.

Nick continued. 'I'll go and have a chat with him. He's apparently asked to see me.'

'Thanks Nick. I'll catch up with you later.' Brian stared into space for a while then swivelled round to face me.

'David. How are you?'

'I'm well thank you.'

'Still enjoying it here? Or are we putting you off hospice care?'

'No, I'm finding it very rewarding. I'm also learning a lot about myself in the process.'

'Not got itchy feet yet? Doesn't the siren call of surgical fame and fortune beckon?'

Gosh, does he know too? He can't know. Am I going mad? I tried not to sound embarrassed or guilty. 'Well, I don't know.'

He laughed. 'Listen, don't worry my boy. I'm not trying to put you on the spot. Glad to hear all's well. I wonder, would you do me a favour? We've got this case conference today about Marilyn, which I can't make. Would you represent me and give the medical side of the case? In situations such as this when there is disagreement within the team about what to do, the final decision rests with me. I'm delegating that to you. You know Marilyn very well, and you've been around here long enough for my way of thinking and doing things to rub off on you. I'm happy to trust your instinct on this.'

'Yes, of course. Thank you.' I was a little overwhelmed.

'Cathy will be there to back you up. And I'm sure you'll both be of the same mind.' He got up to leave. 'Thank you David. I'll see you later.'

I sat there for a moment, taking in the compliment I had just received and pondering the responsibility

I had now shouldered. Sheila turned to look at me. 'Oh David! Well done. Brian must think very highly of you. You'll be heading for a consultant post here before you know it!' I blushed. 'Hey, what about Mr Fleming? Isn't that weird!' Her face was a mixture of horror and amazement. She didn't seem to expect a reply, but turned back to whatever she had on the desk in front of her.

Later that afternoon we gathered in the large sitting room for the case conference. The room was filled with a buzz of conversation and laughter. There was representation from pretty much the whole multi-disciplinary team, including Sharon, Nick, Helen, various nurses who were caring for Marilyn, the physio-therapist, one of the complementary therapists, Cathy and myself. I was very grateful that Cathy was chairing the meeting. She brought the gathering to order.

'Thank you all for coming. As you know the crux of the matter we need to decide upon is whether Marilyn should stay here at the hospice for however long it takes for her to deteriorate and die, or whether we feel we should press for her to be discharged to a nursing home.' It had been established that she could not manage at home any longer, so that was no longer an option.

'We know that Marilyn and her sister really want her to stay here.' There was no need for either of them to be at the meeting, as it was a matter that we had to decide as a team, and it centred on whether her needs were such that they could only be met in the hospice.

'Now it needs to be acknowledged that Marilyn isn't always the easiest person to look after and get alongside, but we mustn't let that colour our judgement about what is best for her. I know it won't, but it is helpful to state that.'

There was a difference of opinion within the team about what to do. Even the auxiliary nurses, who were often a good barometer of general feeling, and whose instinct about patients was usually trustworthy, were divided about the appropriateness of keeping her here. There were some who felt that she was manipulative and that it was not right that she should stay while others who were in similar situations were made to move on.

Cathy continued. 'Perhaps it would be helpful to start with a summary of her medical condition. David, would you mind?'

'Her cancer is quite advanced in that she has extensive local recurrence of her disease in the abdomen and pelvis. As far as we are aware she has not had any spread anywhere else. The pelvic disease is causing the swelling in her legs. There is no more active treatment available. Although she is experiencing significant disability, her blood tests are pretty good at the moment and there is no expectation that she is dying imminently. Prognosis is always difficult to be sure about but it could be anything from a few weeks to a few months.'

'So if we decide she should stay, we might be talking about her being with us for several months before she dies?' Helen knew this but was stating the point for the benefit of everyone involved.

'That's right,' I replied.

Cathy again. 'The question is whether she could receive the care she needs in a nursing home environment. She clearly has major nursing needs. Her main physical symptom problem remains the pain, but her complex psychological responses have a bearing on this too.'

There followed prolonged discussion ranging over each of these areas. There was no disputing the fact that her nursing care could be provided in a nursing home. The areas of contention were the pain control and her complex behavioural responses, and there were varying shades of opinion on these. It gradually became evident that we would not be able to reach a consensus.

After almost three quarters of an hour of debate Cathy sought to bring us to a decision. 'I think we need to accept that we won't all agree on what we should do in this situation. This meeting has given an opportunity for opinions and feelings to be aired, but we really need to decide one way or another, and then get behind the decision as a team. Normally Brian would make the final call, and in this instance he has delegated this authority to David.' She turned towards me with a smile. 'David, having heard all the arguments, what is your feeling?'

I felt remarkably calm and composed despite having the spotlight turned on me. I paused to gather my thoughts. 'I think we can accept that her nursing care could be provided elsewhere. I know some have argued the same about her pain control. And in one sense that's right. We are not anticipating any major changes in her medication or our approach to her pain control, but we know that she expresses a lot of her psychological distress as pain. We've got to know her pretty well over the course of several admissions, and I think we've learned how to manage this distress. My concern, were she to go to a nursing home, is that her expressions of pain would be met by increases in her medication. After all, we've seen this time and again as the factor in precipitating her admission here. I think that she would probably die sooner at a nursing home than she would if she continued to be looked after here. I think her complex pain and psychological symptoms warrant ongoing hospice care. I feel she should probably stay here, for as long as it takes.'

There was silence for a few seconds and then some nodding of heads. I suddenly felt very self-conscious. Cathy broke the silence. 'Thank you David. We will take that as the collective decision of this meeting. Might I also suggest that we agree to hold a meeting every two weeks so as to give staff a forum to which they can bring issues regarding Marilyn's ongoing care? But we will not revisit the decision to let her stay.' There was general agreement. 'Thank you all for coming.'

The meeting closed and people returned to their activities. Nick winked at me as he got up to leave. As I headed for the door Cathy came over and squeezed my arm. 'Well done David. The right decision.'

I emerged into the corridor feeling quite drained. Sandy, one of the staff nurses, met me as I was making my way back to the office. 'David, just to let you know. Percy Fleming has died.' I stopped in my tracks, a shiver down my spine.

'What? Really? How? What happened?' I was bewildered and trying to connect the thoughts that were flitting through my mind and engage them to my mouth.

'He collapsed and died on the way to the bathroom. Complained of sudden pain in his chest and went blue. He probably had a pulmonary embolism.'

163

❦

'Finally Dr Trevelyan, what do you think is the most important quality that one should demonstrate in order to be a successful surgeon?' It was the chairman of the panel who fired the last salvo.

I thought for a moment. 'Well it depends what you mean by successful. I think the most important quality we can bring, as in any field of medicine, is compassion.'

'Compassion?'

'Yes. We are dealing with fellow human beings who are often vulnerable and scared. They trust their lives to us, their future. Many are aware, though they may not voice it, that the moment they go under the anaesthetic may be the last conscious moment they experience. And occasionally when they wake up, it won't be to a sense of relief but to some bad news that they may or may not have been expecting or afraid of, and which we have to break to them. And then more than ever they need us to be not a white coat or technician but a compassionate human being.'

He held my gaze for a moment after I had finished and then glanced at some of the other members on the panel. 'Thank you Dr Trevelyan. That concludes our questions. Do you have any questions for us?'

'Thank you. My questions have already been answered during my pre-interview visit.'

'Well then, it remains for me to bid you good day. We will notify you of the outcome later today.' Smiles and handshakes all round, some of them rather stiff.

I emerged into the waiting room, picked up my belongings and nodded to the next candidate who was nervously fingering the end of his tie. I was one of the earliest to be interviewed and I'd decided not to hang around for the verdict as I wanted to get back in time for Helen's leaving do that afternoon. During the two-hour drive back I reflected on the process. As ever it had been a daunting experience. A long table with seven panel members, each taking turns to probe and expose. I guess I had done reasonably well. I was able to answer all the questions reasonably intelligently, and they seemed happy with my previous experience, though the decision to take the post in the hospice had raised a few eyebrows. I had visited the department the previous week, and the whole set up was pretty impressive – but then that was usually to be expected in such a large teaching hospital. There seemed a distinct lack of warmth, however, compared to the environment I was currently used to. No one at the hospice was aware that I was visiting or attending for interview, and I had simply requested the time off as annual leave.

I finally swung into the hospice car park just after lunch. As I came in through the entrance Cathy was emerging from the staff dining room. 'Hello David. Have you come in for Helen's tea party?'

'Yes. I didn't want to miss it.'

'Oh Good. Can I have a quick word? There's something I'd like you to do when we all meet up with her.' I followed her to her office, intrigued.

At three that afternoon we all congregated in the large sitting room. There were trays of cakes and hot drinks, which and Sheila and Cathy began to distribute. The room was overflowing with staff of all disciplines. Helen had not wanted an evening do, and preferred minimal fuss, but she wasn't going to get away with no celebration. Cathy brought the room to order and thanked everyone for coming. Helen had been close to tears for several minutes but at that point she then broke down, overwhelmed by the whole event. A number of the other nursing staff were also fighting back tears.

'Oh dear! This is not meant to be upsetting!' said Cathy, proffering a box of tissues.

'I'm sorry,' Helen replied. 'You are all so kind. I've loved working here, with such a great team. This place has felt like my home all these years. I don't really want to be going.'

Cathy knelt in front of her while Nick held her around the shoulders. 'Perhaps we could adjourn for five minutes while Helen gathers herself?' Some of us exited the room while others chatted among themselves.

After a few minutes Cathy came out and beckoned us all back in. 'I think we are okay now.' There followed a speech by Cathy thanking Helen and reminiscing about some of the times that were had over the years. Then there was the presentation of the leaving presents, some things for her garden and an album of photographs that the auxiliaries had put together. Helen was suitably touched. 'And now David has something for you.' Cathy motioned towards me.

'Yes. I have some good news hot off the press. Willie has been given a reprieve and reinstated as hospice cat!' Helen beamed with delight and there were cheers and applause all round.

Cathy had shown me the notice after lunch. There had been an acknowledgement of Willie's important role in supporting patients, relatives and friends, and many people had been surprised by the volume of support for him within the staff. The issue of spraying remained, but there was to be guidance on how to minimise the risk of him doing this and a rapid response team with detergent and cloths to deal with any misdemeanours. The trump card, however, had been Helen's suggestion that we try the one avenue of remedy that had not yet been investigated – homeopathy. He was to be seen by a homeopathic vet. This was ironic indeed. Opinion within the team was divided about homeopathic treatments, though everyone accepted that the counselling role of the practitioner was often very therapeutic in itself. Yet the hospice did access homeopathy for those patients who wanted it. And if we implied benefit for our patients, then how could we evict Willie without having tried it for him? It was magnificent! I had really thought that Willie's number was up. Helen could rightly feel proud. It was a fitting end to the celebrations.

People started to melt away back to their work. I went up and gave Helen a hug.

'Thank you David. That's the best news I've had for a long time.'

'Glad to be the bearer of it. When do you actually do your final shift?'

'I've two more weeks left. I finish with a weekend duty.'

'Well, you'll be missed.'

I lingered a little longer and polished off some of the cake. Presently, Sheila came back into the room. 'David, there's a phone call for you in the office. A Mr Hamilton.'

'Oh. Thank you, I'll come straight along.' This was the chairman of the interview panel.

I picked up the phone with bated breath. It was a 'well done, but I'm afraid you didn't get the job' phone call. He was very complimentary about my interview, very impressed by my answer to the final question. But it was a strong field and I was just beaten to the post by one of the other candidates. He wished me well for the future and was certain I'd secure a good post somewhere else. I put the receiver down and stood pensively. I had thought I would be more disappointed, but curiously I wasn't. I was almost relieved.

Marilyn died about a month after the case conference. She stopped wailing once the decision had been made to let her stay at the hospice.

Chapter 6
Days of Wonder

I sat perched on the edge of the open doorway with my right leg hanging down into the void beside the fuselage, and my hands gripping tightly to the edge of the opening. Looking down at the patchwork of fields about three thousand feet below I could see we were approaching the flight school and landing zone beyond. The vibration resonated up through my trunk and arms and seemed to engulf my whole body, masking any contribution of fear or cold to my uncontrollable shaking. My helmet was uncomfortable and the strap was cutting in to the underside of my chin, and the harness was digging into my crotch. The noise was deafening and the force of the icy airflow seemed to suck the breath from my lungs. I felt that if I loosened my grip at all or if there were any sudden tilting of the aircraft I would be swept away. The static line arced up from the pack on my back to the strongpoint just above the doorway above my left shoulder. I hoped it was secure. I looked across to Abby on the other side of the cabin, and she smiled and gave a thumbs-up. The jumpmaster was crouched opposite me in the doorway leaning out, and poised to give the signal. What was I doing here?

We had arrived at the training centre at eight that morning. It was a cold but crisp early winter morning, with not a breath of wind. There were five of us, as one of the members of the public had dropped out. Abby had greeted me warmly, and we all conversed very easily and openly, united by a bond of excitement and apprehension. The instructor was a South African called Kurt and he welcomed us enthusiastically. 'It's a great morning today guys. Weather's perfect. You'll definitely jump today.' After registration and paperwork, we were ushered into a classroom and given an hour of instruction on technique and procedures.

We would be doing a static line jump, where the parachute rip cord was automatically pulled as we fell away from the aircraft. We would also have a reserve parachute in case the first did not open. We were strongly reassured that the likelihood of this happening was negligible. The walls of the room, and indeed most of the centre, were adorned with photographs of skydivers in various poses, on the ground, standing by aircraft and in freefall formations. There was evidently a quasi-community of semi-permanent residents at the centre, whose all-consuming passion was skydiving.

We were then taken to a hangar where we practised parachute landing falls, namely how to land and roll over correctly so as not to break any limbs. Having practised this on mats we then jumped off a small gantry in a controlled descent. Finally, we were shown the aircraft we would be using and Kurt took us through flight and jump procedures. Rather than standing by a door and jumping out as I had anticipated, we would sit on the edge of the open door and push ourselves sideways away from the aircraft. The idea was to spread our arms and legs in the freefall position and count out loud 'one thousand, two thousand, three thousand, four thousand.' On four thousand we were to look up, and if we didn't see an open parachute above us we were to deploy our reserve chute.

It was a long morning and we were grateful to be able to return to the centre canteen for some refreshments and a break. It enabled me, from the safety of small group conversation, to find out some more about Abby. One of three children, she was originally from Wales and then moved to the area when she was at primary school. I thought I had detected a very mild Welsh accent. She had always wanted to be a nurse and came to the hospice shortly after qualifying. Conversation flowed freely in the relaxed atmosphere of a group brought together in a shared experience. It was exhilarating to be close to her, and I was captivated by her every gesture and hung on her every word. I quite forgot the lurking apprehension of what shortly lay ahead of us.

After about half an hour Kurt appeared and intruded on my reverie with a call to action. 'Right guys, time to get some kit on. Follow me.' We all got up and followed him back to the hangar.

Abby fell in beside me. 'Are you looking forward to this David?'

'Well, sort of. A mixture of excitement and apprehension. How about you?'

'Me too. This will be the first time I've been up in an aeroplane.'

'Really?'

'Yes. After this I'll be able to say that I've taken off in a plane, but never landed in one!'

We were issued with jump suits to put on over our clothes and then the main and reserve parachutes were strapped on. We went through the checking procedures on each other's chutes. Finally, we clambered into the Pilatus Porter aircraft and sat on the floor of the cabin with our backs against the cabin wall. The aircraft shuddered as the propellers started up and everything was then drowned out by the noise and vibration of the engines. The side door was slid shut and we taxied to the short runway. Before we knew it we were jolted backwards as the nose lifted high and we were airborne. I looked at the others. They were all staring straight ahead. My mouth went very dry.

The aircraft climbed quickly in a circling ascent before levelling out at the jump height. In a matter of only a few minutes the engines were throttled back and Kurt slid open the door. There was a sudden inrush of wind and it became even noisier. He beckoned me to come across. I had volunteered to jump first. I didn't like the thought of watching the others go while waiting for my turn. As I shuffled forward Kurt took my static line clip and attached it to the strongpoint. I moved right to the edge of the open doorway and swung my leg round and down into the void. I felt like jelly and my stomach was churning.

I seemed to be sitting there for an age but it was probably only a few seconds. Suddenly Kurt gave a thumbs-up and patted me on the shoulder. This was it. I held my breath and shoved off as hard as I could from the edge of the doorway. 'One thousand, two thou.....

Arrgghh!' There was no way I could finish the count out loud. My stomach hit my throat as I plummeted away from the aircraft and the slipstream blasted the air out of my lungs. My mind was numb and everything was a blur. After another second or two I felt a jolt and remembered to look up. There spread gloriously above me was the open canopy.

In moments the sheer panic and overwhelming noise was replaced by an amazing calm and near silence, only broken by the distant noise of the aircraft as it continued on its course high above me. For a while I felt suspended in time, marvelling at the vista stretching out in every direction around me. It didn't last for long, for even floating down on a parachute the ground quickly came up to meet me, and I mentally prepared for the landing technique we had perfected that morning. The landing was remarkably smooth. I rolled over in the short grass and gathered up my chute.

As I stood cradling the gathered bundle in front of me I looked up to see if anyone else was on their way down. There would be two drops on each pass over the airfield and Abby was supposed to be second to jump. I spotted her floating down. She would land about two hundred yards from my position. I started to walk towards her, legs gradually recovering from their jelly-like feeling. Abby landed safely, a perfectly executed parachute landing fall, and was immediately up on her feet. She unstrapped her harness and let out an ecstatic whoop. As I approached her she took off her helmet and shook out her sumptuous blond hair. I stopped, and looked on in wonder. She was sublime, standing there in a jump suit, framed by acres of blue sky and green grass, sunlit hair flowing like silk across her shoulders. It was a picture that would remain forever engraved in my memory. It had all been worth it just for this moment.

She came across and laughed with adrenaline-fuelled excitement. 'We did it! Wasn't that fantastic? We did it David!' She held up her hand for a 'high five'.

We gathered up her parachute and walked together back to the hangar. It was quite a long walk, but I wished it were longer. She couldn't stop talking the whole way back. She was like a little girl that had discovered something amazing and was bubbling over with delight. Back in the hangar we waited for the rest of our group to come in, each one wearing an expression that was a mixture of joy and relief. Before the last one completed the trudge from the landing zone the aircraft had landed and taxied back into the hangar. Kurt jumped out and there was much shaking of hands and slapping of backs. Under his careful supervision we all then had to repack the parachutes before we could repair to the canteen for celebratory refreshments.

The sun was beginning to drop low on the horizon by the time we spilled out and dispersed to our cars. The excitement had given way to tiredness. I was glad it was a Saturday and we still had the rest of the weekend to go. Abby was going on to stay with her sister for the night. I lingered by my car and watched her as she walked over to hers. Before getting in she turned and waved to me. 'See you next week David. Have a good weekend.' With that she was in the car and reversing out of her space. I watched her drive off down the access road. I sighed. What was I to do? This was not in my game plan. By the time we had walked back to the hangar after the jump that afternoon I had realised that I was hopelessly in love with her.

'*This is Mark Jarvis, the drive-time voice of your local radio. It's 8.27 on a beautiful Monday morning. As you know, in our local heroes slot this week we are going to be featuring some of the staff at our local hospice St. Julian's. A number of you have already written and phoned in with some of your stories and comments on your experiences with the hospice, and I'll share some of those later. We're kicking off with one of the nursing sisters, Sarah Wenham, whom I spoke to last week. But first, our thought for the day, and I picked this up from one of the nurses I spoke to during my visit: in caring for others we become better people. In caring for others we become better people. Let us know your thoughts on that, our phone lines are open. And let's hear how I got on with Sarah Wenham.*'

The radio presenter's unfailing morning cheeriness didn't seem to grate as it usually did. I always listened to the station on my drive in to work, the mindless banter that required little engagement of the brain helping to ease me from somnolent stupor to work-readiness, and he often managed to raise at least a smile in me, though Monday mornings tended to have the highest irritation factor.

Perhaps it made a difference now having actually met the man. The hospice was periodically the focus of the media spotlight, and by and large this was welcomed as it helped to maintain public awareness and could provide a much needed boost to donations.

The local media was uniformly sympathetic and always eager to run with anything related to the hospice. Mark Jarvis had visited the previous week to do a series of five recorded interviews across the range of hospice staff, and these were to be featured every day of this week. He was personable and self-effacing, and had demonstrated a genuine interest and concern for our work and the people behind the image.

Perhaps it was the difference in me. Colours were more vivid, scents more intense and melodies more distinctive. I had paused for several minutes on the threshold that morning looking wondrously at the leaves on the trees outside my driveway. Were they always that vibrant? They're beautiful! How could I have missed that before? I had drunk deeply of the chill morning air and revelled in the tingling in my lungs, exhilarated to be alive. I had become a more patient man overnight, making allowance for things that usually irritated me with the condescension of one who had a higher perspective.

The wait for a break in traffic before pulling out of the driveway had become an opportunity to take in the full panoply of life on the street around me. I noticed the kindness of a shopkeeper, opening up at the beginning of his day, to a mother struggling past with a pram and two toddlers who were throwing their coats on the ground. I watched a jogger taking her German Shepherd dog for a run, or was it the other way around? I noticed the weight of the sack over the postman's shoulder as he lugged it from door to door, delivering joy and disappointment, hope and frustration, humour and irritation, in hues of white and grey and brown through mostly faceless letterboxes. There was nothing that could fall through my door today that would dampen my spirits.

'We aim to deliver patient-centred, individualised care. We have a large team of nurses and other professionals that enable us to do that. We are often able to spend more time with people than my colleagues in the hospital are able to do.....'

I wonder which shift she'll be working today. Will she greet me warmly? Will the memories of our shared experience of two days ago even register upon her consciousness today?

'Most patients come in to have symptom problems sorted out. Then we try to get them home again. About half of patients admitted to the hospice will die with us, but many go home again and may end up coming in several times.....'

I've replayed in my mind countless times every detail of our time together. Somehow in the remembering, the others in our party have faded into the background, extras in the drama in which we have become centre stage, the two of us coy protagonists in some Shakespearean drama and destined to be lovers when once the facades are breached and the choreography of desire and wistful longing transcends circumstance and etiquette.

'It is hard sometimes, and some situations affect you more than others. But we are quite a close knit team, and when one of us is finding it hard we support each other. There's also a lot of humour, often black humour, and that releases pressure.....'

I've analysed every remembered gesture, every

nuance of conversation, my heart winging flights of fancy through the ecstasy of hope and possibility. She speaks to me in my sleep, and when I close my eyes I see her face.

'What is often most rewarding is seeing the transformation that happens to some patients. They may come in to the hospice distressed and frightened, but then are able to go home again relaxed and smiling and looking forward to making the most of whatever time is left, supported by carers and family.....'

Does she hold any feelings for me? Have I aroused her interest, or even her curiosity? Could I possibly have a chance? The tension between uncertainty and possibility is torment, but what glorious torment!

I sat for a few minutes in the car before going in, listening to some of the phone calls to the radio station. Caller after caller shared a tale of gilded sadness, effusive in their praise of those that had cared for this husband or that sister. It became almost embarrassing to listen to, layer upon layer of gooey sweet sentiment. Come on, we're not saints! I went in to the hospice reflecting on how far a little kindness and professionalism can go, and I began to feel a little guilty about my reaction. Who was I to belittle the gratitude and heartfelt emotion of those whose lives had been touched by this place? Isn't that what we're all about? I paused on the way down to the office to look at the nursing duty roster, eagerly anticipating Abby's shift. To my great dismay I discovered that she wouldn't be in that day as she had a day off! She was working an early shift the following day, so I would see her in the morning.

Sheila was just finishing on the phone as I came into

the office. She was bouncy and talkative as ever. 'Good morning David! How was the parachute jump? I hear you all came back safely. I bet it was an experience you won't forget in a hurry!'

'Morning Sheila. Yes, back safe and sound. It was a great day. Scary, but fantastic, in many ways.'

'How much have you raised in sponsorship?'

'Well I think I'm in at just over five hundred pounds. I'm not sure about the other four.'

'That's brilliant. Well done.'

'Sheila, do you happen to know, do we get many complaints from patients or relatives?'

'Hardly ever. Of course there's the occasional misunderstanding that is usually cleared up very quickly, but we very rarely get a formal complaint. It's almost always completely the opposite. You've seen the cards we get.'

'Yes I know. I was listening to the radio interview and phone-in just now, and there wasn't a single negative word said.'

'We put the complaints box in the foyer last year, and we hardly ever get anything in it. The last complaint I can remember in there was one a few months ago. It said that they were complaining that we had a complaints box, as there is nothing to complain about!'

She turned back to her typing. I reflected that while it was very pleasing to have such positive feedback, such an atmosphere of affirmation and praise might make it difficult to know if we weren't ever quite doing as good a job as we might or ought.

The morning meeting passed largely over my head, such was my state of euphoria and distraction. I think

I managed to conceal the turmoil of my inner being from all but Cathy, who made one or two comments about having obviously had a good weekend. As ever, her words seemed pregnant with a knowing intuition, but I pretended not to notice. Jackie from fundraising caught me after the meeting to congratulate me on the jump. A photographer from the local newspaper was coming the following day to take a group photograph of the five of us holding a cheque for the total amount raised by our combined jumps. I felt a frisson of excitement, as it would be an opportunity to talk to Abby with minimal risk.

The morning was relatively undemanding as I went round half of the ward with Lucy Danvers while Sally took the other half. The main event of the day was to be the arrival of an electric wheelchair for one of our patients. Nobby Clarke was a spunky Londoner with a peach of a cockney accent. An extremely likeable man, he had endeared himself to all manner of staff within a short time of being admitted. A lifetime of smoking had contributed to severe vascular disease and he had had both legs amputated above the knees about five years before. Confined to a wheelchair ever since, he had always had to rely on someone to push him, as he had also lost a hand in an industrial accident years before. Thankfully, as he put it, it wasn't his drinking hand, and one of his greatest pleasures was to spend time down at the pub. However, he was doted upon by a wife and two daughters and getting away for some time with his friends without one of them was, again as he put it, a rare treat. Sadly, the smoking had dealt him another blow as he had recently been diagnosed with lung cancer. He had come into the hospice for pain control.

The possibility of propelling himself in his wheelchair had always been something he aspired to but their finances didn't stretch very far and it had never seemed a priority until now when suddenly time to enjoy it was limited. The family had no idea it was coming. Staff had picked up on the idea and Sharon had managed to secure a charitable grant to cover part of the cost. The rest was financed by an anonymous donation, though some suspected that the donor was Brian Crosbie. Anyway, at lunchtime today he was going to take delivery of a state-of-the-art electric wheelchair that he could control with his one functioning limb. His wife and daughters had been called in on the pretext of attending a meeting about discharge planning and they and Nobby congregated in the foyer waiting for Sharon to appear. I was tasked with engaging them in conversation while preparations were made out of sight on the ward.

Suddenly Sharon appeared, surrounded by a posse of nursing staff and Sheila in the thick of them, pushing the wheelchair towards us. It had a huge red ribbon tied around it and a placard on it saying 'Nobby Clarke's mean machine'. Four jaws dropped in synchrony as the family tried to take in what was happening. Nobby, for the first time I'd seen it, lost for words, looked on in amazement and tears started rolling down his cheeks. Eventually he broke into a grin and stuck his thumb up, provoking a round of cheering and clapping from assembled onlookers. There were not a few others who found themselves wiping away tears as he was manhandled into the new machine and set off doing circuits of the foyer. Celebrations petered out with much shaking of hands and hugging, and staff drifted back to their duties, leaving Sharon and the family poring over the new contraption and its proud owner.

It was the end of the afternoon, and I was tying up some loose ends before heading home. Sally, who was on call, was in the office preparing to see a late admission. Sarah came in smiling and shaking her head. 'I've just had a call from the police. You'll never guess.'

'What's happened?' I replied.

'Well, a very polite policeman said he was ringing to let me know that Nobby is on the way back to us in a squad car and we mustn't worry because he's fine. Apparently, they were driving along the main road when they spotted him in his wheelchair at the side of the road. It turns out that he was looking for the nearest pub and had made it half way into town before his battery ran out of charge. There he was, happy as Larry, sitting in the chair with traffic passing him in both directions.'

'The crafty devil! He must have slipped out unnoticed after his family left.'

'Do you know what the amazing thing is? When the two young officers heard his story, they loaded him and his chair into the squad car, took him the rest of the way to the pub, and sat with him while he downed a pint!'

'It's 8.29 on this fine Tuesday, and this is Mark Jarvis. Our local heroes this week are the staff of St. Julian's Hospice,

and today we'll be hearing from Sharon Dixon who is part of the social work and bereavement team. Our thought for the day is on the subject of bereavement: we never really die because we live on in the hearts and memories of those who love us.'

That's all very well, but what happens when those who love us die too? Nothing very eternal about that. Or is love itself eternal? When we love someone does that forever change in some way the universe around us? Is there a pool of love? If I love am I drawing on this eternal pool or adding to it? Is there a pool of hate? If so, it must surely be smaller than the pool of love? Which is stronger? Oh shut up David! It's too early in the morning for philosophising.

'We provide practical and emotional support to patients and their families. This can involve a wide range of things such as advising on benefits, arranging care packages or nursing home placement, and even re-housing pets! We are also trained counsellors and can offer emotional support to patients and their families.....'

I dreamt about her again last night. Am I going crazy? I've never been like this before. What if she's not interested in me at all? What if I end up making a big fool of myself?

'We work very closely with the medical and nursing teams to enable a patient to return home safely and comfortably, if that is what they want. A large part of that is ensuring that carers feel able to cope, and there are a number of sources of additional support that can be called upon.....'

I am going to see her today. What do I say? Should I disclose any hint of what I'm feeling? How do we work together if I make a fool of myself? How do we work together if we become an item? What am I doing?

'A large part of my role is in offering bereavement support to loved ones, before and after a patient dies. Although there are many feelings that are common to people who are bereaved, no one experiences it in exactly the same way. We are trained to be good listeners, and often that's all people need. Bereavement can be very isolating, as people find others will avoid them out of embarrassment or awkwardness, not knowing what to say......'

I don't think I'm going to be able to conceal what's going on inside. Someone is going to notice. I've been around others in doctor-nurse liaisons before. I can't bear the thought of whisperings and gossip. David, don't complicate matters, you're moving on from here. Just forget it.

'We deal with a lot of sadness and distress. But although St. Julian's is a place where sad things happen, it is by no means a sad place. There's a lot of laughter......'

I can't forget it. Whatever happens I've been indelibly marked. I've tasted the intoxicating cordial of love, the 'O!' of revelation. I've experienced that heady euphoria where words run out, and to the possibility of which I'd up to now been lost and blind. Whether or not this love is requited, or should I love and lose, I am forever changed, I have joined the ranks of the knowing, and no affection or relationship will ever be the same again.

We gathered at the entrance to the hospice after the morning meeting. As I approached I watched Abby talking excitedly with one of our fellow jumpers. I casually joined the group and exchanged greetings. She looked up and smiled. 'Hello David, good to see you.' There seemed genuine enthusiasm in her voice.

'Have you recovered from the weekend excitement yet?' If she only knew.

'Sort of. A great experience, wasn't it?'

Conversation was cut short by the arrival of Jackie and the photographer. Jackie immediately took control. 'Congratulations everyone, and thank you for a great effort. You raised just over three thousand pounds.' There was general applause and nods of acknowledgement. 'Can we bunch you up? You two, perhaps, kneeling at the front and the other three standing behind, maybe with arms around shoulders at the back?' We dutifully complied. Abby was kneeling in front of me. I could smell a hint of perfume or scented toiletries. 'Yes that looks great.' A few photos, and it was over almost before we knew it. 'Thanks so much everyone.'

The group dispersed and I'd hoped to walk with her back to the ward, but one of the group engaged me in further conversation and before I knew it she was on her way back in. She looked round and smiled again. 'See you later David.' Oh dear, opportunity lost. But what would I have said? She was tantalisingly close, but just out of reach.

I lingered for a while outside, lost in thought. A Rolls Royce Silver Shadow glided into the car park just below me, the sunlight glinting off its highly polished chrome. I gazed admiringly at its sleek and elegant lines. Mike got out and voiced a loud hello. I raised my hand in acknowledgement, and he locked up and made his way up towards me.

Mike Burton was one of our day centre patients. He had run a small business most of his life, and tragically, as too often happens, he had been diagnosed with a terminal illness within a year or two of retiring. His lymphoma was currently in remission, but he knew that he was living on borrowed time. He was a really likeable man who brought a sense of optimism and fun to the day centre which he attended two days a week. I usually met up with him in the early afternoon for a game of chess. He had lost his wife a few years before to breast cancer and they had no children. It had always been a dream to own a Rolls Royce, and when he was diagnosed he cashed in most of his accessible savings and fulfilled his dream. It was his pride and joy and most of those attending on his days had been treated to a ride in it, and he'd taken me out in it too.

'Hello Mike. What's in store for you today?'

'Steak and kidney pie for lunch and then we're going to be treated to a Frank Sinatra tribute. Some crooner from the club circuit.' He raised his eyebrows and then grinned. He had a dry sense of humour and liked to poke fun at some of the day centre activities, but it was all tongue-in-cheek and he never missed a day. 'I'm also helping Alf with his tax return. Are you okay? You're looking far too thoughtful for a beautiful sunny day like this.'

'Yeah you're probably right. I'd better get back and get on with some work.'

'I should say so. You need to do something to justify all that money you docs pull in.' He slapped me on the shoulder.

'I wish! You're the one driving the roller!' He laughed. 'I'll come into the day centre and see you after lunch. I like a bit of Sinatra.'

'Only if you're prepared to join in the sing-along!'

He launched into a rendition of a Sinatra classic, turned and did a shimmy and a shuffle before heading in, singing at the top of his voice.

'Oh what a mover! Eat your heart out Frank!' I shouted after him.

※

'Our local hero this rather damp Wednesday is Dr Sally Marshall of St. Julian's Hospice. Last week was the second time I've met up with Dr Marshall. She's one of the show's veterans, as she featured in our beautiful gardens series a couple of years ago. Here's a thought for you, this one from a philosopher called Nietzsche: he who has a why to live can bear almost any how.'

Did you give him that one Sally? I never knew you were into philosophy. Well, there's a lot I'd disagree with Nietzsche on, but he's probably right there. I've seen enough already in this job to marvel at human resilience.

'We are as much about living as we are about dying. We are trying to improve a person's quality of life by controlling symptoms and meeting their needs, to enable them to live whatever life they have left to the full, and perhaps to find meaning and purpose in their journey.....'

I had a disturbed night last night, tossing and turning. I can't get her scent out of my mind. It permeates my consciousness, evoking strong and sometimes disturbing emotional responses.

'My job is to attend predominantly to physical symptoms such as pain or sickness. But there are many other things that someone with a terminal illness has to contend with, such as emotional, spiritual and social issues, and all these

are important. That's why we work as a team of several disciplines, as no one person can attend to all a patient's needs......'

I've got to snap out of this. I can't concentrate on anything else. Everything I do or think about at the moment is subverted by these new and unruly passions that seem to have exploded into my psyche. I need to get to the hospice, to get to work. I'll be okay if I can refocus on what I know best. Years of patterning by duty and professionalism will fend off the anarchic assaults on my composure.

'I think people sometimes have this idea that if they can get to the hospice then everything will be okay, that we will get rid of their pain and deal with their fear. Thankfully, there is a lot we can do to treat people's symptoms and support them through their illness, but we certainly don't have all the answers to their suffering. We can't always completely eliminate pain or other symptoms, but we can usually improve them and, perhaps more importantly, enable them to cope better......'

Good for you Sally. Does anyone have all the answers to suffering? A quixotic quest for a death, and life for that matter, without suffering fatally misunderstands the human condition. It is also doomed to failure, and its beleaguered pilgrims may gravitate towards the queues of those painting the primrose path to euthanasia. Oh lighten up David! Cynicism is a dull and enervating bedfellow, and not one you've ever moved over for.

'Our work enables us to come alongside people at a unique time in their lives, a time when you can really make a difference. It is demanding, but also very rewarding. People only die once, so you only get one chance to get it

right. How they die can greatly affect how those they leave behind can go on with their lives.....'

It is rewarding, and beguiling to a degree that I hadn't anticipated. Is it the work? Is it the place? Is it the people? Or is it one person in particular?

I had familiarised myself with Abby's shifts for the whole week. She was on an early shift again today, and then afternoon shifts for Thursday and Friday. Brian was doing a ward round today so Sarah accompanied our entourage around the ward, together with another nurse according to whichever bay we were visiting. Abby joined us for her bay, and Brian paused our progress to congratulate her.

'Well done on the jump Abby. I heard all about the day from David here.' He turned to acknowledge me. 'I hear you've still to land in a plane?'

There was that smile again. 'Thank you Dr Crosbie. Yes I have the pleasure of a landing still to come.' She flashed a glance at me.

Brian continued. 'I think I prefer landings myself. It's exhilarating to feel the raw power of take off behind you, but I find the gentle glide and moments of relative weightlessness more pleasing and it's always something of a relief to arrive at one's destination. Let me know what you think when you've a landing to compare.'

Abby fell in beside Sarah as we moved from patient to patient, and I did my best to stand as close to her as I could without it being too obvious. If there was any spark of affection over and above that of a colleague, she didn't give anything away. The ward round ended, I returned to the office a little forlorn and disappointed. I sat and wrote in the notes, listening out for the sound of her voice.

The press were back at the hospice that afternoon. The striker from one of the country's top football clubs was coming to see one of our patients. Gary Bailey was a man in his early twenties who had fought a brain tumour for several years. He had been a promising footballer before he was diagnosed, and had continued his involvement to the degree he was able for some time afterwards, helping out with boys' teams and raising money for equipment and pitches through sponsored activities. Football was his life and our visitor today was his sporting idol.

Gary's disease had progressed significantly and he was losing the battle against immobility and dependence. He was now paralysed down one side and his speech was difficult, but his mind was still sharp. He had the rounded face of those who have been on high doses of steroids for some time, and part of his head was shaven after recent surgery to nibble away a little more of the recurrent tumour. He was in the hospice for some respite and to change his anticonvulsant medication as he had been having fits.

Our visiting star had a previous connection with St. Julian's as we had looked after his dying father. When Sharon discovered Gary's passion for his team and the man himself she contacted him to see if he would be willing to pay a surprise visit, and he was only too happy to help. It was quite a coup. I didn't follow football, but I knew who he was. It was also a scoop for the local reporter. Gary had no idea what had been planned.

Kevin arrived in the early afternoon. There was none of the media razzmatazz of his usual public appearances, just him and a friend, possibly a minder, carrying a large holdall. He drove in himself and was met by Sharon and the local photographer. Some more of the staff on duty had gathered inside the foyer. There were some introductions, and he chatted for a while with some of the assembly, renewing old acquaintances from the time he used to visit his father. There was then a pause outside the single room that Gary occupied until a suitable moment to go in. Gary's parents had been briefed and were waiting in the room with him. I went in first and prepared the ground.

'Hello Gary, I know we saw you this morning, but there's something I need to tell you.' He was sitting in the recliner chair, listening to the radio through earphones. The proud parents were sitting on the edge of the bed next to him.

'Here, let me take those off you so you can speak to Dr David.' His mother relieved him of the earphones and I knelt in front of him.

'Gary, I know you are a great football fan. And I also know that there is one footballer in particular who is a bit of a hero to you.' He nodded hesitantly. With such a puffy face normal facial reactions are blunted, but Gary spoke volumes with his eyes. He looked puzzled. 'Well, we've got a surprise for you today.' He raised his eyebrows. 'Gary there's someone we'd like you to meet.' I got up and moved aside, motioning to the door.

The hero himself came in first with a big grin on his face and stood for a moment to allow the unveiling to sink in. It took a few seconds for Gary to process what he was seeing. Then his eyes widened and his jaw dropped and he started trembling. He made an effort to get up, forgetting in the intensity of the moment that he couldn't manage this unaided. His parents got up and moved away from the bed, making way for the star of the moment. Kevin came and crouched in front of Gary and stretched out his hand in greeting.

'Hello Gary. It is such a privilege to meet you. I've heard all about what an amazing guy you are.'

There was no hint of staged or counterfeit emotion; he seemed truly humbled by the man in the chair before him. Tears welled up briefly in Gary's eyes as he squeezed his hand enthusiastically. They exchanged some small talk, and then the holdall was brought in. It was of course full of goodies, football memorabilia of all kinds, much of which was autographed. This was also the cue for the photographer to get to work. Kevin then asked if he could have some time alone with Gary. 'We're going to talk about football.' He winked at Gary and we all filed out leaving the pair together.

It was almost an hour later that the door opened and Kevin emerged smiling. 'Thanks guys. We're done now.' He beckoned us back in. Gary's parents shook his hand and thanked him before rejoining their son. 'I have to go now Gary, but could I ask you to do something for me before I do?' Gary nodded. Kevin produced a pennant from the side pocket of the holdall and handed it to Gary together with a pen. 'Would you mind letting me have your autograph?'

A little later than normal today, we're going to our local hero slot. I spoke to Rev Nick Hardy of St. Julian's Hospice, or 'Nic the Vic' as he's affectionately known. Here's a thought from the Vic himself: if we can face our

own mortality and deal with death, it releases us to truly live. Shall we have that again? If we can face our own mortality and deal with death, it releases us to truly live. Let us know what you think.'

That's easy to say and less easy to do in a death denying society like ours. Death is hidden away, sanitised, handed over to professionals and certainly not talked about. It's easy to imagine that it's not something that is going to happen to me.

'As with many hospices, St. Julian's has a Christian foundation and local churches played an important, but not exclusive, part in our founding and development. But we cater for people of all faiths and none. I have a small team of volunteers who help me, and we aim to support the spiritual needs of our patients.....'

Gosh I'm tired today. I guess the intensity of emotion over the last few days has been draining. Passion exhausts, unless there are fresh springs.

'Spiritual needs go far beyond any religious beliefs. We all have spiritual needs, though we may not all express those in terms of a religious framework. I'm just as happy talking to people about their hobbies and life stories as about doing the religious bit. For some the religious bit is very important.....'

Religion. I wonder what Abby believes. What do I believe for that matter? Perhaps I need to face my own mortality. You can't do this work for long without a growing yearning that there might be something else after death. You also realise that many people have some belief that it is not the end. Eternity is set in the heart of man – didn't someone famous say that?

'Sometimes people have a lot of spiritual pain.

Unresolved guilt, broken relationships, fear of dying, worry about loved ones, anger at God over what is happening – all these and other things besides can cause a lot of turmoil for people nearing death. We try to get alongside and offer support, even if we can't offer answers.....'

I dreamt about her again last night. She was mouthing some words to me but there was no sound and I couldn't make out what it was. Can only she assuage the hunger that is deep within, the ache that won't go away? I'm off my food. I'm probably losing weight. How long can this go on?

'Some people's faith can strengthen them through the dying process, but this is not always the case. Sometimes they can feel God has let them down, or they refuse to come to terms with what is happening because they are expecting a miraculous cure. I've seen people of no faith at all face death with calmness and serenity. Conversely, it is a great sadness to me to see someone of faith who has to be dragged kicking and screaming into heaven.....'

Heaven. The room next door. Over the horizon. And all the other metaphors that populate the poetry. Hope must palliate the pain of loss and separation. I've sensed the stirring of a new kind of hope within myself since working at the hospice.

Sally finished going round the ward before me, and when I returned to the office she had been joined by Lucy Danvers, who had come across from the hospital. They were looking through some paperwork. 'Ah, David, do you want to come and have a look at this as well?' said Sally. I drew up a chair. 'Lucy is going through a new assessment tool that we are going to pilot for the next month.' Sally surreptitiously raised her eyebrows.

There was apparently an increasing proliferation of such tools to assess patients' symptoms and needs, driven partly by the desire to ensure consistent quality of assessment, but also to facilitate the development of a research evidence base. Many people were uneasy about the whole process, fearing that the art of what we do risked being reduced to tick box assessments, guidelines and protocols. Sally certainly didn't share Lucy Danvers' enthusiasm. In this case I could see her point.

Lucy Danvers explained what we were looking at. 'This is a new tool devised to try and assess and document patients' spiritual needs and level of spiritual distress. I'd like to try it out to see if it is user-friendly and yields any valuable information. I'm thinking of doing some research on the area of spiritual distress, perhaps comparing patients' experiences in the hospital with here, but I need some way of measuring it all. I've run it past Nick and he doesn't mind us trying it out. I thought we could use it when we first admit a patient.'

She set about explaining how to use it, and how to score the various sections. She was terribly enthusiastic. I couldn't quite take it all very seriously. It seemed completely artificial to me. The king has got no clothes on - is anyone going to say so? How can one attempt to reduce something as nebulous and expansive as spirituality to scores and grades? I mentally ran through the assessment for myself and was surprised to come out with quite a high level of spiritual distress! Oh well. Sally managed to restrain herself from making any cynical comments.

Lucy Danvers disappeared into the nurses' office to

brief them on the new paperwork. Sally shrugged her shoulders. 'David, Mrs Guthrie, who came in yesterday, needs a paracentesis. Would you mind doing it after lunch? I've got to attend the discharge meeting for Mr Samson.'

'Yes, that's fine.'

A paracentesis is a procedure whereby fluid is drained from the abdomen. In liver disease and some cancers fluid can accumulate within the space around the abdominal organs and cause distension, sometimes huge and tense. It is a fairly straightforward procedure to drain it, though the fluid almost always re-accumulates so drainage becomes a recurrent necessity. I asked one of the auxiliary nurses to get a trolley with the kit ready for early afternoon.

Around two in the afternoon I stuck my head round the door of the nurses' office and asked if anyone was free to assist me with the procedure. Abby looked up. 'Hello David. The auxiliaries are all tied up elsewhere, but I'll give you a hand.'

Yippee! An excuse to spend time with her! Exhilaration coursed through me. 'Brilliant. I'll just get the lignocaine. Meet you by the bed?'

'Will you now doctor? I'll be waiting.' I felt goose pimples on my arms as I went to collect the local anaesthetic from the drug cupboard.

When I got to Mrs Guthrie she was already lying on the bed and Abby was making her comfortable. She was in her seventies and had ovarian cancer. Her abdomen was the size of a full term pregnancy. 'Hello Mrs Guthrie, I'm Dr David Trevelyan. We are going to take some of that fluid off your tummy, if that's alright.'

'Oh thank you doctor. Yes, please do. It is so un-comfortable, I'm not sure I can take another night of it.'

'Have you had this done before?'

'Yes, once in the hospital. It was rather painful.'

'Oh, this shouldn't be painful. The worst bit is when I numb the skin with the local anaesthetic, as that can sting at first. But after that you should just feel some pushing.'

'If you say so doctor. That's fine.'

Abby took her hand. 'You can squeeze my hand while it's being done Elsie. Dr David is very good at this, and it usually doesn't hurt a bit.'

We drew the curtains round and set about preparing the equipment on the trolley. Abby opened the sterile contents out onto the trolley or into my gloved hands. I watched her hands working swiftly and delicately, so close to touching mine but never actually doing so because of the sterile precautions. I mused that no matter how close we got, even touching, there would still have been the barrier of the latex glove between my flesh and hers. In the enclosed space I could detect the scent I had noticed in our earlier encounter. She looked up at one point and caught me gazing at her, but she smiled and carelessly brushed an unruly lock of hair back behind her ear before reaching for a packet of sterile swabs.

'Is that everything?' She frowned, the first time I had seen her do it. 'There's something missing.' She thought for a few moments, while I looked on transfixed and oblivious to what was and wasn't there. 'Ah! The lignocaine. You were going to get that.'

I was jolted out of my reverie. 'Yes. Yes the

lignocaine, I've got it. It's.....Oh! It's in my trouser pocket. I usually put it there to warm up as it stings less than injecting it cold.' I bit my lip and looked sheepish. I had cleaned my hands and was wearing sterile gloves. 'Could you get me some more gloves?'

'No need for that David. I'll get it out of your pocket. Which one?'

'Err.....it's my left pocket. Are you sure?' She gave a look of feigned exasperation and beckoned me closer. I edged around the trolley and presented my left pocket, tilting my left hip towards her. It was only fleeting, but the warmth of her hand against my thigh triggered a cascade of heat that engulfed my whole body. My heart was pounding out of my chest, my head was swimming, and I wanted to shut my eyes but she was looking straight into them and smiling.

'There we are.' She held up the ampoule like some proud trophy.

Afterwards, I couldn't really remember much of the rest of the procedure. I had done so many before that my mind probably didn't need to be engaged, just functioning on autopilot. I couldn't remember anything I had said or done. I could have made a complete fool of myself as far as I knew. I remembered getting to the end and Mrs Guthrie expressing surprise that it was over so easily. I wheeled the trolley out, leaving Abby to tidy up and resettle her on the bed with her drainage bag. As I headed out of the ward I heard Mrs Guthrie say from behind the curtains, 'What a lovely doctor. You know my dear, you two look good together, you really do.'

'*Have you got that Friday feeling? Looking forward to some pampering this weekend? It's the last of our local heroes interviews from St. Julian's today, and we'll be hearing from Katrina Roberts. Katrina is a complementary therapist at the hospice, and pampering is very much a part of her role. Hasn't it been a great week from St. Julian's? Thank you so much for all your phone calls and letters. We've had some heart warming tales and a real insight into the tremendous work that's done by these dedicated staff. And one thing that has come across loud and clear is how much you value these particular local heroes. I must say, spending time this week thinking about caring for those who are dying has made me really appreciate life, so our final thought for this week focuses on the good things that life brings: some of the best things in life may be free, but they are not cheap.'*

My compliments to you Mr Jarvis. You've done justice to a difficult subject this week. Fundraising should be pleased too.

'*I suppose many see us as the icing on the cake of care at the hospice. We provide the luxury element perhaps. We aim to complement the medical and nursing care that patients receive, and we offer a number of therapies, from simple massage to homeopathy.....'*

Yesterday still seems a bit of a haze. I feel I've been walking on air. I slept so soundly last night, the first time in a week.

'*We aim to help patients relax and improve their sense of well-being. This can also help them cope with some of their symptoms. We are also another set of ears, and it's remarkable how often patients will open up to us when they are feeling relaxed and valued. They may tell us things that they haven't yet told anyone else.....'*

I'm full to bursting. I can't keep these emotions to myself, someone's going to notice. I'm going to have to have out with it.

'We are sometimes able offer treatments to a patient's family or carers, and they really appreciate it as it can be very stressful caring for a loved one or watching them struggle. We also support staff members, and many find this invaluable, particularly when we're going through a tough time on the ward.....'

I must come clean with Abby. I need to resolve this. I'll speak to her today.

I knew she was working the afternoon shift, but when would be the best time to draw her aside and speak to her? Perhaps I should catch her during her afternoon break? I could buy her a coffee. What should I say? The morning seemed laboured and drawn out. I felt heavy with the anticipation of what was to come. I would know today. I would show my hand. I would be vulnerable. I would be vulnerable in a way that I had never been before. Part of me was scared.

I got through the morning ward work on autopilot. After attending to urgent tasks I wandered down the path to the side of the hospice that led a hundred yards or so along the crest of the rise through the trees to a viewpoint area overlooking the valley below. It was called 'Lizzie's spot' after one of the early patients at the hospice, and there were some garden benches and tables set out in a semicircle. It was accessible by wheelchair and was somewhere patients could go and feel they were out of the hospice, which wasn't visible from there. Staff would also use it as a place to get some air or eat lunch. I was earlier than the lunch brigade and was able to sit for a while on my own with my thoughts. The sky was leaden and it was cold, and the valley was still and quiet. I hadn't brought a coat and after a while I began to shiver. The first flurries of snow had fallen that morning, the flakes settling just long enough to stake winter's claim.

Just after midday I got up and headed back towards the hospice. As I emerged from the trees I recognised two of the auxiliary nurses just going in to the building, presumably arriving for the afternoon shift. A car pulled in to the car park just below and Abby got out of the passenger side. She waved at the driver and started towards the path but stopped as if she had forgotten something. She signalled to the driver, who had reversed out of the parking spot, to catch their attention before driving off. The car stopped and the window rolled down. I could see now that it was a dark haired man of about my own age. Abby leant into the window and there was conversation for a few seconds. She then kissed him on the cheek and waved as he drove off.

I stopped dead still. A wave of disappointment, despair, longing and frustration all mixed together seemed to engulf me. I felt sick. What colour remained to the landscape around me under the heavy sky dissolved into shades of grey. Oh no! Of course, the likelihood all along was that she would already have someone else, but hope can easily overlook the limitations of a less convenient reality. I watched her wistfully as she walked up the path and into the hospice, out of reach and unattainable. She didn't notice me.

Chapter 7
Light in the Darkness

There had been a heavy snowfall overnight. The roads in to the hospice were passable, as the gritting lorries had been busy, but the car park was treacherous. One of the maintenance team was out shovelling grit onto the access road but had not got as far as the actual car park. I managed to negotiate the surface and avoid sliding into any of the cars that were already parked before coming to rest in a space of my own. Some of the night staff were walking gingerly to their cars to attempt the journey home. I was at least an hour earlier than normal, but it was lighter than it had been on my arrival over the previous few mornings, the white blanket illuminating the landscape against the heavy grey sky. There was a curious stillness, the world's awakening muffled by acres of insulation. I had been on call overnight and had come in early to deal with a crisis.

It was some three weeks since the disappointment. The euphoria had evaporated in an instant leaving a residue of gnawing ache deep within my gut. Occasionally I would salt the wound with a liberal sprinkling of embarrassed self-reproach at my own foolishness. Day after day had merged in a grey continuum of languid functioning – drab, colourless and automatic. I had simply got on with work, nursing my bereavement. I had not seen much of Abby, as I had avoided her out of self-preservation.

This week I had begun to emerge from my melancholy. It was the preparations for Christmas in the hospice that had awakened latent memories, echoes from childhood celebrations that resonated within me every year at this time. I had always loved Christmas. The sense of anticipation, the excitement of giving, the warmth and snugness and safety of the gathered family had imprinted me deeply at an early age, and no matter what I was going through I couldn't help myself but succumb in some way to stirrings of hope and evocations of joy. The disappointment was still there, a cloak that I could put on and in which I could retreat into myself, but increasingly it had been forced to yield to a resurgence of the optimistic and idealistic persona that had always been more truly representative.

Christmas was a particularly poignant time in the hospice, with most patients having to face the fact that it would be their last. For many it had been a marker on their journey through illness, a staging point by which their prognosis was gauged. Would they be around at Christmas? For some its arrival represented a triumph over expectation, while others for whom it had seemed an easily attainable goal struggled with the reality of progressive deterioration, and the countdown to it measured the ebbing away of their strength and vitality. Some, you knew, were hanging on for that milestone before letting go, just as others did for birthdays or weddings or births. There was then the question of whether they would be well enough to be at home, whether they wanted to be at home, or whether they could stay in the safety of the hospice and simply be looked after here.

For families of inpatients there may be the struggle between guilt over not feeling able to cope with care at home and relief that this was one burden they didn't have to shoulder at an already frenetic time of year. For others the sentimental ideal of the 'last Christmas together' would prove as elusive as the 'perfect Christmas' of previous years. Most knew that the glitter of future Christmases would always be dulled by the marking of an anniversary of bereavement. It was a time of year in the hospice when love, always tangible but often self-effacing, needed to be particularly prominent, and displayed in all its colours. And the hospice rose to the moment. It was always a place of warmth and peace and acceptance, but around Christmas there was a new dimension to love, what might be described as an urgent intensity, that was very moving.

I trudged up the path to the entrance, enveloped in silence except for the scrunching of the snow on every footfall. The decorations had gone up over the previous two days. Tinsel and artificial frosting was strewn liberally but tastefully over doorways, windows and various surfaces. There was a large Christmas tree in the foyer, slightly over-decorated for my taste, but impressive nevertheless, and a substantial nativity scene with painted wooden figures to the left as one came in. There was a small tree at the far end by the window in each of the bays, and several of the patients' lockers and beds were adorned with various festive accoutrements. On the back of the door in the nurses' office was a large Christmas tree poster on which staff could write Christmas greetings, for those who wanted to avoid the rather wasteful and unnecessary exchange of cards with other members of the team.

When I arrived at the office two of the day staff were just setting off on the drug round. Sarah was inside talking with one of the auxiliary nurses. 'Morning David. He's in a bed. Two of the girls are cleaning him up. We've got a name, Michael Duggan. He says he's forty-four. We can't get any next of kin or contact details out of him, and he has no address. He says he's been living on the streets for a long time. He's in a bad way.'

'Do we know how long he was lying outside the door?'

'No, not exactly. Obviously, he wasn't there when the night staff came on, and one of the relatives didn't leave until about midnight. So, it'll be sometime between midnight and six-thirty this morning when the kitchen staff arrived and found him. He was pretty well wrapped up though. I expect sleeping out in this kind of weather wasn't new to him. He had a dog with him, a Border Collie cross, in reasonable condition too.'

'Where's the dog now?'

'Chrissie from reception has taken her home for the morning. She's going to feed her and clean her up, and then stop by the vet when it opens to get her checked over.'

Michael Duggan had been found huddled up inside

several layers of clothing and newspaper and under a blanket on the doorstep of the hospice that morning. He was very weak and clearly in pain. He had told the night staff that he was dying and had nowhere else to go. Thankfully we had a bed. I wandered up to the bay and looked in through the curtains round the bed. There was a nondescript pile of clothes on the chair, and the unmistakeable smell of faecal soiling. He was stretched out on the bed with eyes closed and lips moving occasionally in some silent mantra. He was emaciated and unkempt.

The nurses had got him into a gown and one was tenderly washing his dirty macerated feet, while the other was cleaning dried excrement from his upper thighs. There was a nasty sore on his right lower leg that looked infected. They looked up as I came in. I nodded to carry on, and I went round the other side of the bed.

'Mr Duggan.' He opened his eyes and looked at me. He seemed to be looking beyond me. 'Mr Duggan, I'm Dr Trevelyan, David Trevelyan.' There was an acknowledgment before he closed his eyes again. He looked exhausted. 'Mr Duggan, I need to ask you some questions.' He was mouthing something I couldn't make out. Then he managed to get it out.

'Michael.....it's Michael.'

'Okay, Michael. Can you tell me what's been happening to you Michael?'

'I've got cancer and I'm dying.' It came out slowly and with great effort.

'Have you seen a doctor?' He slowly shook his head. 'What makes you think you have cancer?' He started fiddling with his gown, like he was trying to lift it but he barely had the strength to raise his arm.

'You'd better have a look at his abdomen.' Chloe, one of the two nurses, nodded towards the gown. I pulled it up gently. I didn't have to feel it. I could see a craggy mass filling a large part of his abdomen. When I did palpate he was quite tender. I replaced the gown and took his hand. I noticed a tattoo on his shoulder. It was the wings of the Parachute Regiment.

'Michael have you been seen at the hospital about this?' He turned his head towards me and managed to lift it a little way off the bed, pulling me closer.

'No hospitals, no tests. Just help me to die in peace.' I must have looked hesitant. 'Please.' There was intensity in his gaze and he squeezed my hand with a strength that surprised me. 'Please.....promise.' His head dropped back on the pillow, exhausted by the effort, and his grip relaxed. I looked at Chloe.

She whispered, 'Bless him. Goodness knows how he made it to our door.' I looked back at the bedraggled figure. I squeezed his hand and leant closer to his ear.

'Okay Michael. We'll take care of you.' He opened his eyes and tried to smile. Then his face tensed again.

'Bessie.....Bessie.' I looked at Chloe.

'I think Bessie's his dog.'

'She's fine Michael. We are sorting out some food for her. She'll be back with you later.' He nodded and visibly relaxed.

There was much discussion in the morning meeting about our new arrival and what we should do. We would respect his wishes regarding investigations and treatment, and do our best to keep him comfortable.

Cathy would contact the police in case he was on the missing persons register, and we would try to find out as much as he would tell us about his past and any family.

He slept most of the day. When I looked in on him in the late afternoon he had woken and managed a hot drink. He looked better than he had done earlier that morning. He recognised me as I approached. 'Dr Trevelyan. Thank you. Can I see Bessie?' At that moment Chrissie appeared round the door with the dog trotting at her side. When it saw him there was a frenzy of excitement, and pulling on the lead it leapt onto the bed and was all over him. He was clearly in a lot of pain as the animal danced around on top of him, but when we made to get her off he shook his head emphatically. 'No, no it's all right, leave her be.' After the commotion of reunion the dog settled down lying next to him on the bed, eyes gazing intently and adoringly at Michael's face. 'Can she stay with me?'

'Yes. But we'll need to get you on some pain-killers.'

With good nursing care Michael picked up a little over the next few days. We couldn't get him to tell us anything about his past or whether he had anyone who cared about him. The dog rarely left his side, except for short walks with staff. She developed a routine of accompanying them out to Lizzie's spot at lunchtime and mopping up any scraps and titbits. She soon became the darling of the hospice. On ward rounds we would come round the corner into the bay and sometimes the first thing we would see was Bessie sitting up on the bed in front of Michael and obscuring him from view, so it seemed that she, rather than he, was the patient. She evoked an atmosphere of calm in the bay and was a welcome distraction for many visitors to the other patients. When sleeping, Michael would rest his hand on her fur and the pair of them would lay together, a picture of perfect peace, even their breathing patterns in synchrony, tied by some invisible strand of the bond between them.

It was a relief to take the bow and divest myself of the wig and the pillow that was stuffed up the front of my costume. It was the week of the day centre Christmas parties and I had been conscripted into the pantomime that was the traditional entertainment after the roast turkey lunch. It was an opportunity for staff to make fools of themselves for the benefit of those for whom they cared. This year it was a modern take on Aladdin, though the resemblance to the original was strained to say the least. Whatever the storyline it was always adapted to include fairies, and the highlight of the performances would be the appearance of Cliff, the head of maintenance, in a fairy outfit. The sight of a bearded sixteen stone man prancing around in tights and wings and wafting a wand was enough to render the whole assembly helpless with laughter, to the extent that it didn't really matter what the plot was. This was Friday, and thankfully the final performance.

After the cheers and applause died down I headed over to Mike Burton. He waved and applauded as I approached. 'Well done David! It doesn't get any better the second time you see it!'

'Tell me about it! Good to see you Mike. Are you on for some chess today?'

We retreated to some armchairs and tables at the far end of the room, while in the background the pianist and assembled gathering limbered up for some carols. We were quickly into a game. There was never a lot of conversation during these times. We just seemed to enjoy each other's company.

'Are you doing anything this Christmas Mike?'

'I'm going to spend it with my nephew and his family. I've two nieces and they are joining us too with their families. Figure I ought to be with what family I have, seeing as this will be my last.' There was a silent pause for a few seconds. 'I've relapsed. I was at the hospital this week and it's confirmed. I knew I had, as the sweats are back.' He sounded matter of fact. I looked up at him. He didn't raise his head, seemingly focused on the game in front of us. He took a pawn with his knight. Another pause.

Eventually I spoke. 'I'm sorry Mike. I really am.' I looked back at the board. 'Is there any more treatment?'

'Well, they've offered me some more poison, but I've said no. The first lot of chemo wasn't pleasant, but it bought me some quality time, and I've appreciated that. But I don't want any more time in hospitals. They say I've got a few weeks, possibly a few months. I might make the spring, we'll see.'

'If there's anything I can do.' He looked up and winked. We finished our game and spoke no more of it. I got up to return to the ward. He stood up and grasped my hand.

'Have a good one David. See you in the New Year.'

'Thanks Mike. You too.' I watched as he joined a group at one of the lunch tables and jollied them along in the words to one of the carols.

Gordon was in the office when I arrived back on the ward. I must have looked subdued. 'Are you alright David?'

'I'm a bit flat. A friend of mine who attends the day centre has just relapsed. A really nice guy. I'll be okay in a while.'

'I've just seen the new admission, Rev Thomas Brown. He's a retired vicar, that's if one ever does retire from being a vicar. He's extremely distressed. Inconsolable in fact.'

'What's his diagnosis?'

'Carcinoma of the kidney. Progressive disease, and no further treatment options. No physical symptoms to speak of, but gets overwhelmingly distressed when awake.'

'Is it terminal agitation?'

'I don't think so. He doesn't appear to be dying imminently. It has been an increasing problem over the last two weeks. The GP has tried to get to the bottom of what is going on, and has been through a number of medications, but to no avail. His wife is exhausted and very distressed by it all herself.'

'Any abnormal blood tests?'

'We'll repeat them, but no, they've been unremarkable.'

'A drug reaction?'

'He's taking virtually nothing. Certainly nothing that would cause this sort of reaction.'

Just then Nick came in. 'Ah Nick, just the man,'

said Gordon. 'I wonder if you could get involved with this new admission, Rev Brown. High levels of distress, and no one is sure why.'

'Hello Gordon. Yes, Sarah caught me earlier and mentioned him. I don't know him from the fraternity, so I've no insights into previous history, but I'll do what I can. Have you finished with him for the moment, as I could go along and see him shortly?'

'Yes, the nurse is taking some information from his wife, but I've finished. We may have to give him something to settle him, but we'll wait till you've had a chance to speak to him.'

'David, I have something for you.' Nick handed me piece of paper. 'You kindly agreed to do a reading in the Celebration of Lights next week? This is one of the pieces we usually read. It's based on a passage from the beginning of John's Gospel. Is that alright?'

'Yes that's fine. Whatever you'd like me to read Nick.'

Later that afternoon Cathy came in looking for me. 'David. You've got to know Michael pretty well, haven't you? Michael Duggan.'

'As well as any of us I suppose. Not that he's let us in very much.'

'I've had a call from the police station. They think they've found his daughter. Apparently she hasn't seen him since he left home twelve years ago. She filed a missing person report with another force two years ago when she turned eighteen and has been looking for him ever since. She's very keen to see him. Can you go and talk to him?'

'This is going to be interesting. Yes I'll go and see

him now.' So he had a daughter. What kind of Pandora's Box was I going to be opening now, I wondered.

Michael was resting with his eyes closed but he wasn't asleep and he responded as soon as I walked up and sat down. Bessie was tucked in to the angle behind his bent knees.

'Hello Michael. Is it okay to talk for a moment?'

'Sure. I'm not going anywhere.' He smiled.

'We've been contacted about someone who very much wants to come and see you.' He looked puzzled. 'Go on.'

'There is someone who has been looking for you for quite a while, and who claims to be your daughter.'

He stared at me, transfixed for a few moments. Gradually I saw tears begin to well up in his eyes and, when he could hold his composure no longer, he broke down into quiet sobbing. He curled up further in the bed, half burying his face in his arms and continued sobbing for several minutes. His body shuddered occasionally, convulsions of emotion overwhelming him, causing Bessie to look up and whine softly with concern.

When the emotion seemed to be subsiding I reached out and gently touched his arm. 'Do you want to talk about it?' He looked up, and then sat more upright in the bed, his head hanging forward and staring at the dog. He thought for a while, and then he looked across to me again.

'Yes. Perhaps it's time. I haven't talked about it in twelve years. Perhaps it's time.'

It all came out. Very methodically in a steady monotone, as if he had rehearsed it a thousand times over the years. Long military service, back from one combat zone too many with what was obviously post-traumatic stress disorder, though he didn't understand that at the time. Nightmares, mood changes, violent outbursts, with a wife and eight year old girl caught up in the middle of it, till eventually the wife was on the brink of a breakdown herself. He woke up one morning terrified that if he stayed around any longer he was going to harm one or other of them, and he couldn't bear the thought of the monster he had become. So he left, and disappeared out of sight and society.

He lived in a caravan for a while, surviving outside the system doing casual jobs, dealing with his demons. Eventually he ended up on the streets, lost to the world, a world that passed him by unseeing and uncaring. But there was someone who cared, who never stopped caring, it later emerged. While his wife moved on emotionally, his little girl never gave up hope of seeing her daddy again, and cherished in her heart the determination to find him when she was old enough to do so herself.

'My beautiful Jenny. There's not a day gone by when I haven't thought about her. I went back a few months later, and stood at a distance watching the house to see if I could get sight of her coming in or going to school. But they'd moved shortly after I left.'

We both sat in silence for a few minutes after he had finished. He fondled the dog's ears absent-mindedly, far away in thought and memories. Eventually, I spoke up.

'Michael. Can she come and see you?' He looked at me and started to fill up again.

'Yes. Yes please.' The dam burst again and I moved

214

across and took hold of him, sitting on the edge of the bed while he sobbed in my lap.

I emerged emotionally drained, yet with a curious sense of peace. I found Cathy and recounted the gist of the conversation. She would get back in touch with the police and we'd wait for Jenny to make contact. When I got back to the office Nick was talking to Gordon.

'Oh, hello David. I was just about to feed back what I've ascertained from Rev Brown, or rather mainly from his wife. It's very sad really. He turned his back on God and lost his faith some years ago after the death of their grandson from leukaemia. For the last few years of his ministry before he retired he felt he was living a lie, and simply going through the motions. But at that age he couldn't do anything else to earn a living. She says he's been a shell of a man, embittered and cynical. As the reality of death has approached he has felt increasing despair over his life and losses and what lies ahead.'

'So is this spiritual pain?'

'What we're seeing is spiritual turmoil, a mixture of fear, guilt, anger, despair, bereavement, regret, and probably much more. He's in no state to display any rational insight into what he's feeling, he's too caught up in the overwhelming spiritual pain. And it isn't something that drugs are going to sort out, other than sedatives to anaesthetise him from it. And that's what he's desperate for.'

'What did you do?' I asked.

'I spoke to him and prayed with him. I tried to reassure him that though he may feel he's turned his back on God, God hasn't turned his back on him. I'm not sure that any of it got through, but you never know what divine transactions and encounters happen in our sub-consciousness.'

'It must be profoundly damaging to the foundations of your psyche to abandon what you have based your whole life upon,' I mused.

'I'm sure it is, and that's what we are seeing in him. But there is hope David. Do you have a Bible? Read the story of the prodigal son in chapter fifteen of Luke's Gospel. It's about a son who disowns his father and runs off to squander his inheritance. But his father never abandons him emotionally, and is ready and waiting to welcome him back when he comes to his senses. God never turns his back on us; it is we who turn our backs on him. He is always ready to welcome us back. We are all prodigals in one way or another.'

I cleared my throat and looked out at the sea of faces looking expectantly at me. I recognised a few, though it was difficult to remember exactly whose family they were. There were apparently well over two hundred people gathered for the Celebration of Lights. This was an annual event held just before Christmas as an act of remembrance for those who had died in the hospice over the previous year. It provided an opportunity for families to celebrate the lives of loved ones, partake of some refreshments, and meet up again with staff who had been alongside them at a difficult and emotional time of their lives. The day centre was the main venue, with doors opened onto the foyer in order to accommodate the numbers. The service of remembrance was a mixture of readings, prayers and carols, led overall by Nick but with contributions from a number of staff members.

I began to read from the sheet in front of me. The passage was vaguely familiar.

Jesus, the living Word of God, is fully God, and was with God at the beginning of Creation. It was through him that everything was made, and in him all things continue to have their being. He is the Light of the World and he brings life in all its fullness. The Light shines in the darkness, but those who live in darkness don't always understand this light.'

'He came and walked among us in this world, but most of us did not recognise him. Even those who should have been expecting him missed who he was and rejected him. But even now those who receive him and put their trust in him are spiritually reborn, and enter a new relationship with God, living as children of a perfect heavenly Father. This is their spiritual birthright.'

'The living Word took on human form and lived on earth. He came to reveal the love and truth of God, and when we see him we see the glory of God, for he is the perfect representation of God the Father.'

I paused in silence for a while before stepping down from the lectern and resuming my seat to the left. Brian took the stand and read out a prayer, and this was followed by a hymn. This cycle of reading, prayer, and singing continued for another quarter of an hour or so. I watched the faces of the gathered families, young and old, united by a shared experience of grief and brought together in an act of remembrance, a communal act but each one inhabiting a unique landscape of memories.

Many were clearly moved. For some, perhaps, this would be cathartic.

The service ended and the drama moved on to the switching on of the lights. The large glass doors at the back of the day centre were opened out onto the garden area beyond and the assembly filtered out and congregated around the Tree of Lights. This was a large conifer that was decorated with about one hundred and fifty lights, one for every person who had died in the hospice over the year. It was a crisp clear winter's night with a half-moon in a starlit sky. I shivered with the transition from the warmth of the day centre. There was an expectant hush over the whole assembly. Nick read out a short piece of poetry and then signalled to whomever inside was manning the switch. There must have been a dimmer mechanism, as the lights gradually, almost hesitantly, emerged from the darkness till dozens of brilliant new stars were added to the starlit backdrop of the night.

The silence continued for a little while longer before conversations started here and there and some people began to retreat into the warmth. 'I can see Mummy!' I looked round to find a man crouching down with two children, a girl of about eight and a younger boy. The girl was pointing at the tree.

'Daddy I can see Mummy.'

'Which one is Mummy?'

'That one right at the top.'

'You know, I think you're right. That's Mummy.' The girl brought her fists up to her mouth as children sometimes do when they're excited. She then bent down to her brother and pointed back up at the tree.

'Can you see her John? Look, the light at the top.'

I peeled off along the path that ran along the back of the hospice, drinking in the night air and gazing at the panoply of stars overhead. I couldn't face standing around chatting, and the inevitable awkwardness of conversing with people whom I could barely remember, but who would clearly remember me. I would slip back into the building via the main entrance as I didn't want to go home without looking in on Michael Duggan. He had been reunited with his daughter earlier that day.

Cathy and I had met her at the entrance and taken her for a chat before going onto the ward. Jenny was a tall, slim and well-presented young woman, with a quiet self-assurance that would have made up for any deficiencies in style. She had Michael's dark brown hair and his eyes. She appeared remarkably composed for one on such a momentous day. We sat down and shared some tea.

'You've no idea how often I dreamt about this day Dr Trevelyan. Only I didn't expect that the circumstances would be such as they are. Can you tell me, is he very ill?' Her chocolate brown eyes held mine, probing, enquiring, for a moment not so self-assured, perhaps a trace of fear or was it yearning?

'I'm afraid he is. He's picked up since he arrived with us, but the cancer is very advanced and he's lost a lot of weight.' Her eyes dropped and she inhaled deeply. After a moment she looked up again. The self-assurance was back, there was no trace of uncertainty or fear.

'How long do you think he's got?'

'It's difficult to be sure. He's not imminently dying, but in the state he's in it could be anything from a few days to a few weeks.' She did not look away for what seemed like an age. Eventually her eyes began to fill up and a tear over-spilled the corner of one of them. She reached for her bag and started rummaging, presumably for a tissue. Cathy was prepared and plied her with some that she had brought along.

'I'm sorry. I promised myself that tears today would be tears of joy, and there will be plenty of those.' She dabbed at her eyes, and then stretched her back and shoulders as if releasing tension. 'Will he stay here?'

'We are very happy to look after him if he has nowhere else to go.'

'I'm at college in Manchester. I have a small flat. It's barely big enough for me.'

'That's fine. We are very happy to look after him. Do you have anyone to turn to in a situation like this? Any other family around?'

'My mother moved abroad when I left home for university. I have an aunt, but we are not close. I have a few friends. I'll be okay.' There was a pause. It was as if she was searching for the right words, or was it for courage? 'Has he told you anything about what he's been through over the last twelve years?'

'Only a sketchy outline.'

She nodded slowly, looking at the floor. Then she straightened up. She seemed strong again, decisive. 'Can I see him now?'

'Yes of course. He's strong enough to manage in a wheelchair at the moment, so we thought we'd bring him in here to start with, so that you can have a bit of privacy.'

Cathy stayed with Jenny while I went to fetch her father. The nurses were already helping him into the wheelchair when I got to him. He looked at me expectantly. 'Is she here?'

'Yes Michael, she's here, she's found you.'

'David, what's she like?'

I crouched down in front of the chair, my hands on his arms. 'She's lovely Michael, she's really lovely. Come and see for yourself.' I wheeled him to the threshold of the door that was half open and paused. 'Are you ready?'

He looked up and nodded. 'I'm ready.' I pushed the door open and we entered the room. Jenny rose from her seat. 'Jenny? My Jenny?'

Tears started streaming down her smiling face as she stepped across and knelt down before him. 'Daddy.' He tentatively stretched out his hand and touched her cheek, and began to weep. She put her head on his lap and held on to him, repeating softly, 'Daddy.' Cathy and I melted away discreetly and shut the door. They stayed in there for a long time, eventually coming out when Michael was tiring of sitting and needed to get back to bed.

Jenny stayed by his bedside. She was still there when I looked in on him that evening. He was asleep on his back, exhausted after the emotion of the day. Bessie was lying along one side and Jenny was sitting in the chair on the other, holding his hand. She was looking into space when I came up, but then turned to greet me. She spoke softly so as not to disturb her father.

'Dr Trevelyan. You are here late.'

'David. Call me David. Michael does. You are here late too.'

She smiled. She looked tired. 'We have a lot of catching up to do, and very little time. I need to cram twelve years into at most a few weeks. I don't want to miss a moment. I'll head off when everyone settles down for the night.'

'Have you got somewhere to stay?'

'Yes, a bed and breakfast not far from here. I've nothing to get back to Manchester for at the moment.' She turned and watched her father. 'He's had so much pain over these years. I can't imagine. He looks so frail. I remember he used to be so strong, so muscular. He'd lift me up and swing me in his arms as if I was a doll. I have such wonderful memories!'

She reached into her bag and brought out a photograph. It was of a young man in military uniform crouching down with a little girl who was laughing. 'He was away a lot, but we packed a lot in to the times he was at home.'

'It must have hurt when he disappeared.'

'It did. At first I couldn't understand. He had changed. I thought it might be my fault for a while. But gradually I did come to understand.' She took his hand again, and was silent for a while. 'He was a hero you know. And even if he hadn't been, he was always my hero.'

'And you never gave up hoping you'd see him again?'

She looked at me. 'Of course not. He's my dad. For a while after he left I used to leave a light on in my bedroom, to guide him home in case he was lost in the dark. I must have read something similar in a story. Anyway, fairly soon after that we moved. I wondered then how he'd ever find me. But that doesn't matter now. I've found him.'

I got up to go. Bessie looked up and wagged her tail, then settled back down again. I touched Jenny on the shoulder. 'Make sure you get some rest. Goodnight.'

I collected my things and headed out to the car park. The valley was bathed in a silvery half-light from the moon high above. The sky was breathtaking, and even more clearly visible away from the light of the hospice. As I drove out of the car park and down the access road I could see in my mirror the Tree of Lights. Awash with light and standing like a beacon, it remained visible for well over a mile down the main road.

❧

'Are you going to make my daddy better?' I crouched down by the low table at which she was seated.

'We're going to try to make him feel better,' I replied.

'My mummy says that Daddy is going to heaven.' The uncomplicated directness of children was always disarming, no matter how much one expected it.

Daisy was the seven-year old daughter of one of our inpatients. Ian Prentice was a man in his early thirties who was dying of cancer of the rectum that had spread to his liver and lungs. He had a wife, Sandra, and two children – Daisy and Oliver, who was four. Sandra had coped admirably looking after him at home, but with his recent deterioration coinciding with Christmas holidays the whole family was finding it too much of a strain, and he was admitted for what would probably be terminal care.

The poignancy of imminent loss always seemed that much more affecting when there were young children involved, for staff as well as those who would

223

be left behind. Sandra was finding it particularly hard today as it was Christmas Eve. She had broken down in reception and Sharon had come to the rescue with tea and company. I was minding the children for a while, so she could have a cry and unburden. Oliver was playing with a train set.

'Heaven must be a nice place to go.' Daisy was very matter of fact, intent on colouring in a picture that she was working on. 'Grown-ups are always saying 'Good Heavens', so it must be a nice place to go. Do you like my drawing?'

'Can I have a look?' She slid it across proudly.

'It's an angel, sitting on Daddy's bed.'

'That's beautifully drawn. I always thought angels had butterfly wings.'

'That's fairies, silly!' She rolled her eyes and looked exasperated. 'They're not real.'

'Unlike angels?'

'That's right.'

'How do you know? Have you seen an angel?'

'Of course! How else would I know how to draw one? This is the one that sits on Daddy's bed.'

'I see.....'

'At home I sometimes sneak into Daddy's bedroom when he's sleeping and Mummy's busy, and I see the angel on the end of his bed. He smiles at me, and sometimes he puts his finger on his lips like this so I won't make any noise.' She put her finger to her lips and went 'shhhh.' 'Have you ever seen an angel?'

'I don't think so. You must be very lucky. Or perhaps they only appear to people who have been especially good?'

'Hmmm. I didn't think of that. Perhaps you're right.' She pulled back her piece of paper and resumed her colouring.

One of the auxiliary nurses came up. 'Shall I relieve you David?'

'Thanks Debbie. I ought to get back to the ward, though I must say I'm rather enjoying myself.' Oliver was still playing in the corner, oblivious to our conversation. Daisy was biting her lip, a picture of concentration. 'Daisy I have to go and do some work now. Thank you for letting me talk to you and see your picture. Debbie would like to sit with you for a while till your mummy gets back. I'll see you later.'

'Oh that's okay.' She looked up, smiling broadly, and waved goodbye.

There was a relaxed atmosphere on the ward. There were no admissions expected and two people were being discharged home in time for Christmas, though we were going to hold the bed open for one of them as it was anticipated that the stay at home might be precarious. It was often difficult to discharge anyone in the run-up to, and over, the Christmas period as there was less care available in the community at this time. Having said that, there tended to be less demand for beds over Christmas and the hospice usually closed at least one bay to enable the unit to run slightly understaffed. This year Ian Prentice would occupy this bay on his own and we had moved a large table in so that the family could have Christmas lunch and tea and spend the whole day together.

One of the sitting rooms was given over as a den for those staff who were on duty over the holiday.

A television had been installed and the room was already filling up with boxes of chocolates, cakes and other goodies that were usually donated by patients and families. I had volunteered to work Christmas Day and Boxing Day, as I had no family of my own. Besides, work was still the safest distraction from my lingering heartache over Abby, even though the ache was intensified every time I saw her. I had managed up to now to avoid too prolonged an exposure. She was working a late shift today and was then off for a week.

There was a festive atmosphere in the staff restaurant at lunchtime. There was relaxed laughter, sharing of plans for the next few days, and discussions about presents. While lunchtimes were often animated and light-hearted, it occurred to me that what I was witnessing here was on a different level, untouched, or at least touched to a lesser degree than usual, by the tragedy that was a constant backdrop outside this room. Presently, Sharon appeared and sat down at the end of our table. She had a large envelope that usually signified a collection.

'Collecting for something Sharon?' Nick interrupted his flow to greet her.

'Yes. A bit of a last minute idea that Cathy and I came up with.'

'Sounds intriguing.'

'Well, you know we are making a family room out of the empty bay for the Prentices? We thought we could buy a few small stocking fillers for the children and hang a couple of stockings for them at the end of Ian's bed for when they come in the morning. I'm going to nip out later this afternoon and pick up some odds and ends; you know just a few treats.'

'An excellent idea.' Nick reached into his pocket and added a contribution. He was followed by several others who had access to money there and then. I contributed too.

'How did it go with Sandra?' I asked.

'She's feeling a bit better. She is very resilient.'

Conversation continued, but the spell had been broken. The reminder of someone else's pain had broken in. 'Well, better get back to business.' Nick got up, and I gathered together some of the dirty dishes to return to the serving hatch. 'Don't forget hospice carols at three, for anyone who would like to come.'

The ward work petered out by early afternoon. Sally was on call that night and suggested that I push off early as there was little point in all of us hanging around for the sake of it. I wanted to stay for the carols, so I wandered around the ward looking in on patients, making a mental note of whether or not I thought they might die before I got in the next day. I stopped for a while to talk to Michael and Jenny. He was still comfortable and able to sit out for short periods, but he was getting weaker. He would make it through Christmas.

At three in the afternoon I joined those assembling in the day centre, lots of clinical and office staff, some families who were visiting, and a few patients who could manage to walk or sit in a wheelchair. Nick welcomed everyone to the informal gathering. Brian read something and spoke for a few minutes on a Christmas theme, and then we went into the carols to the accompaniment of the piano. I sang heartily for the first two carols and then just stood soaking in the atmosphere. I looked around at the faces singing with varying degrees of gusto. Cathy was over by the Christmas tree with Sarah. Roger Forbes had also come to join in. It was a veritable gathering of the hospice circle, a 'family' act of celebration, a marking in some way of interdependence and shared purpose.

I was lost in contemplation when I noticed Abby appear at the back of the gathering. She was looking a little flustered initially, possibly at being late, but quickly relaxed. The remaining carols passed me by almost unnoticed. I was mouthing some of the words half-heartedly, but my attention was on Abby. I couldn't help myself. I would look across and watch her singing and exchanging comments from time to time with one of the auxiliary nurses standing next to her, until I would suddenly become self-conscious and look quickly down at the song sheet in case anyone noticed. The last carol was sung, Brian took to the front and wished everyone a merry Christmas, and then everyone began to melt away. I stood for a while, waiting till most had left before making towards the foyer.

Cathy came up behind me and tapped me on the arm. She beckoned me over to the side away from the stream of people dispersing in various directions. 'David. Why don't you ask her out?'

I felt myself blush. 'Who?'

'Who! Abby of course.'

I sighed. 'How long have you known?'

'Longer than you have.'

'She already has someone else.'

'No, you're mistaken. She's had plenty come along who would like to be, but she's not given her heart to anyone yet.'

'But I saw him. He dropped her off in the car park a while back. She kissed him on the cheek.'

'That was probably her kid brother Jack. They share lifts to work sometimes. He borrows the car. I've dropped her home at the end of a shift myself sometimes when he's got it.' I was stunned, speechless. 'Ask her out.'

Perhaps the regaining of a treasure once thought lost forever increases not for the possessor the intensity of affection or worth but refracts insights into their texture. Renewed hope and possibility rekindled the passions that had so possessed me but blended in new dimensions. There was relief and an unexpected peace, a certainty and solidity to what I felt, like a weighty jewel clasped in my palm against my chest. In their testing in the grinder of loss, my rough-hewn emotions had emerged polished and glistening.

I had an inspiring Christmas, one in which the burden of duty was subsumed by the heady atmosphere of kindness and laughter and the glory of the human spirit. I pulled crackers with Michael and Jenny, witnessed the joy and excitement of small children discovering filled stockings and creating memories to be treasured forever, shared Christmas lunch with colleagues who had become friends, and stayed on far longer into the day than I needed to, soaking up the atmosphere in the den. Brian came in during the afternoon with a hamper for the nurses, apparently an annual ritual. He went round and personally wished every patient a merry Christmas.

We didn't lose anyone on the day, and our first death of the holiday was late on Boxing Day, finally letting go after the milestone was achieved. There was a surge of admissions in the days after Boxing Day, others who had hung on for that last Christmas at home. New Year and the following few days were spent with my parents and friends, and I returned to work on the Friday of the following weekend. I wasn't needed until the Monday but the hospice New Year Ball was on the Saturday, and I wanted to catch up and get my bearings again.

On my way down the ward I looked in on Michael. The bed was empty and freshly made up. Perhaps I had confused which bay he was in, or maybe he had been moved. It took a few seconds for the realisation to dawn on me. He had obviously died. A wave of sadness broke over me and then dissipated in shallows of consolation. He had arrived with us about a month ago and in that time we had been privileged to see reconciliation and wonderful transformation. It was far more than we could have expected on that morning when he turned up in such a state on our doorstep.

I looked in on Cathy as I passed. 'Happy New Year Cathy.' She turned in her chair.

'Bless you David. Did you have a good break?'

'Yes, thank you. Really good. I presume Michael Duggan has died?'

'Late yesterday. Very peacefully. Jenny was with him. She was very grateful. She's coming back in this morning to collect his things and say goodbye.'

'I'll look out for her.'

'Are you going to the Ball tomorrow? Abby will be there.'

I smiled. 'I haven't seen her since Christmas Eve. Yes I'll be there'

'Faint hearts and all that.'

I nodded. 'Understood.'

Jenny arrived late morning with Bessie. When she knew I was back she came to find me in the office. I stood up to greet her, but the dog butted in and I had to squat down and greet her first. Jenny seemed relaxed

'David, I'm so glad to have caught you. I just wanted to thank you for all you have done for Dad and me. You've no idea what the last three weeks has meant to me.'

'Jenny it's been a privilege, it really has. What will you do now?'

'Get back to normal as soon as I'm able. College starts next week, but I'll not go back until the following week. I'll get the funeral out of the way first. I contacted Dad's old regiment and filled them in, and they have been very supportive. They are giving him a military funeral.'

'What will you do with Bessie?'

'I'll keep her. We've grown attached to each other, and I think it'll help me adjust having her with me, as they had such a bond. To love and care for something he loved will keep open that connection.'

'Well, I wish you all the best.' I stretched out my hand to say goodbye.

She hesitated. 'Are we allowed to hug?'

'Oh. That would probably be very unprofessional. But who cares!' We embraced in a lingering hug. Then she stood back and nodded, before looking down at the dog.

'Come on Bessie. Time to go.' She turned to leave and raised her hand in farewell.

'You take care.' I stepped out into the corridor and watched as she walked down towards the reception area, the dog trotting at her side. Sarah appeared and stood with me.

'A remarkable young woman.'

I nodded in agreement. 'Her father's daughter, no doubt.'

❦

I never felt comfortable in a dinner jacket and bow tie, but the occasion merited it and I didn't want to stick out. The hotel was sumptuous. Evening gowns of every description wafted through the reception area like butterflies in a tropical biome. Silk and taffeta, lace and sequins coalesced in a kaleidoscope of movement and colour as guests congregated in the foyer and then moved through into the banqueting suite to find their seats. The large round tables with heavy white cloths were scattered like polka dots on the deep blue carpet that surrounded the large dance floor. A band was tuning up at one end, while at the other a few early arrivals were already sampling the wares at the bar.

The annual New Year Ball was both a celebration and a fundraising event, and was supported by many staff and volunteers and their invited guests. Spouses or partners were welcome, but singleness was no bar to attending and groups of staff would get together to make up a table of eight. I was on the doctors' table. Sally was to my right and Brian's wife to my left. Brian, Gordon and his wife, and Lucy Danvers and her husband made up our circle of eight. Brian's wife was elegant and charming, and clearly adept at social interactions of this kind. She engaged me immediately in conversation, which flowed easily, and I was very grateful as I was not naturally at ease among such large gatherings.

Wine flowed and food plates came and went. Gradually the conversation opened out to involve the whole table, and although great play is made on such occasions of trying to steer clear of 'talking shop', it inevitably settled back on medical anecdote. Brian regaled us with tales of the early days of the hospice, and Gordon shared memories, some frankly hilarious, of his days as a young GP in a remote area of Scotland. With the coffee came a lull in the background music and Roger Forbes took the microphone to offer toasts, proffer thanks and sketch a brief review of the hospice year. Sheila announced the results of some raffles and then the floor was given over to the band once more for the evening's dancing.

I had spotted Abby at the beginning of the evening over at one of the tables populated with nurses who had come without partners. O resplendent vision that had possessed my imagination and perturbed my equilibrium! She was as beautiful and intoxicating as I remembered. Her dress was an olive green, but I can't remember much of the detail as I was thoroughly mesmerised by her face and mannerisms. Throughout the evening I had struggled to concentrate on the company at my table while all the time wanting to look across and watch her. Now the volume of the music had increased I could safely sit back and eschew conversation to observe while others took to the dance floor. After two dances Abby and a group from her table got up and joined in, several of them petering out at one point in laughter over some shared joke, the amusement carrying on as they returned to their table after the dance ended.

How should I get to talk to her? This was such a public arena. Perhaps she would get up and go to the bar at some point. I sat through another dance while most of my table-mates took to the floor. I couldn't stand this any more. I would simply ask her to dance, and blow the attention it might draw. Faint hearts, and all that. I got up and weaved my way between the intervening tables. As I approached she broke off her conversation and smiled broadly.

'Hello David. It's so nice to see you. It seems to have been ages.'

'Hello Abby.' The attention of everyone at the table was upon me. I felt sweat on the back of my neck and my heart was pounding. 'Would you like to dance?'

To my utter relief there wasn't the slightest hesitation. 'Certainly!' With that she got up and came round the table to meet me.

We headed onto the floor and began to dance, me gyrating awkwardly and she moving gracefully and effortlessly. She looked at me almost the whole time, looking down only occasionally as if to check her steps. After a while the tempo suddenly changed. 'Now for a slower one folks. Take your partners in a dance hold and get up close.' I could have sworn I saw Cathy through the bodies coming down from the stage. Several couples peeled away back to their tables leaving about a dozen on the floor. I looked at Abby. She was holding up her arms.

'Well then, shall we David?' She came closer and took one hand, and then put the other on my shoulder. I hesitantly placed my other hand on her waist, and off we went slowly moving in time with the music. She fixed me with her gaze and now her eyes never left my face. An enigmatic smile, the radiant face, the searching and slightly teasing eyes totally enchanted me. I was floating, completely oblivious to everything else around me except the underlying rhythm that governed our movements.

I suddenly felt a deep-seated assurance. 'Abby. You are utterly lovely and you have totally captivated me. I want to reach out to you in a way that you might not welcome.....and I need to know if that's the case.'

She looked into my eyes for a second or two and said nothing. Then she pressed herself closer and rested her cheek against mine. I could feel her hair against my neck and I breathed in her loveliness. 'David..... David.' She spoke softly, almost like a prayer. 'I was beginning to fear you would never ask.'

We held the position throughout another two slow dances, moving as one, without looking at each other, speaking without talking, deep calling unto deep. I felt her breath against me, a slow counterpoint to the rhythm of the dance, and the warmth of her body nestled against mine, and closed my eyes. No anthems of rhapsodic joy, no waterfalls of refreshment, no waves of relief, and no vestments of inner peace could surpass the wordless and inexpressible wonder of those moments. The dances extended to an eternity, yet at the same time ended all too quickly. The tempo changed again and more couples joined the melee. We separated slightly and rested our foreheads together for a moment. I took her hand and led her out of the noise of the hall into the quieter lounge area.

We sat down on a sofa by a large window looking out onto the lights of the city night. 'Abby. I think I've been in love with you since I first set eyes on you. I thought at first it was just an infatuation, but I can't get you out of my mind and my heart, nor do I want to. For weeks I've been.....'

She put her fingers up to my mouth and touched my lips. 'I know. I know. Just hold me.' She leaned her head against my chest and I held her, stroking her hair, and feeling the rise and fall of her chest against my arms. We sat in mostly silent communion watching the night while bathing in glorious light.

Chapter 8
Engravings on the Heart

The large brown paper package was waiting for me on the desk when I arrived in the morning. It was addressed to 'Dr David, St. Julian's Hospice', and when I picked it up it was heavier than I had anticipated. I carefully unwrapped the paper to reveal an exquisite chess set, and it became immediately clear why it was so heavy. The board was made of white onyx and black obsidian squares, with ornately carved pieces in the corresponding stone. I carefully unwrapped each individual piece and marvelled at the skill of the craftsman as I fingered the intricate carving in the cool smoothness of the underlying stone. I set up each piece in its place on the board and sat back to take in the beauty of the assembled whole. Intrigued as to the reason for the gift, if that is what it was, I reached for the envelope that had fallen out during the unveiling, and read the note inside.

'Dear David,
If you are reading this then I will have moved on to better things (I hope!). Please accept this gift as a token of our friendship and as a reminder of the hours we spent

together – I can't tell you how much I appreciated our games. The set is one I picked up some years ago on a trip to Mexico, and I would really like you to have it. I wish you both every blessing in the future, wherever your path leads you.

 Your friend,

 Mike.'

The news of his death did not come as a shock. He had not been to the day centre for a week or two, so I guessed he wasn't well. The present was a surprise, and a humbling one. I noted his reference to 'both'. I had told him about Abby in passing, but he was very insightful. It had led him to talk about his wife and his own marriage that he regarded as having been very blessed. I reflected that he had been one of the most contented men I had come across, with no sense of bitterness or self-pity over his circumstances. He liked people and he enjoyed life, whatever it brought him.

Sally came in and interrupted my musings. 'What a lovely chess set.'

'Yes isn't it. It's a gift from a friend.'

'Are you coming to the meeting? We are ready to get going.'

'Yes, of course. On my way. I'd better quickly pack this away.'

Sheila turned round. 'I'll do that David. You don't want to be late for the meeting.' I thanked her and followed Sally out.

Cathy had assembled the usual crowd. She winked at me as I came in. I nodded. Sarah was administering the teas and coffees. Cathy announced, 'Good morning everyone. Before we start this morning I have something to share with you all, some really fantastic news hot off the press.' She immediately had everyone's attention. She was beaming at me. 'Our own David and Abby are engaged to be married!' There were shrieks of delight and enthusiastic congratulations, as I was deluged with handshakes and hugs and pats on the back. When the commotion had subsided sufficiently Cathy continued. 'Abby is in later today if anyone wants to see the ring, but they were keen that it was made official news this morning.'

Winter had slowly given way to spring and the long dark nights continued their retreat before the vanguard of summer. In the weeks following the ball we had spent time together whenever we could within the constraints of working patterns and other commitments. Long weekend walks through winter landscapes, lazy afternoons snuggled on the sofa, talking and laughing but mainly just being. In better weather I would join her for her break and we would sit in Lizzie's spot, looking out over the valley. We had not yet slept together as she wanted to wait till we were married, and I had not even questioned it as it seemed so right. Although there was no formal engagement until now, it was always assumed. I had known from that first embrace at the dance that this was the girl I would marry, and it was a mutual understanding, an exchanging of hearts and a self-giving of one to another that could not be anything other than total. The consummation of that in the physical would come, but it would be in many ways secondary to, and simply a seal on, what had already been committed. The formal engagement had come that weekend, when we announced it on a visit to her parents and had chosen a ring together. It would be a short engagement, with a wedding in the late summer.

I thanked everyone for their kind words and filled in some of the gaps in their knowledge of our courtship. It came as no surprise to any but the most unobservant that we were seeing each other. Our attachment at the ball had not gone unnoticed and the hospice grapevine was pretty extensive and efficient. It transpired that wiser heads were ahead of the game. Brian was not at the meeting, but came to find me later to congratulate me. 'She's made a landing at last, and an impeccable one at that.'

The meeting moved on to the business of the day. Cathy first updated us on a rumoured royal visit by The Prince of Wales. He was going to be in the area visiting a number of charities, and there was a link with the hospice as it had royal patronage.

'Just to let you know that it has been confirmed that the Prince will be visiting us next Tuesday. He's going to speak to some of the patients and there will be a line-up of staff. There will be some preparations in advance of that, some redecorating and titivating here and there. His security staff will also be visiting sometime in the next few days to check us out.'

There followed some discussion about the politics and etiquette, who would be presenting what and when. Such visits are apparently a potential minefield for staff sensitivities, requiring careful choreography of participation and introductions in order to avoid anyone feeling left out or overlooked. They were rendered even more fraught by the possibility that the visitor might step outside the itinerary or that they might be running late and the schedule need improvising.

Moving on to the patients, the meeting flowed very smoothly. However, there was some protracted discussion about two in particular. Martin Beamish was a man in his fifties with a facial tumour. It had horribly disfigured his face and had eaten away into his jaw and neck. Such patients could end up spending long periods in the hospice, usually in one of the single rooms, as they might require complicated pain control, and the social aspects of disfigurement are often distressing. Martin had remained well nourished by means of a feeding tube and was only now beginning to physically decline, despite the fact that his tumour was well advanced. He was fiercely independent and determined to be normal in the face of his illness, and he eschewed any medication that might render him at all drowsy. Pain control was therefore proving a challenge, and his extensive eroding tumour was proving very difficult to keep covered with dressings.

He maintained what seemed like an almost casual disregard for his disfigurement, and could be seen at times examining his face carefully in the bathroom mirror, but it was more likely an incredibly brave defiance of the cruel ravages of his disease. The problem was that his own apparent lack of squeamishness wasn't generally shared by anyone other than clinical staff, most of whom were no longer shocked by such disfigurements. However, Martin's was extreme, and his tendency to walk around the grounds and other public areas of the hospice with his dressings hanging off had caused distress to some visitors, patients and non-clinical staff.

'We are going to have to talk to him.' Cathy threw it out as a general invitation.

Sarah volunteered. 'I'll have a word with him. I'm sure he'll understand. While we don't want to restrict him, we have nevertheless to be sensitive to others. He can at least wear a towel round his neck if the dressings are coming loose.'

'Thanks Sarah. Moving on to Louie Cosgrove. He's clearly still using cannabis. On a number of occasions the auxiliaries have gone in to his room and have detected clouds of the 'medicinal herb', as he puts it. David, you spoke to him last week about it didn't you?'

Louie Cosgrove was a man in his sixties who was a relic of that very decade. He was a rock star of the hippie generation who had enjoyed a modicum of fame and success with a couple of songs in the charts and a lifestyle that went with it. Charming, but a little chaotic, his brain seemed addled at times by years of pharmacological abuse, and he adopted the role of the naughty miscreant who needed to be tamed but had no real intention or capacity of being so. Sadly, his body was finally being tamed by the ravages of lung cancer, and his pain control was a challenge given his Bohemian ways that defied the application of any systematic treatment regimen. He would come into the hospice for a spell and while under supervision he would regain a measure of symptom control, but it would all go to the wall when he was back at home and left to his own devices. His preferred form of self-medication was with cannabis. He was partial to amphetamines too.

'Yes I did. I re-iterated our position. We could

turn a blind eye as long as he doesn't actually smoke it in the hospice building. You know what he's like. Very charming, submissive and apologetic, he promises not to do anything to put us in an awkward position. And he abides by it for a while, at least as far as the cannabis is concerned. I think he's popping other things much of the time.'

Nick looked perplexed. 'Where is he getting it from? He doesn't go out while he's here.'

'I think his friends bring it in for him.'

'Should we speak to them?'

'We have,' Sarah interjected. 'Coming from the angle of it being difficult to monitor the effects of the prescribed drugs he's taking if we don't know what other drugs he's having. He and they are part of a deeply ingrained culture and I'm not sure the message really gets through.'

I continued. 'The trouble is, he says that the cannabis helps the pain and is the way he deals with his situation. He obviously does it at home.'

There was a pause for thought, and then Cathy spoke. 'While one doesn't want to dismantle his coping mechanisms, we need to have some ground rules about what we feel is acceptable while in our care. Could you revisit that with him David?'

'Certainly. I'll have another word.'

The meeting concluded shortly afterwards. There were more congratulations as we went out and as the news filtered through to the other staff in the vicinity. When I returned to the office Sheila jumped up and greeted me effusively, probing me with questions, some of which I carefully avoided answering. Then she was off out of the office and I expect the whole hospice was then informed within a matter of minutes. All morning the congratulations continued. Around lunchtime Abby called to say that she was on her way in and I went out to the car park to meet her. We kissed.

'Are you okay?' she asked.

'I'm overwhelmed by goodwill. I think I've taken the main force of the wave of excitement, so hopefully you won't find it too overwhelming.'

We walked hand in hand up to the entrance and into the foyer. The two receptionists started clapping as we made our way past and down onto the ward. I squeezed Abby's hand and glanced sideways at her. She smiled back, looking confident and relaxed as ever.

❧

It was a beautiful spring morning and the waxing sun was beginning to have some real warmth to it. I paused as I always did to look out over the valley. I had watched it change through the seasons, each one revealing a different facet of its splendour. Spring brought a renewed awakening from its sleepy stark beauty of winter and there were ever increasing signs of life both on the valley floor and in the air above. I looked up and saw a bird of prey for the first time since late autumn.

Predators come in different guises, and there were others closer to home. I didn't recognise the car that was parked alongside me. Neither did I recognise the two occupants. They were smartly dressed, a man and a woman, and in deep discussion. One held a clipboard and the other was leafing through some documents from a pile of files on his knee. They didn't look like relatives and they certainly weren't members of staff. I shrugged and headed into the hospice, feeling slightly uneasy. It was the day before the royal visit and there was an obvious increase in activity already so early in the day. A stretch of carpet in the foyer was due to be replaced and the maintenance team were putting finishing touches to some paintwork that had been carried out over the weekend.

As I walked down to the office I was greeted by Sarah, who was standing at Cathy's door. 'Morning. Sarah didn't the Prince's security team visit at the end of last week?'

'Yes, they had a quick look round. One of his aides will be in touch later today to finalise one or two details of his visit.'

'Hmm. That's odd.'

'What's odd?'

'I've just seen a couple of official looking people parked in the car park. A man and a woman that I didn't recognise. They were looking at documents.'

Sarah looked at Cathy. 'A man and a woman.'

Cathy bit her lip and looked dismayed. 'Oh you don't think? No, surely not today of all days! Have we not got enough to do with the visit tomorrow?'

'I'll go and look.' Sarah disappeared off to the car park.

'What's the matter? Who are those people?'

Cathy sighed. 'I fear they might be inspectors from the regulatory authority. They do an annual visit, which is usually planned, but can be unannounced. If they are, then Sarah and I are in for a busy day. They are into everything. They want to see policies, procedures, documentary evidence for all sorts of things. And the list gets bigger every year. More and more bureaucratic hoops to jump through, all in the noble aim of ensuring that we are providing care to a high enough standard. The trouble is it all takes a huge amount of work and one wonders whether it actually impacts the care we deliver in any way that justifies that work. You've no idea what a proliferation of policies we've had to write over the last few years.'

Sarah returned. 'It's them, I'm sure of it. I don't know the man, but I recognise the woman from last year.'

'Oh no. She was a real bundle of joy. Spread the word amongst the team, and especially think about anything or anyone we need to do our best to steer them away from.'

There was a pause. 'Louie!' They said it together.

Sarah continued. 'Oh Lord. We need to keep them away from Louie. The girls said they could smell dope again this morning.'

I shook my head. 'Oh dear. I spoke to him last week.'

'He behaved for a few days, but he's relapsed again over the weekend. We should have got him home at the end of the week,' reflected Sarah, forlornly.

Sarah headed off to pass the word while Cathy phoned Brian. He came down and Sarah rejoined them in conference while Sally and I attended the morning meeting. Sure enough, the inspectors announced their arrival at reception about a quarter of an hour later and were brought to Cathy's office, which they used as their base for the day.

Throughout the morning one or other of our two

inspectors popped up in all sorts of places, usually accompanied by Sarah or Cathy, looking through log books and assorted documentation, asking questions about procedures and risk assessments, clinical governance and audit. The photocopier in the nurses' office was working almost non-stop reproducing documentary evidence for them to be able to tick some box in their assessment schedules.

The gentleman was amiable and polite, courteous and apologetic at times for the fact that he was in the way or disrupting normal routines. The lady on the other hand was prickly and officious, never once smiling, her requests and comments curt and her demeanour one of bored irritation. On one occasion I happened upon them Sarah pulled a face behind her back, and more than once I saw Cathy raise her eyes in exasperation as she was sent off brusquely to fetch some other piece of evidence.

I met up with Sarah in the dining room at lunch-time, at which point we were treated to a blow by blow account of some of the irritations of the morning. The male inspector was ensconced in Cathy's office writing up some notes, while 'Cruella', as she had been nicknamed, had repaired to the car to eat lunch and make some phone calls.

'I don't know what her problem is. I think she's worse than last year. It doesn't cost much to be polite, and it makes all the difference.'

Sharon was sympathetic. 'Well, only the afternoon to go and that'll be it for another year.'

'That's unless they find enough things they don't like to warrant an interim inspection before then.'

'Have they picked up on anything?' I asked.

'Only a few small things I think. But you kind of sensed the relish with which she pointed them out.'

Conversation moved onto other things. We had just about finished lunch when we were aware of a commotion out in the foyer, followed shortly afterwards by a scream. We looked at each other momentarily and then all shot up and out into the reception area.

Cruella was thrashing around wildly on the floor while one of the receptionists was trying to give assistance. Other people were converging on the scene from various directions. Standing a few feet back looking rather bemused was Martin Beamish. It transpired that Cruella had wandered into the hospice from the car park and bumped into Martin in the foyer. As usual his dressings were half hanging off, and she got sight of part of the gore that was underneath, at which point she promptly fainted. When she came round about thirty seconds later she woke to see a concerned Martin leaning over her. From that angle the loose dressing did nothing to conceal his face and neck, and she was presented with the full horror of his appearance. She flipped and took several minutes to calm down.

Martin was ushered away back into his room, still bemused by the whole affair. Her colleague was summoned from the ward while Cathy sat with her trying to comfort her. Sarah and I looked at each other and I could see she was trying hard to stifle a giggle. Cruella was too traumatised to continue with the rest of the day, and after cups of tea and sympathy she retreated to the safety of the car while her colleague collected their effects. Cathy escorted him to the entrance and apologised for the upset.

'Don't worry, it couldn't be helped. An unfortunate mishap. We were pretty much done here anyway, and what's left wasn't of great importance. You'll get the report in a couple of weeks, but there are no major problems. That should be it till next year.' He smiled and shook hands. 'Thank you and your staff for your time.....and patience.' He grinned knowingly.

Cathy came over to Sarah and me and gave a big sigh of relief. 'We need tea, and we need it now!'

'I'll get it,' Sarah offered. 'Meet you in the small sitting room.'

Sarah rejoined us carrying a tray and we flopped into the easy chairs. 'What a drama!' We chuckled rather guiltily about the turn of events.

Presently, Brian stuck his head around the door looking jubilant. 'Well done! One visit down, and one to go.'

Cathy laughed. 'Oh Lord. I haven't begun to get my head around tomorrow.'

'I heard about the incident.'

'We were so bothered about Louie that I completely forgot about Martin,' Cathy replied. 'He's quite a liability at the moment. We must make sure he is properly covered up and contained tomorrow afternoon. Perhaps one of the auxiliaries could mind him during the visit.'

Brian went on. 'I've been chatting with Roger and we've had an idea. The royal team had asked whether there was anything official we would like the Prince to do during his visit. It occurred to us that we could get him to officially open our Memorial Garden. It is not quite finished, but we are very close and Cliff thinks his team could tidy it up enough in time for an opening ceremony. It would also provide more of a focus for the photographer.'

The Memorial Garden had been created as a secluded area within the hospice grounds with arbours and water features, a place where relatives could come and reflect. They could, for a fee, have the name of their loved one engraved on a large pebble that was then set within the water features and became part of the fabric of the garden. About a dozen pebbles had already been commissioned and engraved. My initial reaction to the idea had been one of slight cringing, wary of the gooey and exploitative sentimentality around some gardens of remembrance, so wonderfully caricatured in Evelyn Waugh's *The Loved One*. However, once the concept took form in wood and stone and water and foliage, there emerged a space that was understated but beautiful, moving but tasteful, a place of palpable peace and perhaps spiritual closure. I had visited it a few times in various stages of its evolution and had been quietly impressed with the result.

'I think that's a great idea Brian,' said Cathy. We all nodded.

'It'll change the timings a little but I'll run through that with you tomorrow.'

When I came into the hospice the following morning I was struck by the air of calm and unhurried efficiency. Staff members of all disciplines were helping with final preparations for the visit. The reception area and indeed all the public areas looked pristine. The visit was scheduled to begin at two in the afternoon. A briefing for as many staff as could make it was arranged for eleven that morning, and individuals with specific responsibilities were rehearsed separately throughout the morning. A smaller group, comprising mainly senior staff, which would be attending the opening of the Memorial Garden, were taken down to the garden and familiarised with the planned schedule.

The business of the day carried on around the interruptions like water flowing between pebbles on a beach. There was a sense of anticipation and excitement throughout the hospice, particularly among the patients, and even the sickest had rallied somewhat at the prospect of a once in a lifetime occasion. The Prince had specifically asked if he could greet some of the patients by their beds, but would clearly be guided by staff if some were felt to be too unwell for this to be appropriate. We had concerns about Martin, but felt we could not deprive him of this opportunity. We would just have to make sure he was well covered up. Louie, too, was under strict instructions to behave that afternoon.

The buzz continued over lunchtime, and shortly after this some of the local press arrived. At about two the word went round the hospice that the Prince and his entourage had arrived. There was a welcoming party in the reception area, comprising senior staff and the press officer. They then moved down to the Memorial Garden for the ceremony. About a quarter of an hour later they returned to the reception area and the Prince set off down the ward, escorted by Cathy and Brian, and the hospice photographer. Down on the ward we were alerted to his imminent arrival and took up positions. A staff nurse was stationed outside each bay, ready to accompany the party into the bay and introduce the patients. I stood in a line with Sarah, Sally and Sheila just by the nurses' station. Abby was waiting outside her bay further down the ward.

We were waiting for quite a while and it was soon evident that progress was running behind schedule. The Prince was taking longer to talk to patients than had been anticipated. Eventually they emerged from the bay just up from the nurses' station and came to our position. Cathy introduced us in turn. He greeted Sarah first who managed a creditable curtsy and then shook his hand.

'Hello Sarah. So you are one of the senior sisters here. You have a splendid unit, very impressive. How long have you worked here?'

'I've been here about thirteen years.'

'Gosh, you must have seen some changes in that time. Have many of your nursing team been here a long time?'

'Yes, quite a few of our nurses have been here a number of years and are very experienced. We are getting some younger blood in too, which is pleasing. And they seem to want to stay.'

'That's very good to hear. A testament to your team, no doubt.'

He moved on to me and he shook my hand. 'Dr Trevelyan. I'm sorry to pull you all away from your work. Thank you for taking the time to indulge me.'

'Not at all, it's a privilege.'

'I've really enjoyed talking to your patients, all of whom are extremely complimentary about the care.'

'That's very good to hear.'

'I've also had a trip down memory lane today. I clearly remember listening to some of Louie Cosgrove's songs in my younger days. It appears we share an interest in horticulture and alternative therapies, and he was extolling the medicinal properties of a certain herb.'

'Ah. Right'

He smiled. 'Keep up the good work. You are all doing a splendid job here.'

He moved on down the line, exchanging pleasantries with each individual, ensuring that this would be an occasion they would not forget. Then they disappeared into the third bay with Abby. Everyone relaxed. I looked at Sarah. We both gave a stifled and rather shocked laugh. 'Ruddy Louie!'

'Ever a rebel. I wonder what he said.'

❧

Abby and I sat together in Lizzie's spot looking out over the valley. It was her afternoon break and we had the place to ourselves. We were talking about what I should do next. I had continued to keep an eye out for interesting posts, but I hadn't been as assiduous recently as I had earlier on.

'I had a strange dream last night,' I said. 'It was so vivid. Often when you dream the details seem to fade very quickly after waking but I can still see every detail of this one.'

'Sounds intriguing. What was it about?'

'I was walking down to the Memorial Garden. I stood in the middle looking around at the features, and there were dozens of pebbles with names engraved on them. Many were names I recognised from the last few months, though it was hard to recall the faces – you know how it is, how quickly we forget the faces. Anyway I was suddenly aware of a weight in my pocket against my thigh. I reached inside and pulled out another large pebble. It had my name engraved upon it.'

'Your name?'

'Yes. Mr David Trevelyan. It was strange, because I wasn't alarmed at all. I looked at it and fingered it for a while and then slowly bent down and placed it along with the others in one of the features. I stood back and then I woke up.'

Abby thought for a while. 'What do you make of it?'

'I don't know. I do know that I'm no longer so sure about where my career is heading.'

She snuggled up to me. 'David, you know I'll go with you anywhere you want.'

'I know. I don't think I want to take you away from all you know here. My own wander lust has faded somewhat. I'm not as driven as I was. The high flying career in a prestigious surgical unit doesn't seem so important now.'

'I just want you to be happy, whatever you do.'

'This morning I had a call from Bill Thomson, my old consultant at the hospital here. He didn't catch me, but left a message for me to get back to him. I noticed an advert for a registrar post in his team this week, and it may be that he was calling about that.'

'Would you want to go back to your old firm?'

'Well, it's a decent solid job and he's a good boss to work for.'

'Why don't you give him a ring and see what develops?'

'Hmm. Perhaps I should.' I looked at my watch. 'It's time we were getting back.'

I finished off the jobs from the day's activities and then looked at the note I'd been given earlier. What did I have to lose? I decided to ring him and managed to catch him at the end of a ward round. 'Hello David. Good of you to return my call. How are things going?'

'I'm very well, thank you.'

'Glad to hear it. Listen, are you fixed up with a reg post yet?'

'No, nothing so far.'

'Well, my boy, our post is now up for grabs. I know you were keen to move into new pastures, but I thought I'd ring in case you'd changed your mind. There's a very strong chance you would get it if you were interested.'

'Really? Okay. I had noticed the ad, and I have to say I was thinking about it.'

'Well, why don't you think about it some more, and if you want to apply then send me an updated CV? The closing date is next week and interviews at the end of the month.'

'Right. Will do. Thank you very much.'

Sheila was in her element. She was like a busy bee flitting here and there, organising and persuading, enthusing and cajoling. She was also the best person for the task. She knew everybody, was disarmingly forthright and was passionate about the hospice. She was the sort of person without whom great ventures would never get off the ground. The annual hospice summer fete was fast approaching, and Sheila was the dynamic force that would get everything together in the right place on the day.

The doctors had been arm-twisted into running a tombola stand. 'David, I haven't got you down yet on the tombola rota. The prizes are coming in thick and fast. Can I put you down for a couple of shifts? I presume you'll be coming to the fete?'

'Yes, I'll be there. I'm happy to do whatever I can to help.' The truth was I didn't have much choice in the matter. Sheila was very difficult to say no to.

'That's good, I've paired you up with Sally for your first hour and you'll be with Brian for your second. It really is a great event. We get lots of families of patients and supporters, and they really appreciate seeing the docs getting involved.' She disappeared out of the office with her master file to chase up some other aspect of the fete arrangements.

The letter had come that morning. I had opened it with a measure of excitement. It was, as expected, a formal invitation to interview for the registrar post with my old firm. The interview was the following week on the Friday, the day before the fete. I would need to tell Brian.....and Cathy. I would feel awkward otherwise. I would do it after the weekend. The knowledge of it weighed on my mind through the morning meeting, and I was a little distracted.

'Rebecca is deteriorating.' Sarah sounded matter of fact, but her tone was subtly different, forlorn perhaps, edged with regret.

Sally sighed and added, 'Her kidneys are beginning to fail. Nothing too dramatic at the moment, but the slide has begun.'

'She's not going to make the wedding, is she?' Nick was stating a fact rather than seeking opinion. There was silence for a moment, everyone in the meeting processing and reflecting on the inevitability presented to us, dealing in different ways with the rising urge to cry out with fury and anguish against another merciless assault from the terrible engines of disease.

Rebecca Wilson was a thirty-eight year old woman who had advanced cancer of the cervix. She was lovely. In every respect she was lovely, and more than any other patient recently she had pulled the heartstrings of almost everyone involved in her care. Bright and vivacious, gentle and kind, she had fought the cancer for eighteen months enduring surgery and chemotherapy, and she had done pretty well. Then her pelvis filled up with tumour, causing her left leg to swell up and threatening her kidneys. Offered some further chemotherapy, she declined on the basis that it would not cure her and she wanted to spend whatever time she had left at home with her three children rather than be tied in to hospital.

She had been with her partner Douglas for fifteen years and they had boys of fourteen and eleven, and a girl of seven. They had decided to get married and have the wedding they never quite got round to having before. That was another two weeks away. She had coped at home with increasing pain and increasing doses of painkillers for several weeks, remaining active and involved in family activities, but she had begun to struggle and had come in to the hospice over two weeks ago for pain control and to get her as well as possible for the wedding. She may still survive till her planned date, but she would almost certainly not be fit to manage the day that had been planned.

'Does she realise that?' I asked.

Sally looked up. 'Yes. I spoke to her yesterday.'

'How did she take it?'

'Too well. There were a few tears, but she then started to talk about making the best of it. I wanted to scream for her.'

'What about bringing it forward and doing it in the hospice?' Cathy looked over at Nick.

'We could certainly offer that. It's a while since we've done it. It'll need to be a civil ceremony conducted by the Registrar. Time is a bit tight, but they will usually act very quickly to accommodate in such exceptional circumstances. If they want a religious ceremony I could do a separate service of blessing afterwards.'

Sarah added, 'If it was on Saturday they could have the day centre for the celebration afterwards.'

Nick nodded thoughtfully. 'Shall I talk to them this morning?' There was general agreement.

Cathy caught me as I was leaving the meeting. She looked concerned. 'Are you alright David? You didn't seem your usual self this morning.'

'Really? I suppose Rebecca has affected all of us.'

'You didn't seem right before we talked about Rebecca.' I should have known by now that Cathy was not easy to fob off.

'Can we talk in your office?' She led the way and closed the door behind us. 'I need to tell you because it'll weigh on my mind if I don't.'

'Tell me what David?' She looked at me, into me, intently. 'Are you and Abby okay?'

'Oh yes, fine. It's not that.' She looked relieved. 'I've got an interview for a surgical post next week. It's with my old firm, and there's a strong chance I'll get it.'

Her emerald eyes scanned my face and her own face visibly relaxed. She smiled. 'David. I'm very touched that you felt you wanted to tell me. The last thing I or any of us want is for you to feel any pressure of expectation. I happen to believe that you belong here. But that is something that you need to discover for yourself. Whatever you decide to do you'll have our blessing and our love.' She stood up. 'Will you speak to Brian before you go for the interview?' I nodded. She opened the door and I turned to leave. She touched me on the shoulder and I looked round. 'You must follow your heart.' The words seemed to pierce my heart. I nodded hesitantly and left the office.

Rebecca and Douglas were grateful and relieved about the possibility of having a ceremony in the hospice. It remained to be confirmed whether anyone in the Registrar's office would be available to come on a Saturday afternoon at short notice. But, amazingly, that confirmation did come by the end of the afternoon. Wedding fever overtook some quarters of the hospice and was a welcome diversion for the family and those most closely involved with Rebecca's care. These included Abby, her principal nurse, and Tina who was also working in that bay. Hasty phone calls, cleverly improvised wedding plans, and adjustments to the dress necessitated by the effects of advancing illness dominated the next couple of days.

The civil ceremony would take place in the day centre with all the guests in attendance. The couple and close family, together with some invited members of staff, would then move to the chapel for a short service of blessing while the day centre was transformed into a reception venue. It was felt that Rebecca could probably manage most of the afternoon in a wheelchair, though the whole schedule could be negotiated with her in her bed if she felt less well on the day. She had agreed to have a short course of steroids to give her a boost and help her appetite over the weekend of celebration. It was my weekend on call and both Abby and Tina would also be on shift on Saturday.

It was a relief when the day arrived and Rebecca felt well. The steroids were doing their job. It was always a worry in people who are so unwell that something might happen before they got to their goal. I busied myself on the ward throughout the morning. Tina came in before her shift started in order to help Rebecca get ready. She had also arranged for a hairdresser friend to come in as a surprise and make up her hair. Lunch and staff handovers out of the way, guests started arriving in the day centre from about two in readiness for the civil ceremony at two-thirty.

I had a quick look without wanting to get in the way. Douglas and the children were standing at one side talking to his parents. One of the tables had been placed at the front and a lady who I presumed was the Registrar was leafing through some paperwork. Rows of chairs were set out on either side of an improvised aisle demarcated by two lines of freestanding floral displays. A photographer was hovering and taking photos of some of those arriving.

I wandered back down onto the ward to check on

Abby. She and Tina were putting finishing touches to Rebecca's appearance while her father sat patiently to one side. The other ladies in the bay were chipping in with complimentary comments and encouraging banter. Everyone loves a wedding. Eventually word came down to say that everyone was assembled and ready to go. Abby set off pushing her in the wheelchair up the corridor, accompanied by Rebecca's father and Tina. Sounds of a wedding march came from the direction of the foyer. I watched them go and then ducked in to the office to finish off some notes. I would join them in about half an hour for the blessing, at Rebecca's invitation.

The newlyweds emerged into the foyer and there were hugs and quick refreshments. Abby fetched some extra painkiller for the bride who was beginning to look a little uncomfortable. After a few minutes to recover, the small bridal party adjourned to the chapel while a small army of helpers set about rearranging chairs and setting out tables. Nick ushered them in and Abby, Tina and I slipped in at the back. Rebecca was looking relaxed - the painkiller was obviously working. Douglas sat in a chair alongside her wheelchair and they held hands. The service was short and moving. I was lost in thought, absorbed with watching the couple. They looked peaceful, radiant, just as any other couple on any other wedding day. It was poignant and uplifting. A flag of defiance, planted in the territory of the enemy that was eroding the ground from beneath them. I reflected on the dignity, resilience and fortitude of enduring love that transcends and transforms.

As I emerged from my contemplation Nick was reading something.

'*For now our vision is blurred and our perspective distorted, but the time will come when we will see things clearly. Now there is much that we don't understand, or only understand partially, but the time will come when we will understand fully. Until that time faith, hope and love are three things that sustain us and give us meaning; they are strong and enduring. And of these, love is the strongest and most sustaining.*'

I looked at Abby. She had tear-filled eyes. I reached out next to me and took her hand. She looked at me and smiled, causing a tear to overspill and run down her cheek.

❧

It had been a strange week, one in which I felt at times almost detached and looking in on all that was going on around me. The interview at the end of the week was a backdrop to the scenes played out before me, and everything I saw and heard and experienced in the hospice was thrown into greater relief, and took on a greater intensity. I was both excited and apprehensive, decided and yet uncertain, confident and yet filled with doubt. Like an important exam or difficult hurdle to surmount it evoked that curious contradiction of wanting to get to it and know the outcome, but at the same time dreading it and wishing it away. It was a week of vivid dreams, mostly involving Abby, but the details would always fade shortly after waking.

I had met up with Brian over coffee mid week. He showed me the reference he had written for me. It was glowing. I didn't know what to say.

'David, it's been a pleasure to have you here these last months. You have been a real blessing to us all.'

'Thank you. It is something I would not have wanted to miss.'

'Whether or not you are successful on Friday I'm sure you would make a fine surgeon and excel in your career. Are you sure that is still what you want?'

'I think so. It's always been the plan.'

'We will of course support you in whatever you want to do. You should know, however, that you are a natural at hospice work and this job is yours as long as you want it.'

'Thank you Brian. I've been overwhelmed by the goodwill I've experienced here.'

'I know that this is not mainstream medicine and many would be of the opinion that choosing to do this line of work is to sideline your career in a backwater of the profession. But we are an emerging specialty, and the time will come when caring for the dying will become a political imperative, and we will become mainstream. The transition to that is going to be difficult and not without risk. We will need gifted and committed people to manage that transition, and in particular to preserve the essence of what is hospice in the face of increasing bureaucracy that comes with systematisation of care. We mustn't lose the art of caring in the science of healthcare. And as you've no doubt discovered, we have the privilege of getting alongside people and making a difference in ways that few other specialties can. Just think about that before Friday. I know you will.' He got up to go. 'All the best for the interview. And I hope you get the outcome that you want.'

His words were in my mind as I drove to the hospital.

Abby had phoned me first thing. It was her day off but she was going in to the hospice to help set up the stalls for the fete. She was enthusiastic and encouraging, and even now her words of reassurance resonated within me. 'I'll be waiting for you. Love you.'

I was early, so I went on to the ward to say hello to familiar faces, but there weren't as many as I had anticipated, such is the turnover of staff. The ward sister greeted me warmly, and we exchanged news from the last few months. She was excited to hear about my engagement. The surroundings were so familiar, evoking not specific memories but a general remembrance. It dawned on me, as I sat at the nurses' station for a while and watched the activity, that this remembrance carried a heaviness with it. This was no longer a place I felt at home; perhaps I'd never really felt at home.

There were two other candidates and I was last to go in. Bill Thomson greeted me enthusiastically and introduced me to the panel. It was smaller, less formal than my previous interview. It went smoothly, very smoothly. I can't remember much of the detail. I do remember feeling very relaxed. It was over before I knew it. Bill looked at each of the panel members and each nodded in agreement. He turned back to me.

'David, I don't think we need to waste any more time. You were by far the strongest candidate on paper and you outshone the others in the interview as well. Many congratulations. We'd like to offer you the post!'

❦

As I drove up the access road and past the side of

the hospice I could see lots of activity in the grounds at the back. A banner had been erected over the main gate advertising the summer fete. I parked the car and took off my jacket and tie before heading up towards the entrance. I followed the path round the side and I paused at the corner. Stalls of different descriptions were at various stages of assembly. Cliff and one of his team were fooling around with the stocks and wet sponges. Some patients and their families were sitting out enjoying the sunny afternoon and watching what was going on. I spotted Cathy and Abby sorting through some boxes of tablecloths and coverings. A sigh of contentment came involuntarily from within.

I started to walk over to Abby. She looked up and waved excitedly. Cathy stopped what she was doing and stood up too. Abby came across to meet me, and we hugged. She looked expectantly into my face.

'Well. How did it go?'

'Extremely well. I got what I wanted.'

'They offered you the job?'

'Yes they did.....but I turned it down. I'm staying here.' She smiled her lovely captivating smile and pressed close to me. I nuzzled her hair, inhaling deeply. I looked across at Cathy. She nodded. I didn't have to tell her. She already knew.

That night I had a dream. There was a large pebble on the ground in front of me. I heard a voice behind me say, 'Pick it up.' As I bent down I realised it was the same stone I had seen before with my name on it, only it was a little less pristine, more weather beaten, and my name was no longer there. The voice spoke again. 'Turn it over. There is something wonderful written on the other side.' I started to turn it in my hands and as I did so it became clean and bright again, as it had been in my first dream. I turned it over and cradled it in my hands and read what was engraved on the other side. And it was wonderful.